ALSO BY IVAN KLÍMA

A Ship Named Hope
My Merry Mornings
My First Loves
A Summer Affair
Love and Garbage
Judge on Trial

MY GOLDEN TRADES

IVAN KLÍMA

*Translated from the Czech
by Paul Wilson*

CHARLES SCRIBNER'S SONS

New York   London   Toronto   Sydney   Tokyo   Singapore

CHARLES SCRIBNER'S SONS
Rockefeller Center
1230 Avenue of the Americas
New York, New York 10020

Manufactured in the United States of America

10 9 8 7 6 5 4 3 2 1

Library of Congress Cataloging-in-Publication Data
Klíma, Ivan.
    My golden trades / Ivan Klíma : translated from the
Czech by Paul Wilson.
        p.   cm.
    ISBN 0-684-19727-8
    1. Klíma, Ivan.   I. Title.
PG5039.21.L5M95   1994
891.8'635—dc20   94-5757

CONTENTS

THE SMUGGLER'S STORY

I HEARD A familiar voice coming over the phone. 'Santa Claus here. Got an hour this afternoon?'

I had.

'Sensational,' said the voice on the other end, in an inimitable accent that could only belong to someone with a Mexican father and an Indian mother. Then he hung up. He obviously believed that the briefer our conversation was, the less suspicion it would arouse in anyone listening in. Whenever he announced himself as Santa Claus, it meant that he'd returned from one of his frequent business trips abroad and was bringing me books.

It was eleven-thirty and snowing heavily. My wife had taken the car earlier that morning, and it would be noon before I could reach her. I'm not very fond of driving, but I had no idea how many bags of contraband St Nicholas had purchased and brought in. He was hard to fathom. There could well be more than I could carry.

I had met Nicholas by accident. The water-pump on my ancient Renault had given up and, after the car had been immobile in the garage for three months, someone gave me Nicholas's name and address, saying that he often travelled out of the country and would certainly bring me

11

a new pump.

Why should he do that, when he didn't even know me?

He would do it because I was a writer. He loved literature or, to be more precise, he worshipped his wife, who loved literature.

And how would I pay him?

I wasn't to worry about that: for a rich businessman a spare part was no more than a kilo of apples would be for me. Give him a signed copy of one of your books. Or invite him to lunch.

I hesitated for almost a month, but when the water pump for my car was still unavailable, I rang the stranger's doorbell.

In a week I not only had my pump, I had a package of books as well.

He smiled. He was tall, greying, and had a dark complexion. He said it was a pleasure to be able to help me. He held art in the highest esteem, he said, and he understood what a difficult situation I was in.

I gave one of my books to him, with a dedication, and I invited him and his wife to dinner.

Having grown up in an era of paranoia, I was guarded during their visit and did not reveal the secrets of my writing—the only secrets I could have betrayed. But Nicholas did not pry. For a while, he spoke about the world of business, something that for me was exotic and far away. After that his wife, Angela, did most of the talking. She was at least twenty years younger than he was and looked like the angel in her name. We talked about Borges, Márquez and most of all about Cortázar's *Rayuela*, which both of us admired though we disagreed somewhat over the scene in which the heroine crawls across some rickety

12

boards stretched between two windows four storeys above the ground merely to satisfy the whims of two strange and indolent men, bringing them a package of *mate* and a handful of nails across the abyss in the punishing heat. Angela saw in that scene an image of the slavish position of women in her country, while I argued that the scene was meant to represent the heroine's inability to choose between the two men. At the same time, I suggested, the author was paying tribute to women for their courage: women are generally capable of taking risks; men can only admire them for it.

Angela conversed and listened with an intensity that had inspired me to talk about writing, which I normally avoid doing. The conversation seemed to make her happy, and her husband looked content as well.

A month later he unexpectedly called and brought me a package of books, most of which were in Czech. He even brought two or three copies of the same books. He knew, he said, that some of my colleagues were in the same position as I was, and he was sure the books would interest us.

Certainly, but what gave him the idea to bring them to us?

Angela claimed that this was the only way we'd ever get to see such books. I allowed that this was so, thanked him, and distributed the books among my friends.

Some time later he brought me two parcels, not only books this time but also a few magazines, which were even harder to come by. I was delighted, but at the same time I began to feel slightly afraid.

I remembered how, 247 years ago, Jiřík Vostrý, a Protestant missionary, had been caught trying to smuggle forbidden books from Saxony into Bohemia. They threw him straight into prison but, of course, what interested them most was who the books were for. The jailer pretended to be a friend and told the young, inexperienced smuggler that he would take a letter out for him. That letter, which I recently read in a collection of documents in Litomyšl, spoke to me in a language I knew well:

> Kladivo,
>
> I am writing to you from my prison cell with a plea. Should there be any books still in your possession I pray you hide them safely away. And make this known to those you know. I, a prisoner in the name of the Lord, pray you to do this in His name. I assure you I have betrayed no one, so look that you comport yourself likewise. Read this letter, and then give it to him who is faithful . . .

My wife wasn't at work; she had just gone to pick up the washing from the laundry. Another delay.

I was anxious because Nicholas had asked me to come in the afternoon, when he wasn't usually at home. He was probably worried that if he left it till the evening, when he came home from work, he could be followed. It occasionally happened to him, as it did to every foreigner—and to everyone else in the country. His tail would stick with him right up to the building where he lived and then stay there, watching, or at the most retreat to the tennis-courts at the top of the street. From there, it was easy to keep an eye not only on the matches but also on the entrance to Nicholas's building. There they would stay until they were relieved or called off. I would certainly not want to appear in their sight, let alone be caught carrying off a bag of books.

I don't know if I can speak for Nicholas, but personally I had never imagined that one day I would take up smuggling. By the rules that apply in most of the world, smugglers are devious people, with a close knowledge of their territory and their pursuers; men and women with nerves of steel and contempt for the law, both the kind that is written in the statute book and the kind that, although it is not written down anywhere, we sense stands above our every action. I have contempt for neither kind of law, but in our situation, where they contradicted each other, I had to choose between them. Thus, despite my natural disinclination, I have more than once found myself prepared to receive smuggled goods. I find consolation in the fact that, in the conditions prevailing here, it is rare for someone to be doing what he was trained to do, or what he is suited for.

Not long ago Nicholas brought me enough books to fill two bags. Dragging them on to the tram, I looked so suspicious, so desperate even, that people began staring at me, which didn't add to my peace of mind. To make matters worse a man I'd noticed earlier got into the same car as I did. I put one of the bags on my lap and put the other one under the seat so I wouldn't look so burdened. At the same time, I racked my brains trying to think what I'd do and say if the man really was who I feared he was. What if he wanted to search my bags? As it turned out, he didn't, but when I got out of the car I was so preoccupied that I forgot about the bag under the seat. I was already on my way out when a kind woman called me back. Is there any way I can thank her enough? In the bag I was apparently determined to leave behind on the tram were all

15

my identification papers. I don't know how I'd have explained the contents of the bag to those who consider all books that have not passed through a censor's hands to be contraband.

The thing I'd almost done startled and frightened me. I began thinking I should ask Nicholas not to bring me any more books, but I was ashamed to refuse gifts offered to me with such magnanimity just because of my fear. Beyond that, the books seemed to me the last bridge to a part of the world that was fading ever more rapidly from view.

As more items are prohibited, more amateurs take up smuggling. I learned this in the ghetto during the war, where almost everything became unobtainable—rice, cocoa, cigarette-lighters, writing-paper, coffee and candles, not to mention jewellery, cigarettes or money. Even the most decent, law-abiding souls decided to ignore such perverted regulations. Where the law goes berserk, all of us become felons. My father, a scholar led by the very essence of his work to be a man of anxious propriety, brought within the ghetto walls a roll of thousand-crown notes and for the first time in his life was confronted with the basic problem every smuggler faces: where to hide his stash.

In the room we were forced to live in at the time, there was only a single piece of furniture—an old sideboard with many battered drawers. When the drawer on the extreme left was pulled out, a small depression could be felt on the side wall, a flaw left by the cabinet-maker. It proved an ideal hiding place for our treasure. The opening for the drawer was so narrow that only a child's arm could reach in, so I was given the task of placing the roll of money into the depression. I wasn't to breathe a word of what I had done to anyone, nor was I allowed to get fat, or the hiding

16

place would have become inaccessible. I carried out my task faithfully, and thus at the age of ten found myself a member of the criminal fraternity.

I entered that company in the firm conviction that I had done good work.

It was two-thirty when I finally reached Nicholas's house. It was still snowing heavily. Here, on the outskirts of the city, the snow did not melt, but settled thickly on tree branches and the roof-tops. The chain-link fence surrounding the tennis-courts stretched like a swag of lace between iron poles. In the middle of the road, cars had made deep ruts in the snow. I knew this end of the city well. My first love had lived not far from here and we had often wandered the neighbouring streets looking for dark corners where we could embrace. Right now I wasn't thinking about that. Right now the world had become an alien and hostile place, and everyone in it was a potential threat.

You should always mentally rehearse how you would behave and what you would say if you were arrested. It wasn't hard to guess what they would ask.

'What books have you brought with you?' the investigator asked the twenty-seven-year-old smuggler of subversive books, Jiřík Vostrý, on 19 April, 1732.

'I have brought three. One: *The New Testament*; Two: *On True Christianity*; Three: *Two Countrymen Converse on the Subject of Faith*.'

'Where are those books now and for whom were they intended?'

'*On True Christianity* was received by Litochlev; he gave me one score and ten groschen for it. *Two Countrymen Converse*, that went to Kaliban, a miller from Kamenné

Sedliště. And the third remained in my pocket; it was confiscated when I was taken.'

'At first you claimed you traded only with Litochleb in Morašice and Kladivo in Lubný. Now you tell me you also called upon the miller in Sedliště?'

'I did. I had forgotten.'

'And how did you come by the knowledge that the miller of Sedliště also cleaved to your cause?'

'I was told he had knowledge of our faith. Litochlev told me.'

'What did you do when you were with this miller, this Kaliban? What was your talk about?'

'Our talk was of God. He told me his people were in sore need of help, for they were weak in the faith. I assured him the Lord God would give them strength.'

'And what else?'

'I don't remember.'

'Who else did you speak with? Who were you going to see? What others have knowledge of your faith?'

'I know none.'

That was two and a half centuries ago. It's exactly the same now, right down to the inaccuracies in the report. How well I know it! They are incapable of setting down names correctly.

I took a careful look around the tennis-courts. Two mothers were pushing prams alongside the lace fence. No one else was in sight. But there was a delivery van parked at the top of the street. The spies could easily be secreted inside with their cameras. I studied the vehicle. Though I couldn't see inside, it appeared cold and empty.

The street I now entered was a dead end—a perfect trap. I had to walk past three small villas before I got to the building where Nicholas lived. I looked around once more. A snow-covered Saab was parked by the kerb opposite his house—but that belonged here. A short distance down the street, however, I saw a caravan that hadn't been here two months ago.

That frightened me.

I don't feel a great affinity for those who smuggled books into this country before the Edict of Toleration of 1781, subversive books which the authorities of that time thought should have been burned. Or at least—unlike those book smugglers of old—I don't hold printed paper in such high regard. The things we write are no longer prompted by God and therefore they are as we ourselves are: good and evil, sometimes wise, and often foolish. Censorship may add to a book's appeal, but it can add nothing to its wisdom.

I walked over to the caravan. The snow around it was untouched, and the boarded window on the windward side was completely covered with sticky snow; there was no opening through which a hidden camera might peer. I went up to the main entrance to Nicholas's building. I was just reaching out to ring the bell when I realized I'd forgotten to take a final look around. I withdrew my hand, stared a moment longer at the column of name-plates by the gate, even though I normally pay no attention to them. Then I turned around slowly. The windows of the building across the street were dark, the curtains drawn. If anyone were hiding behind them, I had no hope of seeing. An elderly lady leading a reddish boxer was walking in my direction from the tiny park. The dog stopped and plunged his muzzle into the snow; the lady bent over him. I could still pretend that I hadn't found the name I was looking for and stroll over to the main entrance of the next apartment building, but I suddenly felt disgusted at the comedy I'd been playing to this innocent old woman. I pressed the doorbell.

Ten years ago my wife and I went on a cruise to Israel, our first visit to that part of the world. The trip had been my wife's idea and she had triumphed over the customary reluctance of officials to permit such journeys to happen. She had moved about the ship in a state of rapture. She was delighted to discover that there were several Israeli citizens on board and she immediately set about to make friends. Her favourite was a black-haired, dark-skinned Levantine woman, who reminded me of the gypsies that ran carnival merry-go-rounds. She taught my wife Israeli songs and won her heart. It turned out that the woman's gesture was not entirely altruistic. As we neared Haifa, she came forward with a request. She was taking her mother a small rug from Greece. Nothing special, but customs officials tend to be more difficult with their own citizens than with foreigners. Could my wife take the carpet through customs for her? The Levantine thrust at my wife a roll of something that weighed more than all our baggage put together. It was carefully wrapped in dark brown paper.

I asked my wife if she was aware that the parcel might well contain a disassembled machine-gun or cocaine or a stolen Leonardo or gold bars, but she was positive the parcel contained nothing but a carpet. Why should her new friend lie to her? I tried to explain that she could be the victim of a professional smuggler and that it would be prudent either to return the parcel or at least to unwrap it and see what was really inside.

My wife said that she would never stoop to open someone else's parcel.

Meanwhile the boat had docked and the owner of the parcel had vanished into the crowd of passengers. We could leave the parcel on the boat, throw it overboard or carry it through customs. My wife was never particularly strong, but she refused to let me carry the parcel because I didn't trust its contents. She heaved it on to her shoulder and, bending under its weight, walked down the gangplank.

We entered an enormous hall where there was a crowd of people, some in uniform and some not. It became clear that the most thorough customs inspection I had ever witnessed was taking place. We approached a long counter where, under the customs officers' gaze, people were being asked to empty their suitcases, hand luggage and purses. I watched with astonishment the transformation this wrought in my wife. She straightened up so that the heavy roll on her shoulders seemed almost to float, and then with an expression of confidence and certainty that only the utter absence of guilt can produce, she stepped up to the counter. When she was asked what was in the parcel on her shoulder, she replied that it was a carpet for an acquaintance.

They waved us through the barrier.

We will never know what it was we were actually carrying, but I understood then what sort of face a good smuggler should put on. I also knew that given my anxieties, I would never make the grade.

Angela came to the gate, greeted the woman with the dog and held her mouth up to be kissed.

On a bench in the hall inside their flat were three bags, crammed full. 'These are for you,' she said. 'Would you like tea?'

It would have been impolite to pick up the bags and scoot out of the door with them, as I had hoped to do. I could see Angela wanted me to sit and talk with her for a while. She must have been bored, spending all those hours alone in a strange flat on the edge of a strange city in the middle of a strange land and among people whose language she did not understand. I peered into one of the bags and saw the flash of shiny covers, but I overcame the desire to kneel down beside the bag and begin rummaging inside. This time I had been bold enough to give Nicholas a list of some books I particularly wanted to read. Had he managed to get them? I pulled the zip shut and went to wait for the tea.

Angela came in with a silver tray holding a teapot. She poured me a cup of *mate*.

Angela is Argentinian, and whenever I find myself near her, I'm always subliminally aware of the distance she has travelled to appear before me. Between us lay jungles and wide rivers, the pampas; a landscape I will almost certainly never behold.

She sat down opposite me, poured herself a glass of wine, tossed back her long black hair so that it fell over her left shoulder down to her waist, removed her glasses and looked at me intently. The colour and shape of her eyes revealed some of her ancestors to be Indians. Angela should have married a poet, not a businessman. Had she done so, either she would have been happy or she would have discovered that poets are people just as businessmen are, and that you can be as happy or as miserable with them as you can with anyone else.

I knew that her journey away from her country—and thus to Nicholas—had not been easy.

Borders, or rather their guardians, present barriers not only to smugglers and fleeing criminals. Of course, the more ruthless the guardians, the more inventive and daring those who feel themselves imprisoned by the border guards become. They dig tunnels under the walls or barbed wire, they sew together hot-air balloons from bed-sheets, they construct trolleys to run along high-tension wires, and they fling themselves against the barbed wire, knowing that they will most likely be shot. They undergo all this in order to carry themselves across the invisible borderline, over the prison wall. For a moment, a man transforms himself into a thing, turns himself into a piece of contraband, in the hope that he may never again be an object of arbitrary power.

Angela said that her escape from her country had been less dramatic. Her friends got her a false passport. But she still occasionally dreamed about a moment when an armed guard at the border takes her passport, looks at the photograph, then at her face, and nods to someone invisible. From a concealed place, some monster with foam dripping from his fangs comes roaring out, grabs her and drags her off. Sometimes she is taken to the very border, which runs along a narrow path on a ridge of mountain peaks. On each side an abyss drops away, and she knows that they will fling her down on one side or the other.

She poured me more tea, more wine for herself, and began to talk about her life before she left her country.

Her father was a colonel in the army. Their household had servants, but it was loveless. Her father behaved in a military fashion: he was courtly and selfless to others, but arrogant and unyielding towards his own. He expected Angela's mother to ensure that everything was done to his satisfaction. When she became seriously ill, he took it as a personal affront. He ignored his wife's suffering, refused to change his ways or even to give up drinking with his companions. He was drunk when she died. After she was gone, he began to miss her, or at least to miss the care she took of him. He drank more, hung around the casinos, and eventually squandered his house and his reputation. He moved into a tiny, ramshackle structure on the fringes of Rosario. They let the maid go. Angela was only twelve at the time, but she devoted herself to her father, making sure he always found everything in order, that he always had his evening meal. She wanted to recreate a feeling of home—but he scarcely took any notice. Except once, when he came back from the casino in a particularly elated mood. He pulled a fistful of banknotes from his pocket, probably money he had won at baccarat or poker, and forced her to accept them, saying she deserved it. He didn't understand her at all.

I had no idea why Angela was telling this to me today, but I listened to her attentively, and would have listened with more compassion had my mental clock not reminded me of the danger of staying too long. A professional smuggler, I felt, wouldn't linger knowing his mortal enemies could be approaching.

The poverty they found themselves in, Angela continued, had a profound effect on her brother. He studied law, but then left school and began to work in the unions. Several times she went to see him address meetings. He captivated his audience like the lead actor in a drama. But this wasn't theatre. One day her brother didn't come home. She never heard from him again. For a long time, she consoled herself with the thought that he was in hiding somewhere, but then one by one his companions began to disappear, most of them without a trace. They only ever found one of them. His mutilated body was washed up by the Paraná River. The corpse had its eyes poked out and there were patches of burned skin on its chest. From that day on, waking or sleeping, Angela could not get out of her mind an image of her brother with his arms and legs bound together, and strange men beating and torturing him. She saw the iron rod being driven into his eyes.

I could see her pain and suffering. And instead of taking advantage of the falling darkness and creeping away with the bags of books, I reached out my hand to stroke her long hair, forgetting that in ancient myths, long hair was a harbinger of danger.

It seems to me that there is a raging demon, a monstrous cloud of our own creation, wandering the earth. Its shadow falls on different parts of the world, sometimes darkening whole continents. The cloud had been suspended above Angela's country. God knows where it would stop next.

'I had to run away,' she whispered, as though she were apologizing. 'They wipe out entire families, and even burn down their houses.' At first it was not easy, then she met Nicholas. Nicholas is an exceptional person; perhaps he shouldn't be a businessman at all, because he has a need to help others. Did I know that his mother knew Gandhi personally, and took part in most of his non-violent actions?

Eventually, what had to happen did happen—outside I heard the sound of an approaching car.

Angela ran to the window. 'Nicholas,' she announced. 'It looks like he's being followed. And I kept you here so long!'

It no longer made any sense to hurry. I sat talking to Nicholas for a while, then arranged to stop by for the bags in three days so I wouldn't be showing up here too often. I

25

thanked Nicholas for everything he was doing for me. He smiled. 'They're only books,' he said, and we parted.

The men who had tailed Nicholas were waiting in a car by the tennis-courts. When I walked out through the gate, they turned their headlights on, perhaps to let me know they were there, or perhaps just to get a better look at me.

Through the windows of the neighbouring houses the blue light of television screens glowed. 'Why do people watch television?' Nicholas had once asked me in amazement. 'They must know they're being lied to.'

I suddenly realized why he smuggled in all those books. Though a foreigner, he divined that those books—mostly written by Czechs, and banned by our overlords—belonged to us. Like his mother, he believed in non-violent resistance.

During the war the rooms in which we were imprisoned were patrolled by three especially well-trained spies. Accompanied by an armed man, these Three Fates, or Three Sowbugs, as they were called, would usually sweep in early in the morning, before the men had gone to work, and search our rooms for contraband. They emptied suitcases, burrowed into sheets, slit open straw mattresses and eiderdowns, felt coatsleeves, poured sugar, ersatz coffee or other luxuries on to the floor, and even prised up floorboards. They rarely discovered anything. But anyone found guilty was sent away to a place where only gas chambers awaited them.

One morning they came bursting in on us. I was still asleep and when I saw them in that first moment of awakening, anxiety gripped me by the throat. I had to get up, dress, all the time looking on while they worked. I knew all too well where the contraband was hidden—the roll of banknotes burned a hole in the wood and fell to my feet like ash—but I also knew that I must not look in that direction. So I stared at the wall in front of me, and occasionally stole a glance at those three women absorbed in their unwomanly work. Sidelong, I saw them only as strange, moving monsters with fuzzy outlines.

Until they approached the sideboard that is; then I suddenly saw them sharply: three fat ugly old women, one of whom was just opening the fateful drawer. I remember noticing clearly her chubby hands and realizing at that moment that not one of the women could have reached into our hiding place. I felt the joyous laughter of relief rising within me. I was able to suppress it, but it rang inside me all the time those women were rummaging among our things. It was a laughter which, on that occasion at least, ushered death from our door.

I walked casually back to my car. I might have left it there, walked past the tennis-court and run down some of the steep lanes on the hillside, but if they were determined to follow me there was little I could do to escape. Moreover, I didn't have a single illegal item on me. I wasn't carrying rice or cocoa or writing-paper. But the definition of contraband changes with the wandering of that monstrous cloud. The current definition took greatest exception to ideas, that is, to anything that could disseminate them. Instead of being entrusted to three fat women, the search for contraband was now conducted by entire special departments provided with expensive but effective technology. Everything was done to ensure that not a single impulse of the spirit nor the sound of pure speech could ever occur in the territory they controlled.

Normally, I don't even notice the activities of these departments, or at least I try not to let them get to me. I don't want them to smother my world. Occasionally, however, they make an appearance. I open my eyes in the morning and see them slitting open my books, dusting white powder on my floor, reading my letters. Or I hear about the flames they leave behind in their footsteps. Or they emerge from the darkness and shine their lights on me, reminders of death with whom they are allied. At such moments, I am possessed by a will to resist; I must do something quickly— to show myself that I am still alive, that the world in which I move is still human. I am prepared to weave in and out of the lights that pursue me, to seek out a secret hiding place, and when it seems at last that I have deceived their vigilance, I hear inside me the laughter of relief.

I knocked the snow off my boots, swung my arms back and forth to let them know that my hands were empty. I unlocked the car and got in. I had to drive past them; there was no other way out. They started off behind me.

I shouldn't have cared. There was nothing in the car but a basket of damp laundry my wife had picked up. They could have noted down my registration number before I drove off.

So why were they following me? Did they know something about those occasional bags full of books? Or did they not know, but suspect something else? Or was it that they didn't know, and suspected nothing in particular, but were merely running a routine check on Nicholas to see who he associated with? Who did Nicholas associate with? I had no idea.

They were keeping close. They had a better, newer car than I did, and it was equipped with a two-way radio they could use to call for help, or to send instructions ahead to stop me at the first major intersection. Nevertheless, I longed to escape them.

I drove slowly through the fresh drifts of snow. At the first junction I braked, and my followers came to a halt behind me. The street I was intending to take climbed steeply up to the top of a hill. Several cars were descending towards the junction, and I waited until they were very close, then I moved out, stepped on the accelerator, and roared up the hill. Halfway up, I looked around. They hadn't managed to get away; they were still waiting until the cars descending the slippery hill had cleared the junction. I managed to reach the next corner before I saw them in the distance.

For a while I wound through some narrow back streets, constantly turning corners until, yes, there was a building I knew, with a wide gate leading to a large inner courtyard. As far as I could remember there was, or had been, a small park inside. There was even a bench hidden under the trees where my first love and I had necked. I drove through the gate. The trees had grown and there were more cars than I remembered, but I managed to find an empty space and parked in it. I walked back to the gate, and watched the street outside. They was no sign of them.

I got into my car again and, on a sudden whim, drove directly to the place where they would least expect to find me.

I stopped in front of Nicholas's house.

'What an idea,' said Angela, surprised to see me. 'You'd have probably tried to walk across those planks, too,' she added, referring to our conversation about Cortázar. Nicholas took one of the bags and carried it out for me.

I threw the bags on the floor between the front and back seats, then got in and drove off, taking the route I had followed a while before, except that instead of turning up the hill, I drove down it towards my home. The only problem was that to get there I had to drive right across the city. If they wanted to, they could certainly find me somewhere along the way. Returning for the bags probably hadn't been a very wise thing to do. I could still hear Angela's excited voice evoking images of bloody faces, tortured bodies and burning homes.

Night was falling and the snow was beginning to freeze. As I drove around a corner the car went into a dangerous skid. All it needed was a car coming in the other direction: a collision would have brought out the very people I wanted to avoid. It was better not to think about it. A pair of headlights glared in my rear-view mirror. Was it them? What should I do now that I was really carrying smuggled goods? I drove on, watching the mirror. I tried, without success, to determine how many people were in the car, and what kind of people they were. Not looking where I was driving, I hit a large pothole in the middle of the road; the suspension complained and the basket of laundry slid forward and bumped into the back of my seat. I slowed down. I was in danger of becoming paranoid. I turned on to a main street that would take me to the river. There were several cars behind me now, as well as in front. It made no sense to try to keep track of them.

Last spring, outside the house where I live, two workmen were repairing a fence. They were a product of our era. They drank beer, stood by the fence and enjoyed the spring sun, delighted that they'd been sent to work in such a pretty and remote part of town. They managed to spread work that should have taken two days over the whole week. Occasionally they would ring my doorbell and offer to drink coffee with me, or something stronger. One day, when the

30

bell rang just before noon, I assumed it was them again and toyed with the idea of pretending I hadn't heard them.

Outside the door stood a short, pale man. Even before I spoke, I could see he was a foreigner. He wanted to be reassured that he wasn't putting me in any danger by coming in. Once inside the door, he asked me if I was always so closely watched. He'd been trying to visit me for three days.

He was a young priest and he'd smuggled in several books for me that were as innocent as he was. When he saw the two men lounging about, never actually working but never going far from my gate, he assumed they were secret policemen. He'd buried the books under some leaves in a nearby wood.

On the way to the wood I explained his mistake to him.

He laughed and, as if to apologize, remarked that when a man enters the kingdom of Satan, he expects to see devils at every turn.

Paranoia is something that diseased spirits succumb to, but if we live in a diseased world it requires ever greater efforts to banish sinister expectations.

I saw them from a distance. The yellow car was parked by the edge of the road, and one of the uniformed officers was signalling to me in the regulation manner with a luminous baton.

Of course. Why should they chase me when they could simply lie in wait? The road was like a mountain pass—the only route a smuggler can take, and where he is most frequently apprehended.

I stopped.

'Road check. Could I see your documents , please?'

I turned off the engine and got out of the car. The road

31

was covered in slush; the salt truck must already have gone by. The man in the uniform leafed through my I.D.

The advantage that Jiřík Vostrý—arrested two and a half centuries ago with three books—had over me is that I had three bags of books. My only advantage might have been that I was older and therefore more experienced. I knew that I should speak as little as possible, mention no names, never get into an argument or try to persuade them of anything, even if they looked as though they were listening with interest or sympathy. What a person says in good confidence is bound to be turned against him or, what is worse, against those close to him.

'Who were you with in Pardubice, and why did you go there?' they asked Jiřík Vostrý.

'I went there to do trade in textiles,' was the excuse he came up with.

I was coming from the laundry, but this would not explain anything if I was caught with the evidence.

About a month ago, they sent a young woman to jail for a year for typing copies of several books like the ones now in my possession. Her books would not have quarter-filled one of my bags. She had two small children; usually the court took such factors into account and handed down a suspended sentence. On this occasion her crime had obviously been of such a serious and dangerous nature that it warranted more.

'You were with someone, and also brought some books with you,' they said to Jiřík Vostrý.

'I was with no one, nor did I bring any books with me. I was searched at the customs house.'

'Who brought you here to the jail?'

'Some four men.'

'What did you say to them on the way?'

'I said that in our country we do not bow to the cross, for that is idolatry.'

In his zeal he had said more than he should have and they—for it is part of their nature—reported everything. The smuggler of long ago had a difficult time; he had also entrusted his jailer with the secret letter.

'Is it true that from the magistrate's jail you sent a letter alerting someone to danger?'

'My message was that if they had books they ought to put them away.'

'And whom did you so advise?'

'Litochleb and Kladivo and also Kaliban, the miller from Sedliště.'

'Is this the message?' [*Exhibitae eidem schedulae, quae in allegatis lit. A et B videntur.*]

'It is.'

'Through whose offices did you write and send this letter?'

'The jailer led me to believe he would deliver it.'

'You must have been here bearing books before; and you must also know of people who cleave to your faith.'

'I know nothing; nor of anyone.'

The worst crime of all was to circulate forbidden books. Three young men from the place where Jiřík Vostrý was apprehended 247 years ago were recently given a total of six and a half years in prison for the same activity.

'Aren't you employed anywhere?' asked the officer leafing through my I.D. He seemed surprised. He was rather heavily built. There was a small moustache under his nose.

'I'm free-lance.'

He looked at me suspiciously, as if this was the first time

he had heard the expression. Perhaps he simply did not like the word 'free'. Could I prove that? he asked.

I handed him a piece of paper confirming that I was covered by social insurance.

He pretended to examine the paper, then folded it and handed it back to me. He kept my other documents. 'Have you had anything to drink, sir?'

I hadn't. I had no intention of tempting fate any more than necessary.

He put on an expression that suggested he did not entirely believe me. Then he asked me to turn on the headlights.

They were working properly.

Could he see my first-aid kit?

I would have to open the back door. I saw with relief that the laundry basket almost completely covered the bags containing the books. But in my excitement I could not remember where I kept my first-aid kit. I groped haphazardly under the seat, trying to shield the books with my body.

The uniformed men watched with interest. 'Do you know what they call the first-aid kit, sir?' the one who had not previously spoken asked. 'I'll tell you. They call it "handy". And do you know why?'

I was forced to listen to the etymology of the word 'handy'.

'Why aren't you carrying your laundry in the boot?' said the first officer, suddenly bringing the conversation to its point.

About five years ago, my theatrical agent from the United States came to see me. She was an older woman who had been born in Europe and had experienced all that continent's cultural benefits, including a concentration camp. In other words she was well equipped to understand the course of events that had determined my life. I needed to send a letter to a friend in Switzerland. The content of the letter was harmless even with regard to our vigilant laws, but the notion that a third party might read it disturbed me. I asked my American friend if she would take the letter across the border for me. At the airport, however, she was subjected to a thorough search. When she was forced to take the letter from her pocket, she tore open the envelope and, before they were able to snatch the letter from her hand, she put it into her mouth and, before the customs officers' eyes, chewed and swallowed it.

Could I eat three bags of books?

My only consolation was the knowledge that the worst cloud had already passed over our country: they wouldn't put out my eyes.

I finally found the first-aid kit and handed it to the officer with the moustache. 'My spare tyre is in the boot.' I said, by way of explanation.

'Could you show us?'

The first-aid kit under a pile of rags; bags on the floor; a basket full of laundry on the seat; the spare tyre in the boot. Sir, there's something about you we don't like. Put the spare where it belongs. Put the first-aid kit in the glove-compartment. And take those bags and put them in the boot. Here, we'll help you. My goodness, sir, these bags weigh a ton. What on earth do you have in them?

Both officers leaned into the boot and tested the depth of the tread on my spare tyre. 'I'm not surprised you keep this hidden, sir. When was the last time you put any air in it?'

'A few days ago.' I could not understand why they were

putting off the moment when they would display interest in what they were really after.

'A few days ago. Would you mind checking the pressure for us?'

I had a gauge in a compartment next to the steering-wheel. Regardless of the pressure it always gave a reading of two atmospheres.

'You're in luck,' one of them said, looking sceptically at the needle, which was pointing reliably to the two.

'You may close the boot,' said the other one.

'Get back in to the car,' said the first.

Suddenly I understood the mystery of this pointless and rather protracted game. Their orders were to stop me and detain me. The officers who were really interested in me and my contraband had, for some reason, been held up. When they arrived and saw my bags, they would be delighted: Surely you don't mean to tell me someone put these bags in your car without your knowledge, sir?

Indeed, such a claim would not sound credible. Where, then, had I got the bags from? It's odd that although we've had 247 years to work on it, we have not yet come up with even a slightly probable reply to a highly probable question.

What alibi could I come up with on the spur of the moment? I had brought them from home, where a stranger had left them. But why would I have them in my car now? In a rush, I weighed various unconvincing explanations in my mind. I just put them there and then forgot about them? I wanted to store them at a relative's flat, then changed my mind? I was on my way to hand them in to the authorities?

He opens one of them. I realize I've made another irretrievable mistake. I'd spent the whole afternoon with Angela and without so much as glancing into the three bags. Unlike Jiřík Vostrý, I didn't know what books I had on my hands. I might have had magazines in the bags; they tend to get very upset about magazines.

So you're bringing them from home. Well, what about this one? And with great distaste, he spells out the name of the author and the title. Is this your book?

It's my book.

Who did you get it from?

I was given it. That's not against the law.

And did you read it?

I have a lot of books I haven't managed to read yet.

You might at least have unwrapped it, he says, looking at me disapprovingly. You've left it all wrapped up like a piece of cheese. Not only that, you've got two copies of it. He rummages around in the bag some more and corrects himself: Three! Where were you taking these bags?

For years now I've had a running debate with those who liken books to explosives or drugs. During that time, I've prepared a lengthy speech in which I defend freedom of creation, which is part of a dignified and truthful life. But I have never had the occasion to deliver the speech. The temptation to do it now is powerful. But I mustn't succumb. To entrust my own convictions to these men in uniform would be just as silly now as it was two and a half centuries ago.

The two of them were talking something over; perhaps they were radioing in a query. It seemed undignified to watch.

When the others, whom they are clearly waiting for, come, I should at least pose them a question: Why, by what authority, do you of all people, who are so convinced that the life of man is limited to this insignificant little patch of time when he dwells upon the earth, transform our lives into a suffocating mixture of lies, filth and repression?

No one else comes, but the two uniformed officers return to my car.

'Sir, are you aware of which traffic regulation you've broken?' They wait for a moment, and then the one with the moustache tries to help out: 'When you stopped, did you turn out your lights?'

'Was I driving without my headlights on?' It was not my negligence that astonished me, but the fact that they had spent so long in coming up with something so trivial.

'That's right, sir. And in this weather. Do you know that this could have cost you your license?' The two of them watched me, and when I didn't protest, the one with the moustache asked: 'Are you willing to pay us a hundred crown fine on the spot?'

I took out a big, green banknote and then, with dismay, I realized that I was handing it over far too willingly.

They gave me the requisite ticket from their booklet, and wished me a good trip. From their expressions I could tell that this had made them feel good; they'd done some useful work.

My wife was waiting impatiently, afraid that something bad had happened. We carried the bags into the room, and I unwrapped the books, which smelled of newness. The titles promised the intellectual consolation of pure, original language.

I opened one of the volumes, but I was unable to concentrate on the contents.

Nicholas had indeed bought two, or even three copies of some of the books. That meant that the next day, I would be a messenger and go to Morašice, to Lubný, and then to see Kaliban in Kamenné Sedliště.

What was Jiřík Vostrý's fate? They let him go, of course. The eighteenth century wasn't the middle ages, after all. The archives have preserved a later report of him. The incorrigible smuggler—now thirty years older—was apprehended again. From the interrogation it is clear that in the intervening years Vostrý had not been idle. At one time he had been imprisoned at Lytomyšl where he 'remained for three years less eight weeks.' (We will never know how often, during the rest of those years, he had successfully evaded capture.) He was released for good behaviour, and he rushed home to his wife and children.

No record has been preserved of how he fared in his last trial, but everything suggests that this time he didn't get off so easily. The Edict of Toleration, which made book smuggling pointless for the next two hundred years, was soon to be law. If only Vostrý had been twenty years younger.

But such is the deceitful game of history. People sacrifice their time, put their freedom and even their lives at risk just to cross, or eliminate, borders they know are absurd. And then—often soon afterwards—in a single instant, as a consequence of a single decree, the border disappears without a trace.

In revealing their transience, these borders also seem to expose the futility of all the former sacrifices. But perhaps it is really the other way around: if it weren't for those who, in their battle against borders, risked everything, the borders would not disappear, but would become a net and all of us trapped insects inside.

Suddenly my wife thought of something: 'Did you bring in the laundry basket?'

The basket was still in the car.

It was no longer snowing outside, and stars were shining through ragged, fast flying clouds. The snow sparkled in the light of the streetlamps. In the distance, I could hear a police siren.

I unlocked the garage and pulled the laundry basket out of the car. It seemed unusually heavy and, when I walked up the stairs, something inside it clinked metallically.

I felt like lifting up the laundry to see what was hidden underneath it, but I managed to control my curiosity. I set the basket down on the dining-room table as carefully as possible and went away to read.

The Painter's Story

THIS MORNING, I decided to go to the country. A nice day was forecast, my wife would be at work till evening and, anyway, I didn't feel like writing. Recently, a realization that everything has already been written has made me despondent. All the stories have already been told or filmed or recorded and, even with a hundred heads, I would never discover most of what others have already recounted.

This winter my cousin, who is a painter, offered us the use of her cottage in the town of M. for the year, as she was moving to the other end of the country. My cousin is a beautiful, petite woman, and so is her house. Its one disadvantage is its location: it stands by a busy road where all day long cars and trucks and tractors chase each other up and down. However, the same train that blows its whistle under our window in the city takes us there. All we have to do is pack a book and a sandwich and walk down to the station in time for the next train. The journey takes an hour. The best thing about the cottage, my cousin assured me, were the neighbours. Right next door, for example, an interesting young gypsy couple had moved in.

My cousin's cottage is full of paintings, small paintings, as diminutive as their creator. Most of them depict strange creatures—monsters, witches and vampires—riding around in fancy aerodynamic cars, crawling through the subway or peering through windows into rooms where terrified lovers cower in each other's arms. Her drawers and shelves are crammed with paints, pencils and charcoal sticks.

As a boy I was determined—that is if I didn't become a doctor or a writer—to learn how to paint. I longed to acquire the skill to represent the world in colour. But my life didn't unfold as I had imagined it would. During the war I wasn't allowed to go to school; the only branches of human activity I learned anything about were penal servitude and mass murder. And this happened to me at the most impressionable age, when one finds mystery wherever one looks. Nevertheless it was during the war, when I was interned by the Nazis, that quartos of paper and a set of watercolour paints first came into my possession. The watercolours were the cheapest kind—twelve different shades in a little tin tray—but I soon discovered that the colours could be mixed to make new ones. I painted what I saw: barrack walls and yards, food lines, trains transporting miserable wretches with suitcases and gunnysacks (stuffed, in vain hope, with feather pillows), wooden shacks where they produced mica, and brick fortifications. I had no idea how to handle perspective, but I noticed that the long barrack walls seemed to converge in the distance, so I drew them that way and they at once looked more realistic. I was so excited by my discovery that I drew only houses and walls until I ran out of paper.

After the war, I still believed I would become a painter. The barracks had vanished from my life, and it was more than buildings that attracted me now; it was the faces of girls in my school. In social studies classes or during singing lessons—for which I had no talent—I tried, under my desk, to capture the appearance of those graceful creatures who shared the enclosed world of the classroom with me. Word of my talent got around. Soon the girls were even willing to pose for me—clothed, of course—as long as I gave them the finished painting. Portraiture thus brought me close to the beings for whom I longed; could I have dreamed a finer destiny than to be a painter?

It was eight-thirty in the morning, the train would leave in half an hour, but from the moment I made up my mind to go, I was restless. I locked the door and strolled down our long street to the station. About half-way there, I passed the house that Mr Vondrák had been building during the past five years. Mr Vondrák was a remarkable man, for he was a master of all the necessary trades. He performed the role of bricklayer and carpenter, roofer, electrician, plumber and painter. I had watched him from a distance all those years, waiting for the moment when I would see at least one contractor on the site, but he even stuccoed the walls himself. Sometimes his wife would be there, but she seldom worked, and then only as his assistant. Of course he noticed me; we always greeted each other and sometimes exchanged a few sentences. He would usually complain about something that wasn't available.

A short distance from the level crossing a dove was sitting hunched over in the middle of the pavement. There was something strange about where and how it was sitting, and when I got closer I saw that it was dead. I felt saddened by its dismal end on a filthy pavement. The loneliness of its dying—how will that be any different from the loneliness of my own death? And the pavement—how does that differ from a hospital cell where a priest is not allowed to visit the dying, and relatives are unwelcome?

It is inappropriate to talk of death today. It's as though we're afraid it will threaten the majesty of life. Or is it because there have never been so many desecrated funerals, or so many corpses disposed of with no funeral whatever?

In earlier times, people mourned the animal they had to kill and they shrouded their dead and sent them off with a prayer or at least a ceremony of some kind, for they wished peace to the departing soul. In our century, they have often uncovered the dead and paraded them before the eyes of the mob.

For a decent burial, as for a decent life, you need at the very least some basic human compassion. Antigone gave up her life, but buried her brother with honour. Centuries later, her story still moves us, though we may also feel astonishment at her sacrifice. We no longer see that she died not for the sake of a proper funeral, but for the dignity of human life. How can we understand it, when we have stood by while the bodies of countless brothers and cousins, whom they have tortured, beaten, shot and gassed, have been thrown into common holes in the ground, like garbage? When we have looked on in silence while they scattered the bones and ashes of others over fields and tossed them into rivers? When we have pretended not to hear their voices crying for help?

A dignified funeral and a marked grave express our will to preserve the identity of a person. We erect a stone on which we carve a name and a few numbers, but in fact we are trying to maintain the shape of a former life, a single unrepeatable story. When compassion and the commandment that life should be lived in dignity have been lost, where awareness of the past is lost, there are no stories, there are only cries of horror.

Apart from my cousin, I have several friends who paint. One of them, Karel, caused me to give up all thought of getting any work done today. Yesterday he showed up unexpectedly with a bottle of Rakije he'd brought back from Yugoslavia, poured himself a drink—I refused one—and at once began telling me the depressing story of his trip.

Karel is a thin, gloomy man with a thick artist's beard, the fanatical look of a visionary who has seen the coming apocalypse, and the pale complexion of those who sleep during the day. When he speaks, his voice has the quiet whine of the winter wind blowing through the garden at night, which accentuates his accusatory tone. 'I've been to a lot of galleries, but it never hit me the way it did down there. Do you know where Montenegro is?'

I said I knew roughly where it was.

It's a land of black mountains, he said, and desolate valleys populated by farmers, wine-growers and the occasional shepherd. Sometimes, in those valleys, you come across a town with mosques, minarets and souks. In one such place, in the former royal palace, they'd established a big art gallery. 'I went in just because I had some time to kill and it was terribly hot outside, and when I go through the halls I can't believe what I'm seeing. At a glance there is Braque, Rouault, Munch and Ernst, and over there—I can't believe it—Pollock, Hartung and Reinhardt. They've got Andy Warhol! I look again and I see some of our painters too. From a distance I can see Rada, Filla, a late Muzika. They've given over a whole wall to Medek at the top of his form. Then I put my glasses on to look at the signatures. And you know who had signed them? Some guys called Cvetkovič and Stankovič and Toškovič, one Mrdjan, a Danice. And suddenly, the thing I was most afraid of happened: I found myself hanging there. I couldn't remember when I'd painted this picture, but it was me about five years ago. However, I'd signed my name Kavurič-Kurtovič. I've seen it before,' he complained, 'in Munich and Warsaw and Budapest, everyone hanging there, except they'd confused the signatures. But the tragedy didn't hit me until I was down there in Montenegro. I tell you, my friend, it's all over with painting. There's nothing new to invent. Everyone is ripping off somebody else. A hundred people line up for every idea, and even then they haven't a clue the idea's a hundred years old. A single Mondrian or a single Newman: fantastic—you fall to your knees in wonder; two are OK, and you can even take three, but when you see a hundred of those monochrome canvasses that look like a housepainter did them, each crossed with a white or maybe a black horizontal line, you feel like throwing up, or throwing yourself out of a thirteenth-storey window. It's the end of art. There's nothing behind it: no ideas, no experience, no invention—forget authenticity, that's a joke anyway. These guys are pure con artists, and the only people who call it art are the critics who are just as dishonest.'

That evening, when he'd left, I got out the book of Ecclesiastes which, as I've discovered many times, has everything in it. Sure enough, there it was:

All things are full of labour; man cannot utter it . . . Is there anything whereof it may be said, See, this is new?

It has already been of old time, which was before us.

But so many had written in the same vein, both before and after Ecclesiastes. I admire them for it—Seneca and Suetonius, Chekhov, Wilder, Böll, Dürrenmatt, Greene and Deml—even though they've deprived me of my last crumb of hope that I might still find a story to tell that no one else has told. I admire them for not giving up, for searching the grey tide of words and constantly reiterated tales for undiscovered droplets in that sea in which they stood, as I do, on their toes from dawn to dusk, keeping their eyes and noses, at least, above the surface.

At first, though, I did not care for stories; I was convinced I would become a painter. I had oils, an easel, frames and a roll of canvas. I tried to draw everything that I saw, or even imagined. By now, I had seen the work of real masters, in reproductions and even in the original, but their achievements did not trouble me; the fact that the face I painted was at least a distant reminder of a real face, that my alley of birch trees might have been recognizable as such, filled me with so much satisfaction that I felt myself a companion of the greats.

The girl I was going with at the time loved poetry, white water, quiet corners in parks and Van Gogh, especially his sunflowers. A day before her eighteenth birthday I had a wonderful idea. I had a reproduction of 'The Sunflowers' at home: what if I made her a copy in real oils?

I stretched a canvas and set to work. There wasn't much time, so I decided not to bother with a sketch or an outline, but to start right in painting a flower. I worked my way down towards the vase. Before I started, I had felt there would be nothing simpler than to imitate the energetic, expansive strokes of Van Gogh's brush. Oddly enough, however, my sunflower did not want to look like the one in the reproduction, and the vase refused to fit into the space I had left for it. Shortly before midnight, my brother peered into the kitchen, which I had turned into a studio. He was seven years younger than me and, as a future scholar of the exact sciences, he had a contempt for art. When he saw my desperate attempt to force the vase on to the canvas, he pushed me aside, drew a grid of squares over both the canvas and the reproduction, and then began, mechanically, to fill them in with the appropriate colours and shapes.

The next day, it was his copy of the sunflowers that I gave to my girl-friend. I reaped the praise that did not belong to me and was crushed by the experience. Suddenly, my paintings did not have enough space, enough movement. I wasn't able to say exactly what it was I lacked—perhaps it was narrative. I put the box of paints away in the cellar and, until this spring, I never painted another picture.

Although it was only Friday morning, the train was full of young men and women in army surplus overalls or dirty jeans, off for a weekend ramble in the country. Eventually, I found a seat. Across from me sat three young men who, together, were holding a girl on their laps. A fourth was cradling a guitar. On the overhead racks bottles of beer poked out of worn rucksacks. When they got to their shack, if they had one, the girl would make goulash, and they'd all start to drink the beer. They'd play the guitar and sing songs as they got drunk. Those who got tired of the beer would then make love to the girl. The girl had dishevelled, peroxided hair that half covered her expressionless face. That morning, or more probably the night before, she had outlined her lips with vulgar red lipstick; the red varnish was chipping off her finger-nails. Her hands were dirty, and so was her denim dress. The boys were talking big, tough-guy talk, while she giggled. When one of them touched her breasts, she slapped his hand. But she did not get off their knees.

Twenty years ago, I would have wanted to get to know them. By then, I had stopped painting, but my longing to capture the world around me remained. I began to write. I was obsessed with a desire to know new people, and everywhere I sensed the presence of fresh and exciting stories. I trembled with eagerness to add to the sea that is threatening to engulf us all.

Ecclesiastes talks about this kind of obsession:

The words of a wise man's mouth are gracious; but the lips of a fool will swallow up himself. The beginning of the words of his mouth is foolishness: and the end of his talk is mischievous madness. A fool is also full of words. . . Of making many books there is no end.

If only he had known . . .

Of course there are people who probably don't even have time to observe the sea that is preparing to sweep our humanity away. This occurred to me when, on Saturdays or Sundays I would see Mr Vondrák moving about his house in blue overalls. The overalls had gradually faded as the house grew. Sometimes I heard him whistling somewhere inside the building. It seemed enormous, and I wanted to ask him how it felt to build something that large all by himself, but I was too shy. It wasn't until last month that, for no apparent reason, he suddenly invited me inside and showed me his work. The floor of the entrance hall was covered with smooth, carefully laid linoleum. The radiators were impeccably installed, the windows closed with exemplary precision. The walls were straight and the corners right-angled. I wanted to know where he had learned all these skills. He replied that he worked as a graphic designer in advertising. I asked him about his work, but he avoided giving me an answer. I don't think he was trying to hide anything from me; it was more that he didn't seem to know what to say about it. He had poured his life into building this house. He talked to me about pipes of different dimensions and the difficulties of getting the right tiles. I noticed that not a single window looked out on to the street; they all opened out on the garden. As soon as we reached the attic, he asked me to wait at the top stair. Then he ran downstairs, I heard a door opening and suddenly the house was filled with cathedral-like tones. I looked in vain for its source. When Mr Vondrák didn't return, I went to look for him so I could compliment him on his fine sound system. As I walked down the stairs, I realized that the music was coming from somewhere in the basement. So I went down, and there, on the concrete floor, was a harmonium, and behind it, in his now faded overalls, sat Mr Vondrák the advertising designer, his head tossed back, playing Bach. 'I'm practising for the house-warming,' he said.

Several days later he finally broke down and used the services of professionals; these were equipped with a removal van. His furniture was ordinary, even a little scratched and worn. That evening, however, Roman candles flared merrily over the street.

The kids got off the train before I did. Novels and articles have already been written about them; they've been interviewed and made the subject of documentaries, and not just in our country, of course. They've been studied by sociologists, psychologists and criminologists, and spoken about with understanding, pity and disgust; everyone has tried to capture or at least caricature their faces. I refer anyone interested in them to the relevant literature.

It occurs to me that we are approaching a frontier. We have used up not only most of our fuel, our non-ferrous metals, our drinking water, our clean air; we've used up our stories as well. There is nothing new to add.

So they won't have to admit that fact, authors invent things out of desperation; they describe how the child hero is buried in the earth up to his neck and how the crows circle around him, ready to peck out his eyes. Or they force him to watch as the father offers his under-age daughter to a goat as a sexual object. They have the hero experience an orgasm while raping a sixty-year-old woman connected to a life-support system. Or they try to excite the reader with a tale of a man deprived of his manhood by a bolt of lightning. These authors may think that they have, indeed, found a new story, or at least a new dimension of horror and ugliness, but they only think this because they've forgotten the ancient tales of Oedipus or Tantalus. They have not read their Suetonius and they haven't experienced a fraction of what Dostoyevsky, Solzhenitsyn, Čosić or Kulka have gone through, and with them dozens or rather millions of others. Stories cannot be woven from horrors or ugliness, nor from perversion or debauchery. There are still people who long for solidarity and know that life without dignity is not real life, but I'm afraid their number is diminishing, just as real craftsmen and their apprentices, mendicant friars, sailors, merchants and travellers who walked or went on horseback are dying out. And I'm not surprised at the diminishment: most people have long ago been swept away in the tide of the mundane, though they stood defiantly on their tiptoes.

As I approached my cousin's house, I saw her smiling gypsy neighbour hanging out the washing.

I had first come here to see my cousin back in the winter, and the neighbour was hanging out the washing then too. The moment she saw me—a complete stranger— she waved to me, and I waved back. And then she shrugged her shoulders, as if to say: It's too late. You should have come sooner. And she smiled a broad smile, as if to add: But we'll see if we can do something about it. She was scarcely eighteen.

I saw her husband soon afterwards. An enormous moustache sprouted under his nose and a beer belly hung over his belt. He had gigantic hands. I would not have wanted to be caught in their grip.

My cousin noticed that I enjoyed watching those two, and she told me his name was Sandor and that he worked on the collective farm. Her name was Marie. They had married very young—when she was fifteen—and now they had two daughters. A pity I'd missed the gypsy wedding, she said. Then she took a small painting out of a wooden chest. It depicted several svelte little witches stepping out of an automobile to join their companions in a dance. Among the witches I recognized our young neighbour.

'Why did you paint her that way?' I asked.

'She's in the right company,' my cousin declared, arousing my curiosity even further.

I spent the night in my cousin's cottage, and the next day I saw the husband, Sandor, dressed fit to kill, hurrying to catch the train.

No sooner had the train rattled off than a greying, elegant man appeared at the fence. The young mother ran out of the house, but I couldn't hear what they were talking about, though I could occasionally hear high, flirtatious female laughter.

'Sandor won't be back until late tonight,' my cousin remarked. 'By then everything will be back to normal.'

Soon after, the woman, bundled up in a big woollen scarf, left the house with her children and went off with the man.

But at noon, unexpectedly, the husband returned. I happened to see him hurrying home from the station. He was gripping two parcels in his enormous hands. He banged on the gate for a while, and when no one came to open it for him, he unlocked it himself. And then, though two walls separated us, I heard him calling her name. He repeated it several times, his voice rising, finally, to an inarticulate roar. At least it seemed that way to me, though perhaps he was only shouting from a more distant room.

I began to anticipate a possible story in which passions are carried far above the surface of things: free, destructive, enthralling—until I began to worry that it might all come to a head in mindless violence.

A while later Sandor appeared, no longer in his Sunday clothes. He had put on a red windbreaker, and was pulling a sleigh behind him. I didn't understand what the sleigh was for. God knows what, or whom and in what state, he was preparing to drag off.

I watched in astonishment as he walked towards a hillside, where children were playing in the snow. Then I could see his red windbreaker swooping down the hill.

In the early evening, I saw him in the pub. The landlord

brought him beer, and I heard him say out loud, to amuse the other tables, 'You look a little the worse for wear, Sandor.'

The gypsy took a drink. 'You should've seen the dream I had!' And he started telling them about it. An army officer had sent him up to Mars and ordered him to come back to earth on foot. 'And the cocksucker only gave me three days to do it. I had to run so fast I was dying of thirst.' He finished off his beer, then added bitterly, 'And I still have to write it down.'

My cousin explained that, because of their youth, her neighbours had been required to take marriage counselling before the wedding. There they'd been taught how to build their relationship, and had also been alerted to the meaning of dreams, in which the repressed subconscious speaks; if it remained mute, they were told, it could drive one to commit indiscretions. Sandor had been so startled by the notion of a subconscious that he agreed to write his dreams down, and then take them to the psychologist from time to time. But Sandor didn't usually dream, except about food and the army. 'So I sometimes lend him one of my dreams about monsters,' my cousin concluded, 'and he chops my wood in return.'

That's the way it goes. My story of the gypsies had been killed before it had a chance to be born. Not even Shakespeare, had he lived to see it, would have known what to do. The moment Desdemona insisted that Othello see a marriage counsellor, Shakespeare would have given up. Nevertheless, though I now expected no writing to come of it, I accepted my cousin's offer to use her cottage. The countryside was pretty, and the evening mist still smelled sweet.

I stepped into the cottage and was met with the usual smell of paint, primer and turpentine.

I didn't stay inside for long. I took a sketch-pad and pastels and set out into the countryside. It was a cloudless September day, and the wooded hilltops on the horizon shimmered in the haze; shades of yellow and brown were beginning to dominate the landscape. I walked through a colony of small weekend cottages where the diligent owners were working to keep their tiny plots and gardens in perfect order. The air here was full of the scent of autumn flowers, ripening fruit and fresh coats of paint. A little past the colony I could see some shacks inhabited by the kind of kids I'd seen on the train. The smell of wood-smoke emanated from them, and a girl not unlike the one in my compartment on the train was pumping water into a tub. I greeted her. She turned to look at me, and her eyes were red—from crying, or from the smoke. She looked at me for a moment, then nodded and turned back to her tub.

Beyond the shacks, meadows rose gently to woodland. There, the railway passed through a shallow valley. I walked up to the first trees and looked for a view I would enjoy drawing. I draw mostly landscapes now. Even my wife likes them. She claims that they express the more pleasant, comforting, less contradictory part of my personality.

The sun poured down on the land, a nearby hill rose steeply against the sky, a pond sparkled at the bottom of it. Several willows dipped their branches in its water, and a narrow, sandy pathway ran from the water towards me; it was lined with low shrubs, among which, closer to me, rose a mature mountain ash, its crown laden with reddish-orange fruit. I found a warm stone, sat down and began to

57

sketch the outline of the distant hill.

'And the only thing that really grabbed me,' my friend Karel had said yesterday, reminiscing about his visit to the gallery in Montenegro, 'apart from Hegedušič, who's dead now anyway, was old Generalič. You look at his cat sitting in the window, with a couple of apples and onions in front of it, and you say to yourself: This guy is incredibly inventive. He can't help it, he's a true primitive. He doesn't think about things, he doesn't make anything up, he just paints. There's one where he's got this plucked cockerel hanging on a hook. Can you think of a more eloquent image of the modern world? A greater disgrace to life than a bird stripped of its feathers? It's the image of man who has nothing left: no God, no hope. But Generalič doesn't know about any of this; he just thinks he's painted a plucked rooster in his village. Tell me, does it make any sense to go on making an effort? Wouldn't it be better to admit honestly that we haven't got what it takes any more? And now tell me,' he said, stretching out his bony hand towards me, 'does anyone have what it takes any more?'

Ecclesiastes has an answer to that: 'He that observeth the wind shall not sow; and he that regardeth the clouds shall not reap.'

I expect that the landscape in front of me had been painted by several painters already. And the number of times photographers had immortalized it would be hard to guess at. I could, to distinguish myself somewhat, treat it as a cubist would, or a surrealist—paint a dead dove in the foreground instead of the mountain ash, perhaps. I could pretend that I saw the landscape in completely different colours from those a camera would see, but why? If I were a painter, I would probably feel the same kind of despair

58

that my friend Karel feels when he sees that he has barely been able to go beyond the limits others have reached before him. Fortunately, thanks to the spoiled sunflowers, I had been able to rid myself for ever of the responsibility of thinking up something new, at least in paint. I could, in all good conscience, delight in the fact that my mountain ash would at least faintly resemble the mountain ash I was looking at now, and that one day, when I looked at my picture again, the pleasure of this moment would perhaps come to mind.

A train gave a long whistle, and then I could hear the rattling of the carriages as though it were right behind me.

Sometimes I think that the furious hunt for novelty is diseased and self-destructive. We have declared progress to be our idol. Progress we understand to be something new, something that has never been here before and thus must be better than everything we have. It doesn't matter whether we move in the sphere of technology, science, the organization of society or the arts. The discovery of something new was always reserved for the genius; today all you need is a school-leaving certificate or at least a month-long training course and a good supply of arrogance. Perhaps we'd be better off if we worried less about whether we'd seen and expressed ourselves in a new way, and worried more about whether what we have seen and expressed is of use to anyone at all.

Something in the woods behind me snapped. I turned around. A girl in a denim skirt and blouse was approaching—at first sight a twin of the two girls I had seen today: the one in the train, and the one by the pump. She saw me. For a moment she stared at me, and it seemed that she too had red eyes, although most likely my own

59

vision was clouded by a red mist. She stopped abruptly, turned and hurried away down to the valley where the railway track was.

The girl would also have looked good in my picture; I could have painted her leaning against the trunk of the mountain ash, staring at me with her reddened eyes. But what kind of expression did she have, exactly? Lately, girls' faces have begun to seem less expressive, and more and more often I meet young girls who have no expression at all.

Recently in a doctor's waiting-room I picked up a magazine from the table and read that 'extensive cablization is an inseparable aspect of all electrification; the successful development of scientific and technological evolution requires tireless and qualified knowledge . . . ' Language deprived of meaning—I dare not say beauty— and amplified by countless loudspeakers is pouring over the countryside, seeping into our homes, our spirits, our lungs, until we are stifled. I'm not sure that we could find even one brave girl who would bury us with dignity once our suffering is at an end.

How can we achieve real solidarity when we cannot even speak to each other?

Not long ago Karel brought me a poem by a friend of his who had hung himself a short while before. The poem went like this:

1. . . *this day*
2. . . *this morning*
3. . . *this forenoon*
4. . . *this noon*
5. . . *this afternoon*
6. . . *this evening*

7. . . *this dusk*
8. . . *this night*
9. . . *yes, just then*
10. . . *it happened*

It was his last poem. He believed that precisely by using such spare language he could stand up to the poisoned waves; he was constructing a raft on which to sail closer to others. Then he realized that he could not make himself heard even from this craft, and he gave up. They threw him into a mass grave, and that was the end of it.

A train whistled in the distance, but I paid no attention to it.

A handful of people despair at the barrier they see surrounding them. They believe they must get beyond it, or their lives on earth will have been in vain. But what of the rest? What of those who have never heard a kind word or a whisper of hope? The loudspeakers roar and the picture tubes cast their pallid glow.

The train's horn sounded close by, unexpectedly, insistently, and at the same time the brakes squealed; then I heard, or thought I heard, a brief, piercing scream. Then there was silence. I couldn't see it, but I knew that the train had come to a halt.

I stood up, as though that would better enable me to determine what had happened. The silence persisted; somewhere nearby a woodpecker started up. The scream had evidently sprung from my imagination, for it didn't seem possible that a human voice could reach me all the way from the valley, especially not over the sound of the train's horn.

I sat down again, gathered my pencils together, put the paper into a folder and set off towards the track.

The train was still standing there. It was a freight train.

I stood on a ledge of rock that overlooked the rails. From that height I could see three men leaning over a woman's body; the body did not have a head. The men were carefully avoiding a pool of blood which had soaked the girl's blue blouse and skirt. If I'd walked around the spur of rock, I could have gone down to the track, but it wouldn't have made any sense. There was no help I could offer.

One of the men climbed into the engine and came back with a piece of light-coloured rag. He shook it out, then he laid it over the body. It was a small rag, and it only covered the upper part of the corpse. The men talked for a while; the sound of their voices reached me, but I could not understand individual words. Then two of the men climbed up the ladder into the engine. The third man stood motionless by the body, as though unable to move, then he took a few uncertain steps to one side. The two men in the engine were shouting at him to get back in the train; then they climbed down, took him under the arms and pushed him with their combined strength up the ladder. A moment later, the train began to move.

What could I do? I turned my eyes to the heavens, hoping they were not empty, and whispered a prayer.

I went back to the cottage, put the paints away, and gazed for a while at my sketch. Then I crumpled it and threw it into the waste basket. In the distance, I could hear the siren of an ambulance, or perhaps a police car.

I had not done anything wrong, but I could not get rid of the idea of the utter futility of my painting. If only I had known that the girl had decided to give up. Yet what could I have done? One tries so often to speak, but is not heard. I would like to have found or merely repeated a word of hope: 'Be not over much wicked, neither be thou foolish;

why shoulds't thou die before thy time?'

The monsters my cousin had left grinned down at me from the walls, and I couldn't stay here any longer.

Outside, there were several women standing around the fence of my smiling neighbour. 'Have you heard?' they called to me.

Imprudently, from a childish desire to display my masculine superiority, I revealed that I had even seen the body lying on the tracks. Moreover, I said, I was probably the last person to see the poor girl alive.

They immediately wanted to know everything I'd seen and what she looked like, because so far, they said, no one had any idea who the dead girl was. I disappointed them. I knew nothing except that the girl had reminded me of lots of other girls; she looked so ordinary: nothing about her had struck me.

Did I think she was from the village or one of the cottage colonies nearby? Or was she a complete stranger?

I didn't know, I said, but I was sure I had never seen her before. Yet as soon as I said that out loud, I realized I wasn't sure even of that. Since I wasn't certain what she looked like, how could I be certain I'd never seen her?

They were disappointed, but even so they tried to persuade me that it was my duty to go to the police station and declare myself as a witness.

I thanked them for the advice, but I knew that, in any case, they would not allow me to bury her.

When I got home, my wife greeted me with a great sense of relief. She said that all afternoon she'd had ugly premonitions. When she had come home from work that afternoon and there was an ambulance in the street, she was terrified that something had happened to me. But it had been for the man who had recently finished building the house in our street.

'What happened to him?'

A heart attack, she said. And the poor man had worked so hard. 'And what did you do?' she wanted to know. 'Did you go mushroom hunting?'

Suddenly, what I'd experienced seemed so improbable and unreal that I began to doubt it had actually happened. But I certainly did not want to talk about it. My wife would not have been able to sleep.

I said that the mushrooms weren't growing, and that I'd painted a picture but it hadn't worked out.

That evening, when my wife was already in bed, the doorbell rang.

It was an older woman in a headscarf—obviously a woman from the country. Embarrassed that she was disturbing me at such a late hour, she tried to persuade me that I knew her, that we'd met each other in the shop in M., and she'd seen me several times with a sketch-pad—once I'd even done a picture of her cottage.

I could recall none of this, but I nodded and invited her in.

She refused to sit down. She didn't want to take up any of my time, but they had told her that I was the one who had last seen the—she groped for the right expression—the one the train ran over, and so she had to talk to me. Every Friday her daughter came home from school for the weekend. Today she hadn't come back, and she wasn't at the school.

I tried to reassure her that her daughter would certainly turn up. And in any case, I couldn't help her. I had scarcely laid eyes on the girl in question.

That didn't matter; she'd show me a photograph. I'd certainly recognize her if I'd seen her. She began to rummage in her handbag, searching with increasing desperation among the things she kept there, but she couldn't find the photograph. Obviously she'd been so upset she'd left it at home.

I told her it was better that way, because the photograph would only reinforce an image I couldn't be sure of anyway.

But she had to know the truth. Sometimes the girl comes home, sometimes she stays with friends. Sometimes she even disappears for a whole week. She's a bit of a—nomad.

'There now, you see? That probably explains it,' I reassured her.

'What should I do, then?'

'Well, if you think it is your daughter, perhaps you should ask to see the body.'

She'd already been there and looked at the body; I couldn't imagine how hideous it was. No one could recognize her. No one! 'For a while I thought it was her—her poor little body, at least, but then I thought the legs were too long. If you could see how mangled she was.' The woman began to cry.

I said I thought the girl couldn't have fallen under the train by accident. Did she think her daughter had any reason to do something like that?

'Who knows?' she sobbed. 'You know what they're like! They don't take life seriously. They probably don't even know why they're alive!' She began searching in her handbag again. 'Do you think you could go back with me? I have a car.'

'It wouldn't make any sense. Even if you show me a photograph, I still won't be sure. But when they showed you the body, you must have seen how she was dressed. Did your daughter ever wear a denim skirt, for instance?'

'They all dress alike, don't they. And if you could have seen the dress, it was soaked in blood. The blouse didn't look like one of hers, but the girls are always wearing each others' clothes. You're a painter, aren't you?' she said, suddenly. 'Couldn't you draw what she looked like?'

I said I wasn't really a painter, and in any case I'd hardly be able to draw someone I'd only caught a glimpse of. 'Was she wearing a ring?'

'No. Besides, they'd steal it anyway.'

'Did she have any birthmarks?'

She shook her head. 'But you saw her. You were the only one who saw her.'

'I would like to help you, really,' I said. 'But I don't remember what she looked like.'

'You won't come with me?' She walked to the door. 'What am I supposed to do, just wait?' She stopped once more in the doorway. 'If it was her, I'll have to arrange the funeral.'

I'd forgotten about that.

She noticed me hesitate. 'Couldn't you just try. . . ?'

I led her into the dining-room, then went into my room and pulled out a piece of paper. The mountain ash danced red before my eyes. Then I saw the expressionless face of the girl in the train, and I couldn't shake it. The garden was bathed in moonlight. Several quick clouds scudded across the sky. The weather was changing. The wind whistled somewhere in the eaves like a squeaky pump. Now, when I half-closed my eyes, I could see the uncertain appearance of the other girl with the bucket. The branches of the trees trembled slightly.

What was the point? They would have to identify her by something, the doctors, the police, the mother herself.

Somewhere far below me the familiar train sounded its horn. Then the branches cracked quietly. I turned around suddenly and she was standing there, several steps away. Her dishevelled hair tumbled over her low forehead and her left ear. She had a large ring in her left ear. Was it plastic, or perhaps ceramic? Her reddish eyes were set far apart, her eyebrows short and inexpressive, as though she'd two-thirds plucked them. Her nose was blunt, and her mouth was disproportionately small for her over-large chin. The chin, jutting forward, was the most expressive thing about her face, if anything was at all expressive about it. And then, of course, the eyes. Not their colour, but the look in them, a look of desperate anxiety. Eyes that had just caught sight of the sea. The sea that threatens to engulf us all; a sea the colour of blood.

I looked at the picture before me with astonishment and mistrust. Where had that face come from? From what depths had it emerged, and what did it have to do with any actual appearance? Had the visitor suggested it to me? Was I not merely depicting one of my own anxious, subconscious memories? I shoved the sheet with its portrait under a stack of scrap paper. I went back into the dining-room. 'Unfortunately,' I said, 'I really can't remember. Please go home. Perhaps your daughter is waiting for you already.'

'Do you think so?'

I walked her to the door.

'Who was that,' my wife wanted to know.

'Just a customer,' I said. 'She wanted me to draw her a picture.'

'At this time of night?'

'People are strange.'

'You see,' said my wife. 'I'm always telling you your pictures are good. They express . . . '

'I know,' I interrupted. 'But that wasn't why. I'll explain tomorrow.'

'I keep thinking about the man down the road,' said my wife. 'He spent so many years building the house, and now, when he had finally finished . . . ' And, she added, that kind of thing happens a lot. People who put an enormous amount of effort into achieving something often collapse when they finally reach their goal.

It's probably true. It must be awful to finish a work and then not have the strength to go on to the next thing. I imagined Mr Vondrák one evening climbing up to the highest stair in his new house, certain that he had spent the last five years wisely and well—the water wouldn't reach him here—and at that moment, he saw it: the sea he had tried to escape from, and for which he had had no time until now. It was here, its waves were rushing around his ears, and at that moment, his heart gave out.

A man should not build himself a house and, if he does, he should not complete that last step, because from that vantage point, he will see it.

Ecclesiastes writes about this:

I made me great works; I builded me houses; I planted me vineyards: I made me gardens and orchards . . . Then I looked on all the works that my hands had wrought, and on that labour that I had laboured to do: and behold, all was vanity and vexation of the spirit . . .

In some cases, people don't even begin the work before they realize that their strength has gone. They glimpse the sea and understand that they cannot swim across. The waves roar round them. They call for help, knowing that no one hears them, and give up. So they run into the woods, see a railway track, lie down on it and wait. That is their story—their one, unrepeatable story. Several sentences long.

Who will bury her? This disturbed me.

I slowly fell asleep. If the dead girl remained unidentified, I will take a stone and place it in the ground near the tracks. And I saw myself transferring her face, or what I think was her face, into a piece of granite. That much, at least.

Then I remembered the dead dove, the one that gave up this morning. I had picked it up, so it wouldn't just lie there on the asphalt pavement, and as I picked it up, the grey feathers fell from its body like autumn leaves from a tree, and I didn't know what to do with it, because I didn't just want to toss it, naked, into the dustbin. So I carried it to a patch of long grass that was growing beside the path, and I set it down there and watched the leaves of grass rise trembling above it, as if to cover its nakedness.

Ecclesiastes also says:

And whatsoever mine eyes desired I kept not from them, I withheld not my heart from any joy; for my heart rejoiced in all my labour: and this was my portion of all my labour.

THE ARCHAEOLOGIST'S STORY

THE SUN HAD already warmed the caravan. I opened the metal locker where the workers usually put their clothes, and took out two paintbrushes, a scraper and a bundle of paper bags. I was thirsty. There was nothing to drink, but there were a few apples on the table that the foreman, Vítek, had brought from his garden. I slipped one into my pocket, took a bite of another and stepped out of the caravan with my small load. I hid the key behind one of the rear wheels—exactly the same place they hide the key from potential burglars in every caravan I've ever known—then I followed the path that wound among piles of excavated earth and puddles from the recent rains. From here you could see a spruce wood on the opposite hillside and practically all of the construction site, but you couldn't see the burial grounds. The metal shells of future buildings were radiating heat, and I was suddenly aware that the construction site, where at least a hundred people were supposed to be working, was silent, more silent than the burial grounds, where there are never more than five of us at any one time.

I had no particular feelings one way of the other about archaeology; it certainly wasn't one of my hobbies. In high school, one of my classmates had longed to be an archaeologist. We were close friends for a while, and he would drag me around the old Celtic settlements near Prague. He even persuaded me to carry a small pick and trowel in my rucksack. Every so often we would dig a scrap of baked clay out of the ground, and my friend would lecture me excitedly on the people who had made it. Thanks to his enthusiasm, I knew something, at least, about the funnel-shaped-cup culture, the globular-amphorae culture and the scroll culture, the Řivňa and Únětice cultures, and the people who made braided ceramics. But my friend was not allowed to study archaeology. His parents owned a small private laundry and at that time the authorities still took a dim view of such enterprises. Over the years, I had managed to forget almost everything he'd told me about ancient potters or Celtic settlements. All that remained in my memory were the poetic associations in the names of those ancient cultures.

History, on the other hand, has always interested me— and the mystery of where man first came from, where he made his first appearance on earth. I mean on the earth in general, and in particular in the place where I live.

The path led me alongside the portable units used by the construction workers. From here you could see the burial ground and the people who were working there: Lída, the archaeologist who was guiding our mole-like labours, her assistant from the museum, Petra, and the volunteer, Masenka, who at that moment was wheeling away a barrow-full of earth. She was the only person moving on the entire construction site.

In the portable changing-room there was running water. I squeezed between chaotic piles of scrap metal and lumber, and past a table piled with yesterday's unwashed thermoses, filthy plates and utensils caked with old food. I found a half-empty glass of beer with a drowned wasp floating it in, poured the contents on the floor and stepped into the washroom. The water that emerged from the tap looked as though it were mixed with blood. Only one of the three sinks worked, and it did not seem that anyone had cleaned it in the two years the construction site had been there. It was covered with a layer of rust and slimy grease. I rinsed the glass out as thoroughly as I could and filled it with water.

We don't know a lot about the Celts who once lived in our country; that much I learned from my high-school classmate. They left no written records. Caesar, who fought the Celts for many years, tells us that Celtic priests—the Druids—considered it a sin to put down anything of what they knew in written form. What we know about them was passed on to us by others—by foreigners or enemies like Caesar, who also tells us what is so often repeated about the Celts, that they were an immensely religious people who believed in the transmigration of souls after death, and who worshipped their gods with human sacrifices. *Natio est omnis Gallorum admodum dedita religionibus . . . aut pro victimis homines immolant aut se immolaturos vovent . . .* But I certainly wouldn't want the main written evidence of our own lives to come from the notebooks of some marshal who happened to be commander-in-chief of an invading army.

Historians prefer the testimony of archaeologists. Unfortunately, archaeologists derive most of their knowledge of the Celts from graves. I am sceptical of the notion that we can know much of life from the grave, though I admit that the way we bury our dead today reveals much about how relationships among the living have deteriorated.

Long before Caesar encountered religion in its Druidic form, the Celts worshipped both their heroes and the forces of nature: the goddess Mother Earth being foremost of those. Everything that surrounded them was an expression of spirits, whose voices they tried to hear and understand.

I'd love to know what those voices sounded like. Did they sound like the howling of the wind, like birdsong or the buzzing of bees? Or were they like the pounding of metal, as might have suited that age of metalworkers? Or did they perhaps come to man as invisible and inaudible vibrations, filling him with anxiety, love and portentous dreams—and do they sound essentially the same today?

'Did you find everything?' Lída, our boss, put down the scraper she was using to remove a thin layer of dirt from the grave. She was young, although her hair was prematurely grey, befitting her dignified bearing and her position.

I handed her the instruments, she gave me her customary smile and immediately divided the bundle of paper bags in half and handed one lot to Petra, who began putting lumps of clay into them. The lumps were lightly veined with tiny fragments of bone. 'Wonderful old fellows, aren't they?'

'That's all you've found?' I asked, mainly out of politeness.

'That's about it. A few bits of carbon. It's not going to be a good day. Just like all this week. I had a feeling it would be this way when I got up this morning.' Petra has a figure like the women on the fresco from Pyl: narrow waist and large breasts, black eyebrows that almost met over her nose, and almond eyes—just like a Greek woman. 'Like last week, as soon as I saw Lída by the bus, I told her, "Today we're uncovering a treasure."'

Last Monday, at the edge of the uncovered part of the burial ground, they had unearthed a bronze needle, a buckle and part of a hollow tube that looked more than anything else like a bronze syringe. They couldn't say what it had been used for, and rather than trying to concoct a hypothesis that would have upset all our notions of ancient medicine—which I would have enjoyed—they wrapped everything in cotton wool, put it in a box, and we took it all the way to the next district where, in the middle of a wheat-field, a group of pensioners were digging under the guidance of a professor from the Academy.

Lída and Petra had talked all the way about their discoveries while I observed the countryside, which was still covered with trackless, uninhabited forests. It was here, mostly in the upland areas, that the Celts had built their settlements. They had lived here for centuries, and their spirits lived here with them. Then they suddenly vanished. But had they really left no more behind them than these few fragments and shards we were now discovering in their graves?

The professor knew her bronzes, and she received us warmly. She showed us the grave-site they'd uncovered in the field, swept clean of the last scrap of earth, and a large vessel still embedded in the ground. Then she offered us cakes. She couldn't be sure to what use the little tube had been put. 'You'll have to be satisfied with having uncovered something unique,' she had said to Lída. Lída had flushed with delight.

I went over to the next partially uncovered grave-site,

took a pick, and began to dig.

Masha came back with the empty barrow. With a shovel, she carefully removed the clay I'd loosened, then thoroughly examined each shovelful with her eyes and her fingers.

'Masha, are you hungry?' I asked, pulling the apple out of my pocket.

'Thanks, that's awfully kind of you. It's as hot as the Sahara out here,' she said, wiping the sweat from her forehead. 'If only we could find something. Petra says we won't uncover a single bone today.'

Masha is just seventeen. She has a wide, good-natured face, large, curious eyes and rather thick legs. Two days ago she rode through the back gate in the fence surrounding the building site on a bicycle that looked cobbled together from spare parts. She stopped at the edge of the grave-site, hesitating a while before daring to offer her services.

'If you work for us, you won't make enough to cover your petrol,' said Lída, pointing to the engineless machine.

Masha laughed. She said she was mainly concerned about getting the proper stamp in her I.D.

'But I found a bone a while ago,' she announced to me proudly. 'Just a tiny little fragment. Lída thinks it's from a skull.'

'Congratulations, Masha!'

'As a matter of fact, it made me feel kind of sad.'

'Why?'

'Because someone was once alive, and whether he was miserable or whether he was happy, it was all the same to them, wasn't it? And now all that's left of him is this tiny little bone—I almost missed it.'

'And what about his soul?'

'Do you think he had one?'

'The Celts believed that souls migrated into new bodies.'

'Do you believe that?'

'I don't suppose I do.'

When I was a boy I was bothered by the question of whether the unbelievers and pre-Christian souls would experience salvation and resurrection. The previous night I had been reading an ancient edition of Eusebius's *History of the Christian Church*. Sixteen hundred years ago, the author had written on that very theme, about how Jesus had descended into hell, having destroyed its gates, which for ages had been unmoveable, and how on the third day he arose from the dead, and resurrected with him the other dead, who had remained in the earth from ancient times. Today I no longer worry about such questions. I've realized that everything that has ever been preached over the centuries about the soul or about God, about the origins of the world or of life, is merely intimations, fragments or shards of something that goes far beyond our proud reason; our imagination can only seek in vain for words or images which might compose the fragments into a whole. And I am amazed by how readily that which we declare to be a sign of God's will or intervention is delineated by human time and human dimensions. Even those I consider wise cling desperately to fragments and persuade themselves, and others, that they have the whole vessel. I have been coming to terms with my own being and my future non-being all my life. The self-assurance of those who claim to know, even roughly, how it was and how it will be awakens my mistrust.

'Sometimes I think nothing has any meaning,' Masha

said, waving towards the stones that outlined our grave-site. 'Actually, I wrote a story about it.' She blushed.

'You write stories?'

'Sometimes, only when I get certain ideas.'

'What was the story about?'

'Someone poisoned my cat a little while ago. He was a beautiful tom, really adorable. Everyone said he was the most adorable creature they'd ever seen. I decided that it must have been done by someone really hungry for revenge . . .'

Vítek, the foreman, who was walking by the next grave, stopped and interrupted our literary discussion with a down-to-earth question: 'What colour was the cat?'

'He was a strange kind of yellowish-brown. He looked like a miniature lion.'

'Do you know who did him in?'

'That's just it; I don't know who could have done such a thing. It's like the Vietnamese. Those poor people are so far from home, and no one likes them. In our town, whenever you go into a store and ask for something they don't have, the shopkeepers tell you that the Vietnamese have bought it all.'

'Don't talk to me about those little gooks!' snapped the foreman angrily. 'I'd like to see you when one of them goes crazy. One of them here went after the section chief with a pick-axe. It took three men to hold the bastard back.'

As though they had sensed we were talking about them, two Vietnamese in overalls approached us with a swinging gait they had adopted from their Czech co-workers. They were gaunt and slightly built, one was half a head shorter than the other. They stopped at the edge of our grave-site and observed us for a while with polite interest. Then finally one of them asked: 'So, did anything you find today, *madame?*'

'Nothing!' said Lída, looking up from the grave.

'Not yet a Celtic jewel, even?' asked the shorter one. His intonation was a remarkable blend of the orient and Pilsen.

'Not a single thing,' said Lída.

'It is regretful,' replied the Vietnamese. 'Truthfully. We were forward looking.'

'Curious little buggers, aren't they?' said the foreman as soon as the Vietnamese had wandered off. 'They get hammered every morning. They drink a bottle of beer for breakfast and can't hold it—I'm afraid to send them up on the scaffolding.' He took his pick and with delicate, almost gentle blows, broke the hard, compacted clay. He was the one who had accidentally discovered the burial ground. Last spring, when a bulldozer was digging a trench for the foundations, Vítek noticed something glittering in the piles of earth. He picked it up, rinsed it in water—and found himself holding a golden ear-ring. Not the kind they make today; a solid, heavy thing. The foreman had not been surprised at his discovery: a gypsy woman had predicted he'd find treasure three times in his lifetime. Of course, she hadn't necessarily meant a treasure of precious metal. As soon as he made his discovery, Vítek took the golden ring to a museum, where it caused a great commotion. The trinket came from the young Halstat period, or even from the early Laten period. It was a magnificent example of its kind. He may have chanced upon a whole Celtic burial ground, they said, and warned him to take a good look at everything the bulldozer turned up.

Vítek started looking carefully, but then the archaeologist

81

had arrived in the corner of the site, along with her assistants and some amateur enthusiasts, and they began to dig. Foreman Vítek became an enthusiastic amateur. He lived nearby, and he continued to draw wages even when he was digging here. Deep down, he was hoping to find the other ear-ring; on top of that, he was rather fond of Mrs Petra.

So far, no one had found the other ear-ring, nor any other trace of gold. The most likely explanation was that the Celtic goddess Nerthus, Mother Earth, had planted the ear-ring there to prevent the last remains of a people who had worshipped her and made sacrifices to her from being scattered by a bulldozer.

'All the same, I'm telling you,' the foreman went on, 'these little gooks—it's the start of a whole new wave of immigration.'

'Whatever do you mean by that?' asked Lída.

'They've come here from the east, haven't they? There's more of them around than dog-shit on the pavement. A week ago in our housing estate, the building inspector just okayed two new dormitories; they've already filled them.'

'You mustn't look at it like that,' Lída objected. 'They work here, after all, and they've got to live somewhere.'

'And our people are all moving west,' Vítek continued, pursuing his theory. 'Can you imagine what the place would be like if the borders weren't wired up?'

'Dear God, where do you dredge up ideas like that?' said Petra at last. Vítek's remonstrances had been directed chiefly at her.

'You're the one always telling me how nations migrate,' said Vítek in his own defence, 'how these Celts suddenly disappeared.'

'But that was under completely different circumstances,' said Petra, and sighed, perhaps regretting the passing of those circumstances.

The Celts really had vanished. For centuries, they had worked on their fortified settlements, clearing the woods, grazing their herds. Some of the graves testified to the wealth of their princes, but as the beginning of the millennium from which we date our era approached, the earth seemed to have swallowed them up.

Were they wiped out by a plague? Or did they think the soil would no longer support them and so moved west with their herds, their tools and their clay vessels filled with grain? Or were they slaughtered or driven out by the wild warriors who lived to the north and east?

It occurred to me that if we admit the influence of what is called the *genius loci,* we may retrospectively conjecture about the events that took place. Perhaps one of the neighbouring rulers—more powerful, or maybe just more determined than the rest—brought his army to the very borders of our basin. Perhaps he would not even have had to enter the territory in arms because the local inhabitants respected the commands of their chieftains and Druids not to provoke the enemy, but rather to overwhelm him with their discipline, and with unexpected kindness. The conqueror would perhaps have summoned the chieftains and arrogantly demanded their submission in exchange for which he—the invader—would promise to protect their territory against invasion.

The chieftains would have weighed their options carefully before accepting subjection and protection. A treaty of vassalage was perhaps written—emphasizing that the signatories were entering into vassalage voluntarily—

and signed in a big ceremony. It wouldn't matter whether the signatories knew how to read and write. The treaty—like all such treaties—would be binding only on the subject peoples regardless of whether they even knew the treaty existed, let alone whether they had accepted and signed it.

We might surmise that the people were not happy about this state of affairs. Some of them rebelled and were killed, others packed up their meagre belongings and struck out for the west or the south through the nearly impenetrable forests. In those idyllic times, when free movement was hindered only by lack of roads and the only impediments were bears or wolf packs, whole tribes could simply leave. But because we are considering what we have called the influence of a *genius loci*, we ought also to assume that not all of the subjected people withdrew, or were slaughtered; some must have simply adapted so completely to their conquerors that no one could have told master from slave when living, let alone in the grave.

And thus the Celts vanished from the places where we live today, and all that remained were burial grounds containing the ashes of their ancestors; and perhaps the gods and goddesses and spirits who had become too attached to the rivers and mountains and trees and rocks.

With a deafening roar of jet engines, a squadron of fighter planes chased each other across the sky. It was impossible to tell at that speed whether they belonged to the Celts or their conquerors. In any case, it made no difference. Masha dropped her knife and brush, looked up in alarm and put her hands over her ears.

The beautiful Petra also stopped digging. 'Yesterday we had Civil Defence exercises,' she said. 'An officer with a lot of brass on his shoulders came and gave us a pep-talk about what to do if the bomb went off. He was pretty optimistic about our prospects, because—he kept assuring us—in the event of a nuclear war, we'd be issued with plastic coats and masks that you could put on in twenty seconds. He brought a set with him all wrapped up to show us how it worked. So he gazes out of the window and suddenly shouts: Fire-flash, south-south-west, approximately twenty kilometres away! He grabs the parcel, but he can't get the knot undone. He tries to break the string, but he can't do that either. He ends up having to borrow a knife from someone just so he can show us the protective gear. The fool has gone into a nuclear war without even taking a penknife! And you know what he says? He says, "Strictly speaking, comrades, I'm already dead. You see, a mere length of hempen twine can cost a man his life!"'

'He didn't really say, "strictly speaking" and "hempen twine"?' asked Vítek.

'"Strictly speaking, hempen twine",' Petra repeated. 'You don't think I'd make something like that up, do you? I couldn't if I tried.'

Lída stood up in her grave and wiped the sweat and dust from her forehead. 'I guess it's time to photograph this now,' she said, pointing to the grave that she and Petra had carefully swept clean. She pulled a camera out of a bucket and looked around for the best spot from which to immortalize the grave-site. 'You know who called me at five o'clock this morning?' she said, suddenly remembering. 'The professor. She said our discovery wouldn't let her sleep. And then, when she finally dropped off, she dreamt about the thing.' Lída turned the wheelbarrow over and stood on it. The grave in front of her was as clean as a table ready to be set, but at the same time it was bare, empty, and as hot as a patch of earth after a fire.

'So, what was it?' asked Petra.

'She claims it was a handle.'

'A handle? Who's she kidding!' said Vítek. 'What did they need a handle for?'

'Maybe for a chisel,' explained Lída. 'Or for some special kind of knife.'

'Do you think it could have been a sacrificial knife?' Masha set down the brush she was using to clean the cracks between the rocks.

'A sacrificial knife would probably have been bigger.' Lída jumped down, turned the wheelbarrow upright, pushed it over to the other side, and then got up on it again. 'Anyway, it's difficult for anyone to say with any certainty now.'

'That's awful,' Masha whispered to me. 'I touched that handle yesterday, too. And they might have used it to kill people with.'

'The blood would have dried up long ago,' I reassured her.

'But what if there was a curse on the thing?'

'Do you believe in curses?'

She shrugged her shoulders. 'Don't you?'

'Not really.'

'Do you think they . . . aren't they watching what we're doing here?'

'Who, the dead?'

'The ones buried here.'

'Are you afraid they might take revenge on us?'

'When they dug that Tollund man out of the peat bog, one of the excavators suddenly dropped dead on the spot.

I read about it. It couldn't just have been a coincidence. The man who had written the story was there—he said that the old gods demanded a life in exchange for that ancient man.'

'That sounds like a pretty human notion of what the gods expect.'

'So you think there's nothing, then?'

I didn't understand her.

'I mean, you die and then—nothing?' she explained.

'There's no answer to that.'

'Why not?'

'There's no answer that you can put into words.'

'I know—I ask a lot of dumb questions. It drives my parents mad.'

'Words come from experience, that's what I meant to say. When we talk about something that no one has ever experienced, words can only be misleading.'

'That's interesting, what you say. Does that mean you can't even write about it?' Masha filled the wheelbarrow right to the brim with earth. 'I'd still like to see him—the Tollund man, I mean. They say he has a beautiful head.'

I trundled the wheelbarrow off to a nearby pile.

We are all waiting for some message of hope, hope for our life here, and perhaps even more, for eternity. We want assurances that we will be saved from the laws of nature, where everything is subject to extinction; assurances that the life in us has strived for something new, and thus that death has no dominion over us. From ancient times, people have offered bloody sacrifices, even human sacrifices, to the gods, expecting hope in return. Finally they, or some of them anyway, found consolation in a God who accepted the sacrifice of his own Son, and in return gave them hope once and for all. At the same time other people, who had never heard of this God worshipped by the Israelites—nor of his Son who said: 'Heaven and earth shall pass away, but my words shall never pass away'—sacrificed one of their own people and threw his body into the Tollund bog.

The man on the cross looks down upon us in countless forms. The man from the Tollund Fen, the noose removed from around his beautiful head, with that magnificent high-bridged nose, was put on display in a provincial museum. The meaning of sacrifice has been lost today; we continue to wait for some more persuasive, more logical and more understandable prophesy. We await this news from priests, from astrologers, from political leaders, from philosophers and from writers. And many, longing to win the favour of those who wait, say: 'May you be saved!' And others cry, 'There is no heaven except on this earth, except in this life.' Still others skilfully divert attention and seek a substitute hope. Very few have the courage to stand up and say, 'Beloved, there is no answer. Insofar as death can be conquered, insofar as man is truly endowed with something denied to other forms of life, it can only exist in a dimension for which we lack words.' But such answers, no matter how true, would interest or satisfy no one.

'What do you want to be, anyway, Masha?' I asked when I came back.

'I wanted to study archaeology. But they're probably not going to open the faculty this year, or next year either.'

'Of course they won't,' said Lída from the next grave-site. 'They say archaeology has no practical use. It is uneconomic.'

'And what draws you to archaeology, if it makes you think such thoughts?' I asked Masha.

'I like the idea of finding gifts in graves. Each of those things must have been rare and special for those people, and yet they put them into the grave along with their dead. I like the idea that people used to be so fond of each other.' She continued piling the earth into the wheelbarrow. 'When Mum and Dad got divorced,' she said quietly, 'they sued each other for possession of the TV and the cutlery. They couldn't have done that if they'd known how people used to ... Archaeologists have to be kinder than that; at least I can't imagine a bad archaeologist.' Masha dropped her shovel and quickly covered her ears as the squadron of unidentifiable jet fighters screamed over our heads again.

'When you tell it, it's a fantastic joke,' said Petra, returning to her nuclear war story. 'A mask and a coat! I saw on German television what would happen if the rockets started flying. It was such fun I didn't have the heart to send the kids to bed. What if the whole thing just blew up that night? I'm not kidding, I had this stupid idea: let them live a little. I let them eat a whole ice-cream cake for a snack.'

'Do you think it could start suddenly, just like that?' said Masha. She was clearly alarmed.

'Why not?' said the foreman. 'It could start by accident.'

'I've already talked things over with Joe,' Petra continued. 'We're going to apply to emigrate to New Zealand.'

'Oh, sure, the whole country's just waiting for you to show up down there,' said Vítek. He sounded as though he'd taken the idea as a personal insult, as though she'd decided to move away from him.

'If not New Zealand, somewhere else. It could scarcely be worse than it is here.'

'It wouldn't be any more use than a fart in a hurricane,

Petra,' said Vítek vengefully. 'When those bombs start exploding, where'll you hide? Radiation will be everywhere, it'll be winter all over the world, because the sun will never make it through that cloud of ash.'

'Well, what of it?' insisted Petra. 'So I'll freeze somewhere. Is it better to stay here like a calf waiting to be slaughtered? Look at those fools, always putting on such a show.' She pointed at the squadron of jets flying straight towards us. So far, they were completely silent.

Masha was furiously sweeping the grave-site with a straw whisk. 'What will you do if you don't get to study archaeology?' I asked.

'I don't know. Maybe I could still study literature.'

'Do you think there's a connection?' I said, surprised. 'Or is it because you think that writers are good people too?'

'Don't you think they're good?'

'I prefer not to make judgements about people in advance,' I said.

Not long ago, my friend the priest told me what one of our own chieftains—who had refused to sign the latest solemn treaty of vassalage and protection—had told him just before his death: 'You Christians are making one big mistake. You look on all people as your neighbours and you don't understand that once in a while, you have to deal with the devil.'

I respect that chieftain, because he rejected that ill-fated tendency to which the spirits of our homeland seduce us. At the same time, I would not want the human world to be reduced to angels and devils, to those who have seen truth and those who are in error, to those who are with me and those who go for my throat. Though when I think of all the things I've witnessed in my life, I really don't know why man thinks he is endowed with qualities that rank him above all other living things.

'I know a few wonderful people,' I said cautiously, 'and they are neither archaeologists nor writers.'

'As a matter of fact there is a connection,' said Masha, returning to my previous question. 'A friend of mine and I went for an outing a little way past Konstantinky. Do you know that area?'

'A little.'

'And we found a fragment of something on a hilltop. They were widening the road. The piece was traced with old-fashioned decoration. It must have been in the ground for a length of time that I could scarcely imagine, and yet, once, someone must have made it. Someone living. Before, in school or in museums, I was never interested in archaeological finds. And now suddenly I felt it was important to find something out about that person, especially since I lived right where he did. So I wrote a story about it.' She blushed.

'What did you call the story?'

'For a long time I couldn't think of a title, and then it came to me: Silence! I tried to imagine what it must have been like back then, and all I could come up with was how awfully silent it must have been everywhere. I got scared just thinking about it. I sent it in to a competition in *Cheb* magazine. They wrote back and said it was sensitively written, but I didn't know how to work with themes properly. They also said it wasn't contemporary enough.'

'I wouldn't take it too much to heart. Maybe they were afraid of silence too.'

'I don't understand what they meant, working with themes.'

91

I would like to have told her that I can only imagine with great difficulty something more hopeless than submitting short stories to a competition, or studying in one of our subjugated universities, but I didn't feel like letting on that I had some connections with that massive literary grave-site. Besides, Masha had thrown down her scraper and was plugging her ears because the squadron of fighters was screaming over our heads again. Whether they belonged to the Celts or to the other side, they certainly drowned out all the voices, the secret ones and the obvious ones.

Years ago I travelled through Scotland. Not because I was interested in the progeny of the Celts; I was drawn, rather, by the barren mountains and lakes celebrated in old songs, and modern myths about primeval monsters. At Inverness I checked in at a small hotel and then set off for a walk in the hills that rose over the town. I only got as far as the outskirts where, through the window of a small house, I heard a woman's voice singing a Scottish song. I'd heard Scottish songs and ballads sung in English, but the woman was singing in Gaelic, and I heard the old melodies as they had sounded originally.

I know that music cannot be expressed in words, just as words cannot express eternity, God, infinity or the soul. So I leaned against the stone fence post, listening to the woman singing, and looked at the rocky, barren mountains. Suddenly, the sun emerged from behind a cloud and illuminated a distant hillside. In the sharp light that defined a strip of rocky ground, I saw a white stone structure. It stood alone in a large field of heather. Even at that distance, I could see that the cracks between the stones were overgrown with moss, there was no glass in the windows, and the walls were strangely distorted. Outside a

92

low doorway, on a bench, sat an old man in a white coat. He was looking towards me. I was overcome with inexpressible excitement: I knew that this house was the place I had been gravitating towards all my life. It was the home I had been looking for. I was expected. I knew that when I stepped over the threshold, the embrace into which I would sink would surround me and fill me with joy once and for ever.

Then the woman came to the end of her song, and everything vanished.

I could have continued my walk into the hills, but I understood that my real reason for coming here had been fulfilled. I could expect nothing more blissful. So I walked back into town, packed my suitcase and went to the station.

Only later did I realize how through the voice, in a land so apparently distant, I had heard the spirit of my true homeland speaking to me. It was a voice that could not reach me at home, for it was drowned out by the shouts and arguments and laughter that fill every homeland. Like Masha, I tried to write about it—several times, in fact—but of course I never found the right words.

'I've just been thinking,' said Vítek, 'that the whole ice age must have been caused by a huge cloud of ashes. What if those people a long time ago were as stupid as we are, and invented everything we have?'

'And you think that they wouldn't have left a trace of themselves behind?' said Lída.

'Why should they? What do you think will be left of all this?' he said, pointing contemptuously at the unfinished structures of iron and steel around him, his own work. 'The rust will eat all this up in a couple of years.'

'Rubbish, Vítek,' said Petra. 'You'll never convince me. How would it be if you just uncover another layer over here for me?' And the foreman obediently took his pick and carefully began to loosen the clay.

The voice through which the spirit of place speaks to those who listen is common to us all; to me and to those people who moved from the backwaters of my homeland more than two millennia ago. By calling it a voice I don't mean anything mystical, a voice of blood and soil. I'm surprised that most people don't hear it, don't feel the natural reasons for affinity with one another. I'm surprised that they invent other reasons, more artificial ones, for sticking together: race, faith or ideas. They are more eager to believe their lives are influenced by the positions of planets than by the shape of the mountains that surround their birthplace, or the height of the heavens above them, or the direction of the winds that bring the clouds.

Is it possible not to feel some affinity for people who have followed every day the meanderings of the same river, climbed the same hills, seen the same flock of birds with each spring, and to whom darkness and light, the cold season and fruitful season, arrived at the same time?

It is probable that very soon we will have altered the courses of all our rivers, cut down all our forests, killed off the migrating birds, and obscured the boundary between day and night; in other words, that we will have broken the ties that bind us to our ancestors, those of our blood and those not of our blood, the tie that binds us to our homeland and therefore to the earth. And then we will have hurled ourselves into the emptiness of the universe.

'Jesus, Mary and Joseph! Look! Come and look!' cried Petra suddenly. And we all rushed out of our graves to see

94

what she'd found.

'Bronze!' she cried. 'I've got something bronze!' She was gripping a kitchen knife and carefully peeling away thin layers of clay.

'My word, there it is,' said Lída, kneeling beside Petra, her gaze fixed on a single place in the grave.

All I could see were several poisonous-looking greenish spots.

Petra got up, sat on one of the stones that edged the grave-site, took a cigarette out of a packet and lit it. Her fingers were trembling. 'This would happen now,' she complained, 'just as I was getting ready to call it a day.'

Lída brought over a box, then she and Petra knelt in the grave and began peeling back thin layers of clay bit by bit. 'It was Mother Earth,' sighed Petra. 'She could feel our strength and enthusiasm running out.' She cut a rectangle of clay out of the earth; a thin, greenish line was visible in it.

'What do you think it is?' whispered Masha.

The knife was very slowly scraping back the clay. The time allotted for our work was gone; the construction workers had suddenly emerged from their hiding places and were trudging along the pathway that led to the back gate.

I gathered up the tools and put them in the wheelbarrow.

The Vietnamese were now all shiny and clean; they had changed out of their overalls and into jeans. They stopped a little way off and spoke together in their impenetrable language. The larger of the two came up and looked curiously into the grave. 'Did you find something for your pleasure, *madame?*'

Petra looked up. She hesitated for a moment, as though

wondering whether they were worthy of hearing such important news. 'A bronze,' she announced dryly.

'After all!' said the man happily. 'Congratulation.' He nodded to his mate, who approached quietly. Then, as if on command, both of them leaned over the grave in unison. Petra leaned slightly to one side and pointed to the thin, green line in the soil. The smaller Vietnamese extended his index finger and declared, in his exotic Pilsen accent: 'I have seen already. When I dig a trench, I find such thing.'

'What did you do with it?' asked Vítek.

'Had no time,' sighed the Vietnamese. 'It was too much shooting.' And then he caught himself, as though he'd revealed too much, nodded his head and hurried away to the gate, followed by his companion.

The bronze needle was almost entirely exposed now. Masha, standing beside me, was scarcely breathing. 'It's beautiful!' Then she stopped. 'I hope it's not another one of those sacrificial knives.'

The notion that not long ago people still offered human sacrifices to the gods appals us, and we feel ennobled at how distant we, as humans, are from that primitive cruelty. But when I think of the endless masses of people sacrificed in my own lifetime, not to the gods, but to the insane visions of those who put themselves in the place of those gods, it doesn't seem to me that we have any reason to feel ennobled at all.

At last Petra carefully liberated that rare object from its grave, laid it in the box and said: 'Tune in tomorrow!' Masha swept the grave-site again, and then the women went to the caravan to change. Vítek the foreman also disappeared so that he could take a quick tour of

inspection around the emptying construction site and still
be able to walk Petra to the bus. Masha came up with her
makeshift bicycle. 'Too bad we didn't find anything,' she
said to me.

'Maybe tomorrow.' I watched as she skillfully
manoeuvred her bicycle around the piles of earth. Perhaps
back then, when she found her first ancient fragment, she
too had heard the voice of the local spirits.

I have suggested that the voices urged us only to submit
or to escape. But I know that's not how it was at all. Most
probably, the voices counselled caution or moderation. The
cowardly took them as an appeal to submit; the restless or
impatient as an invitation to flee. But there must have been
others still who understood that they were to remain, to
hold out and to survive, because without them the land
would remain empty and dumb. Perhaps the graves of
these people will yet be found, or perhaps they were so
poor that there is nothing in their graves at all. But I am
certain that they lived here and remained.

I consider them my true kinsmen: by fate, by place and
by choice.

It was suffocatingly hot in the caravan. I opened the
window as wide as I could and then went to wash in the
bathroom that had never been cleaned.

The construction site was silent. The wretched metal
structures pointlessly rose out of the earth. The piles of dirt
cast long shadows and blushed red in the setting sun. A
short distance beyond the caravan, a huge digger reached
out its long arm towards me. Girders, painted planks and
sheets of plastic lay scattered everywhere on the ground.

I walked back to the caravan, sat down on the steps and
watched evening descend over the piles of earth. A strange

world, where the cleanest, tidiest, most stimulating place is a two-and-a-half-thousand-year-old burial ground. From somewhere in the distance I could hear a dog barking and the faint rumbling of a truck's engine.

Suddenly, from somewhere around the burial ground, I heard a sound—as though someone were pounding metal dustbin lids together. The clatter echoed with improbable force through the silent construction site. I got up from the step and cautiously walked along the empty path to the graves.

The banging continued at the same strength, and fell silent only when I reached the spot from which the graves could be seen. I climbed up on a pile of earth and scrutinized the area in front of me. There was no sign of movement anywhere. No sooner had I started back than the lids began to bang again.

Who knows what the voices of our home spirits sound like; who would be brave enough to claim that he is capable of hearing them?

I sat down on the steps again. A mist was rising off the woods on the opposite hillside. You try to listen all your life, and all that time, you try to distinguish which of the voices you hear are essential, which resonate with your inner self and which are merely empty chatter tempting you into the universal abyss.

The metallic voice sounded for a while longer, and then gradually faded, as though it were disappearing into the depths of the earth. But I could still hear it long after it had fallen quite silent.

THE ENGINE DRIVER'S STORY

THE SEASON OF ballroom dancing was upon us, and crime was on the increase. I have little interest in ballroom dancing—I don't dance. A paedophile was at large in our neighbourhood, and the school had warned us to keep our children off the streets. My daughter told me that, coming back from aerobics with a younger friend, they had seen a stranger by the telephone booth on the corner who asked if they could give him two fifty-heller coins for a crown.

'So what did you do?'

'I only had one,' my daughter told me, 'but he gave me the whole crown for it anyway.'

The man asked them where they lived and where the Nováks lived. As fate would have it, the only Novák in our neighbourhood, Engineer Novák, happened to be walking by and when the girls called to him, the stranger took off. My daughter described him, but her description meant nothing to me.

Not long ago my wife's colleague, who works in a psychiatric institute, invited her to a club meeting for paedophiles. I went along. I was surprised to discover that most of the rehabilitated paedophiles looked not only utterly normal, but even rather sympathetic; they seemed gentle and restrained. Of course, when they behave properly, my wife's colleague informed us, they are allowed to go home for the weekend.

'And they don't do anything wrong?' I asked.

'We tranquillize them before they leave,' she said, to allay my fears. 'But sometimes something goes wrong inside their heads and they don't come back on Monday. In such cases, the institute calls the police at once to avoid possible trouble. But the police have other things on their minds besides chasing after patients from the psychiatric institute, and so paedophiles, along with other escapees and as yet unexposed criminals, have the run of the city. As long as they don't actually assault anyone, no one but anxious parents gives them much thought.'

Since the conversation had turned to the organs of public security, the doctor reminisced about a schizophrenic wrestler who had once been a patient of hers. This wrestler had a theory about life, or rather about death, that interested me the moment I heard it. He thought that death was engaged in an unending struggle for control of the world, and to that end, She hired various assistants. Death and Her assistants moved among us, the living, in constantly changing disguises. On green days, which the wrestler alone was able to determine, they would dress up in police uniforms. That was when they were most dangerous.

The wrestler would never harm a soul, the doctor went on, but on the green days he had to be kept away from policemen in uniform. If he saw one, he would attack. He was a powerful man anyway, but when the fit came upon him his strength was amplified. Not only would he take the officer's pistol and night stick away from him, he would remove his cap, rip off his epaulettes and try to strip him of his uniform. Then he'd throw everything down the sewer or stuff it into a garbage can and run. Most of the time the police caught him, took their private revenge, and then returned him to the institute with a warning.

I asked, not without a certain malicious satisfaction, how often he indulged in such delights. The doctor grew sad. They had scarcely let him out once every six months, and then only when they felt he had become completely quiescent. Last fall, however, he hadn't returned, and they found him a week later with a broken back in a field some distance from the institute.

So, in fact, he hadn't been wrong.

The doctor shrugged her shoulders.

The borderline between the madman and someone with brilliant insight into things that remain a mystery to others is usually infinitesimally narrow.

My daughter is afraid neither of perverts nor of those who should be trying to catch them. She seldom thinks about death, but when she sees through its disguises and glimpses it, she cries. As befits her fourteen years, however, she prefers to giggle even when there is no reason to. She loves driving fast, she's a secret smoker, and whenever she can find the excuse, she hangs out in the evening with fellow students of dubious reputation. When we take her to the theatre, she responds to the performance as though it were real life. Unlike me, she plays the piano, strums the guitar and the mandolin, and knows how to dance. She says that if I were willing, she'd teach me too.

My supply of willingness, however, has been exhausted in other areas.

'So how about it? Are you coming to the ball with us?'

I was trapped. So far, I had managed to avoid going to

balls, but now my friends were trying to persuade me to overcome, just this once, what they called my negative relationship to dancing. I could hardly refuse them. My friends were among those hounded and harassed by the police, in some cases even more than me. My attendance at this particular ball, though the thought annoyed me, had ceased to be a simple matter of my relationship to dancing.

Almost all of my friends had signed Charter 77, which meant that they had committed themselves (in the words of the Charter) 'both individually and as a community to work towards recognition and respect for civic and human rights in our country and in the world.' The authorities were firmly convinced that they and they alone were competent and entitled to protect the people and their rights, and they took the Charter as a declaration of war. The Charter signatories were picked up and interrogated; their flats were searched. When those carrying out orders discovered nothing more incriminating than ideas and books that they alone found offensive, the authorities had the Chartists thrown out of their jobs, put under surveillance, publicly vilified. Their passports and drivers' licences were confiscated, their telephones disconnected. This battle had gone on for a year, one side obstinately demonstrating the justice of their claims, the other side demonstrating their vast superiority in strength. One of my persecuted friends decided that the season of balls would be a good time to have some fun and relax.

The ball they were to attend was organized by the railway workers. Though my friends could not hold a ball on their own, they believed no one could object to their attending a function organized by a group as politically correct as the railway workers.

I suspected that the plan to join the railwaymen for an evening could not remain a secret. I believed my friends were foolish to think that those in disguise would not begrudge them an evening of dancing. My wife and daughter, on the other hand, had begun discussing what they would wear the moment our friends offered us tickets.

The day of the ball was overcast. A chilly wind spread a sheet of smoke, soot and ash over the city, and the streets were covered with a slick film of dirt. Anticipating disaster, I drove with extra care and parked the car as far as possible from the hall where the dance was to take place. My wife had had her high-school graduation dress repaired and altered for the occasion, and she still looked like a young girl. My daughter had made herself a gown of shiny scarlet taffeta. It was her first real evening dress; I could see that she was rehearsing in her mind the moment when she would take off her coat and enter the ballroom.

The women concentrated on negotiating the damp, treacherous pavement while I looked around. I noticed that on Peace Square, where we were headed, white and yellow squad cars bearing the two large, widely ridiculed letters indicating the Public Security forces—VB—were parked in places where it was forbidden to stop. Another white and yellow car, its siren wailing, wheeled into the square and sped up to the hall.

Even I could see that a green day was upon us..

Usually at this time of year, the small park in front of the St Ludmilla Church is empty, but now it was filled with men who, judging from their appearance, were obviously not regulars in the park. Corruption was in the air, and if you listened closely you could hear a quiet scraping sound—the noise of radio interference—like carborundum

105

sliding over a scythe blade or at least over hidden stilettoes. Soon we ran into the first group of friends, who announced that we would not get into the ball. When the people at the door realized we were not railway workers, they would give us our money back and turn us away.

As far as I was concerned, it made no sense to go any further, but my wife and daughter protested. They had finally managed to drag me out to a dance, so we should at least see for ourselves if it was impossible to get in.

My wife took me by one arm, my daughter by the other, and they would almost have persuaded me to pretend to be a railwayman (which, by the way, as a child I had always longed to be) had my friend Pavel not suddenly appeared in the park, supported by his wife.

My friend Pavel is one of those people who are plagued by the notion that they must tell others how to live in order to make the world a better place. That's why he's constantly getting mixed up in politics. He may well have been slightly more involved than others; that would explain why he was the only one who had suffered a blow to the head when, earlier, the mass expulsion of would-be ballroom dancers had taken place.

His driver's licence had long been confiscated, so he was looking for someone to take him to see a doctor.

I had always wanted to be an engine driver. When I was a child, there was nothing exceptional about this: there were almost no cars then, and truck drivers had not yet become an object of childhood dreams. I can no longer say exactly what it was about being an engine driver that attracted me: whether it was the desire to control the motion of an enormous hunk of metal, or the lure of far-away places. Whatever it was, I could stand by the kitchen window for ages, staring down towards the tracks and waiting for a train to appear. Then, when I heard the puffing of the enormous machine in the distance and saw the approaching plume of smoke—and when it was dark outside the smoke was full of swirling sparks as tiny as stars in the sky that glowed and then died—I was gripped by a blissful sense of expectation, as though I were supposed to leave on that train, or as though I were expecting a visitor to arrive on it, perhaps from the heavens themselves, from where the train always seemed to emerge. At the time I did not know of those other freight trains that, on narrow, normal and wide-gauge tracks carried, and would continue to carry throughout most of my life, uncountable numbers of people whom She and her beaters and followers had singled out as victims.

The moment Pavel stepped into the car, he started telling us what had just happened to him, things that to him seemed incomprehensible. Then he stopped. It occurred to him that perhaps it might be better to remain silent about it all in front of my daughter. My daughter, in rather rough terms, reassured him that on the contrary, she found such experiences entertaining; at least they made up, in part, for the ruined evening. She unbuttoned her coat to reveal her ball gown.

I would like to have told my friend something of my wartime experiences, because they had helped me to understand many of the events that came later. I would like to have told him that I had learned how the persecution of a select sample of victims gave Her several advantages. Not only did it arouse fear among other innocent people, but it also gave those who were not included in the sample a sense of satisfaction that they were considered worthy of

107

trust. I would like to have mentioned how this even encouraged the most anxious of citizens to lend a hand, at least in the most inconspicuous of ways, to Her efforts so that with the passage of time remaining silent about Her work became second nature, an understandable and forgivable vice. I could have gone on to suggest that persecution of the innocent also satisfied a degenerate passion that circulates in the blood of many of Her assistants. However, the white and yellow car I could see behind us distracted me.

Before the war, the famous Helada company made soap. Into the long boxes containing their soap, they put pictures of steam and diesel locomotives. They issued an album with spaces into which you were supposed to stick the pictures. I owned the album and gradually filled the spaces in it. When I leafed through the book before going to sleep and saw locomotives in colours I'd never seen them in, locomotives with magnificent red wheels or with blue or green flanks, I was overwhelmed. And I imagined that I was the one who was allowed to move the rods and levers that controlled them.

I drove Pavel and his wife to the nearest health clinic. The yellow and white striped car that had followed us all the way like a faithful hyena parked by the curb behind me. Now that I was no longer distracted by driving, I could observe its crew. There were four of them. The man sitting next to the driver was saying something into his walkie-talkie. When he finished talking, he and the rest of them were obviously waiting for an answer. I imagined I could hear a hollow, loud-speaker voice coming from inside their car. Then one of the men got out, walked around my car and rapped on my window.

I opened it, and he asked to see my documents. My driver's licence was almost new, and the vehicle registration was in order, as was the car. He produced a breathalyser, and I blew into the tube, certain that not the tiniest drop of alcohol was circulating in my blood. He noted my innocence, even thanked me and said goodnight before returning to his car, from where he must have reported the results of his investigation by radio.

My collection was almost complete; I was only missing two cards, both of express-train locomotives. One was called *The Mikado*, the other was nicknamed *Passepartout*. Their stats were printed in my album, but I had no idea what noble shapes and outlines distinguished them from the rest. What good is an incomplete collection? Whenever I opened the album, I saw only those two empty spaces crying out to be filled. We had enough soap at home to last for at least three years. I couldn't get the missing pictures by trading for them at school, so I had already given up hope when our grocer invited me behind the counter and allowed me to open the soap boxes until I found the two missing engines.

The unusual pleasure of being behind a counter was even greater than the joy of at last finding the pictures I needed. I sensed, although I had no way of appreciating my discovery yet, that the man behind the counter, no matter how deeply he might bow to his customers, possessed the power to satisfy people's needs and desires. And anyone who has such power is like a king.

My first encounter with a real engine driver happened not long ago. He brought me a message from a friend of mine who lived outside Prague. The message vouched for its bearer, Martin B., and asked me to lend him something good to read.

Martin B. was not the kind of man I had imagined in my childhood commanding an enormous engine. He seemed too slight, too young, and moreover he was dressed in jeans.

We talked about folk singers. He was proud of his tape collection of protest songs by singers who were mostly silenced, and of his collection of books by banned authors. He or his friends copied out these books by themselves. I expressed surprise that someone so young would devote his time to copying out books by unknown authors.

'You have to do something!' This was the hope that encouraged him and told him his actions had meaning. I nodded and asked him how he liked his work.

My question surprised him. He had never wanted to be an engine driver.

I said that as a boy, I had, very much. What had he wanted to be, then?

He laughed. The only thing he could remember was wanting to go hunting in Alaska. At school, he had directed a play about Jack London. London could not have imagined how anyone could enjoy doing the same thing all his life. They should allow everyone to do one job for a while, and then to do something completely different, or nothing at all. He said he would happily spend half a year working double shifts on the trains if he could spend the same amount of time wandering about the world.

Would he go to Alaska?

He'd go to Denmark first.

Why Denmark?

Because they have a decent government there, he explained. And you can travel through the whole country by bicycle. After a long fast, you have to begin with small mouthfuls. Besides, Hamlet was prince of the Danes.

I could find no fault with his reasons.

He left with a parcel of extremely hard-to-get books. He said that if I really wanted, he would, as a favour, let me ride with him in the engine and allow me to drive it. Of course it would only be a freight train; someone like him could never get a better position; he was not sufficiently committed politically.

I didn't take his offer seriously, but that night I had a dream. I was walking through a desert landscape on a path between a railway line and a high wall. Suddenly, a gate opened in the wall ahead of me and a hissing steam engine emerged. It cut across my path and stopped in front of me.

I realized that this was the train I'd been waiting for and that I should quickly climb aboard one of its cars. Instead, I stared at the locomotive in fascination. It was a steely blue and it seemed to be very light, as if hollow. The front of it looked like any steam locomotive; smoke was even coming out of the smokestack. But the whole rear section looked like the exposed inside of a large clock. Cog-wheels, large and small, gleamed as though cast from pure gold. Through the small window I saw the engine driver's face, and his hands moving nimbly among the rods and levers. I wanted to call out to him, to ask him to let me climb aboard, but before I could bring myself to do it, the train started up and in an instant disappeared in the distance, leaving me alone by the track.

When I told my dream to my non-existent psychoanalyst, he persuaded me that the dream had nothing to do with how I had longed to drive a locomotive. I had merely seen an image of my desperation to overcome the isolation in which I have found myself for some time now. The train, especially this complicated steam engine, represented an

111

unattainable community—shiny and attractive, even though hopelessly outmoded. It symbolized friendship, a sense of belonging, love. I wanted to climb aboard, but the train started up and disappeared, leaving behind the rail of hope as a reminder of missed opportunities.

When did I miss my chance? I can't answer that. People miss opportunities every day. One can only try not to miss them through laziness or fear.

Pavel returned with a bandage around his head. There was an unexpected satisfaction in his expression. The doctor, Pavel claimed, had let it be known he sympathized. Pavel forgot about his pain as soon as he thought others shared it with him.

My wife leaned over to me and whispered an offer to drive if I was too upset.

Why should I have been more upset than her?

She imagines, like most people, that anyone who spends some time in prison or in concentration camps will spend the rest of his days, at least subconsciously, in fear of losing his freedom.

In fact it is usually the other way around. Often it is those who know about prison only from hearsay who fear it most. Fantasy can be more frightening than reality. Or perhaps it is even simpler: those who have made it through once hope they will be able to make it through again; the rest don't know. They have nothing to base their hope on.

My experience of life so far led me to two simple, if contradictory, conclusions. The first one was: everything evil a person can imagine can in fact happen. The second derived from the first: nothing that will happen to me in life can be worse than what has already happened to me.

The yellow and white car continued to follow us,

keeping as close as safety allowed. Perhaps they were afraid we would try to escape, or they wished to frighten me to the point where I would try to lose them. They'd be happy enough to stop me for speeding.

Yet why should we, who had done nothing wrong, try to escape?

I wondered how many such chases and harassments were taking place at that moment? I've heard it said that a crime is committed somewhere on earth every second. Yet there are no generally acceptable definitions of crime. In some places, crimes are kept a secret. Elsewhere it is a crime when a man goes to a railwaymen's ball with his wife and daughter. And who keeps count of crimes perpetrated by criminals artfully disguised as crimefighters?

But it is certain that at any moment, somewhere in the world, there are those who are on the run from robberies, from raped women, from murders and from molested and abused children. The harassment we suffered is worth paying attention to for one reason alone: it was probably the most nonsensical, and therefore the most wasteful crime of all.

'Europe is asking,' Pavel had written in one of his recent *feuilletons*, which the young engine driver and others like him were probably copying out, 'where is the liberty, equality and fraternity for which people bled under the Bastille? It is asking, how is "all power to the Soviets" working, for which people died beneath the Winter Palace? It is asking, when will this game of power end that is keeping us artificially divided, so that we cannot have today what the prophets of happier tomorrows promise for the future?'

Pavel asked these questions in the name of Europe. But

it was Pavel who received a blow to the head. It seems to me that if they beat someone for asking questions, it should at least be his most personal question—especially if he is a writer. If a writer asks in the name of Europe or his country or the people, in whose name should the politicians ask? But then what should a writer do, when the politicians have long ago stopped asking questions and take care only that they may rule without interruption, regardless of how harmful their rule may be?

I drove Pavel and his wife across the city to their home. When we parted, it occurred to me that I should get out with them and put my wife and daughter on a tram, or try to find them a taxi. But I assumed that the men in the yellow and white car were more interested in Pavel, my fractious friend, and that as soon as he got out, they would disappear. So I now looked hopefully into the rear-view mirror.

They were following me. I turned into a narrow side-street. So did they. It seemed I had committed one of the crimes they do not like to leave unpunished: I had expressed my solidarity.

We could have stopped and got out of the car. But one feels a little safer in a car. Many people think of the car as their second home and some prefer it to their real home, which offers them no change, no mystery, not even the excitement of speeding. It depends on the people—and on the car.

I continued on my way home. When I next looked into the rear-view mirror, I saw that another yellow and white car had joined the procession.

Mr Novák, the civil engineer, lived only a few doors from us, but until recently we had never actually talked. He was handsome, and so was his wife. They had three children. They played golf together—at least I would occasionally see them loading golf-clubs into their Škoda. I think he saw his wife as a princess, and had he been a prince he would certainly have wanted to provide her with more than golf; but he was just a civil engineer. Last New Year's Eve, we walked back from the bus-stop together. He'd had a little bit to drink and he was carrying a basket piled high with eggs. He told me that he'd recently been lent one of my books that was circulating in manuscript, and that he'd been waiting for a chance to express his sympathy. He could well imagine what a difficult time I must be having when I couldn't make a living at work I knew how to do.

Then he spoke about his own difficulties, and how often he had to demean himself before dull people he had no respect for, and how he suffered this humiliation only so that he would not lose his pay cheque, which was miserable enough anyway. Was it possible, he asked me, as though I were some clairvoyant, for life to go on in this hopeless way? What, then, was a person here for and why should he stay around?

I wasn't certain if he meant his sojourn in our country, or on this earth.

He slipped a couple of eggs in my pocket, we wished each other a happy new year, and parted.

Several days later I saw him on a bitterly cold morning attending to a shiny Mercedes. He couldn't contain himself and asked me what I thought of it. Seven years old, but in wonderful condition. He and his wife had always longed for such a car and then a once-in-a-lifetime offer to buy this one came up, but he'd had to go so deeply into debt that if anything happened to him in the foreseeable future, his family wouldn't even be able to afford a wreath. And then, with a rag that he'd dipped in some foul-looking chemical substance, he resumed polishing the chrome.

We had already passed through the city centre and through the Vysehrad Tunnel, beyond which was a straight stretch of road running alongside the Vltava river. We were scarcely five minutes from home. It was at this point that the second yellow and white car suddenly accelerated past the first car and past us. For a moment I dared to hope they were leaving us to do something more useful, but then a uniformed arm emerged from the window waving the regulation lollipop stick that meant stop. I braked, and so did the car behind us.

Two uniformed officers got out of the first car and walked towards me. I opened the door.

'Please get out, driver,' said one. 'Your documents.' He spoke to me in the tone he probably used with criminals he was arresting. He was the smaller and rounder of the two. The other one, who was more robustly built, remained a few steps behind him.

I objected that his colleague in the other car, which was still behind us, had already seen my documents.

He was unmoved. He held his palm out and waited until I handed the papers over. He leafed through them for a while, and then he said something that surprised me. 'Sir, the way you've been driving suggests to me you've been drinking. Are you willing to submit to a breathalyser test?'

I protested. After all, I had been tested an hour ago, and since then they'd been constantly on my tail. It was highly unlikely that I would have drunk something while I was driving.

116

'Do you refuse to take the test?'

I sensed a trap, and besides, they were behaving like clowns, not me. I agreed to the test.

When I'd blown into the tube, he took it from me, turned his back, and declared that the tube had turned green. Was I aware of the consequences that this could have for me?

Though I had become used to most things, I was astonished. For years I have tried to stay out of the game that in this country is a substitute for politics, a game which one side plays dishonourably, while the other side, though it plays honourably, plays without hope. I don't take sides. Not out of cowardice or calculation; it's just that I have neither the strength, nor the time, nor the capacity for the game.

I know that bad political policies influence everyone's life, mine included, but I would not dare to claim, not even to myself, that I am sure enough of what are good policies to be able to persuade others.

I am not convinced that one has a right to one's own car or plane, or the satisfaction of all one's needs at a time when most of mankind is hungry. I don't know whose side I should take in the struggles and wars I hear about and read about every day, though I suspect that most of those struggles will soon be forgotten, whereas the stories of Antigone or Hamlet will live as long as humanity itself.

But all my doubts have not stifled within me the awareness that injustice must be resisted.

The tube couldn't have turned green. Show it to me!

He replied that he was not required to show me the tube. So he was, after all, ashamed to confront his claim with reality. He then began, somewhat incoherently, to explain that there were cases of mild intoxication in which the liquid in the tube changed colour only slightly. It made no sense to show the tube to me because to my untrained eye, the colouration would be imperceptible. He was not suggesting that I had drunk a lot, but the tone of the liquid had altered and that meant I had failed in my duty as a driver and become a hazard on the road. His voice cracked. I suddenly saw that he was ashamed. He had been ordered to detain me with a charge of drinking and driving, without regard for the self-respect that he would have to repress to do so. He was not trying to persuade me so much as himself.

He realized that he hadn't been firm enough with me. He was through talking, he said. I'd been drinking and driving and therefore he was confiscating my driver's licence. The persons in the car would have to get out. I was to lock the vehicle, turn the keys over to him, and leave the car parked here until they decided what action to take.

I looked towards my car and saw a golden head of hair in the window: my daughter was anxiously watching a scene that would certainly stick in her memory far more vividly than better plays performed by better actors. Unfortunately, I had a role in this play, and how I acquitted myself would also stick in her memory.

No one was getting out of the car, I said. 'I will not give you my keys, and furthermore I will lodge an official complaint about your behaviour.'

'If you don't hand over your keys, you'll have to come with us.' His voice cracked again.

I didn't care about the keys. I learned long ago that you cannot cling to objects if you don't want to become their slave. But is it the same with one's rights? If you don't cling to your rights, you will gradually be deprived of them, and become a slave all the same.

With a barely perceptible gesture, the second uniformed officer, who had so far stood silently observing all this, motioned the first man aside and stepped into his place. He could see that I was upset, he said. People who are excited behave rashly. I should understand that, at a time like this, it made no sense to argue over petty details. I had become involved in events over which neither I—nor he, for that matter—had any control. They had to take my driver's licence and keys. If I resisted, they would have to detain me, and they'd take my keys anyway and, given the mood that would prevail, I would certainly not be going anywhere for a while. What good would that do? If I surrendered the keys now, I could go home and go to bed, and when the dust had settled I'd get them back. He leaned over to me and said, almost in a whisper: 'Meanwhile . . . you have another set at home, don't you?'

I know that during interrogations the roles are usually divided. One of the interrogators plays the tough guy and the other one tries to gain the confidence of the detainee by kindness. But this was not an interrogation, and it didn't seem to me that these two had been assigned complicated roles. They didn't have the basic props. They didn't have a breathalyser that normal breath would cause to change colour. They had not been taught how to switch a colourless tube for a coloured one. It seemed probable that the man who was talking to me now genuinely wanted to save himself some work, and me some unpleasantness.

But I still could not overcome my feelings of resistance and disgust. Should one submit to a false accusation only to avoid greater unpleasantness? If I acquiesced now, how could I later ask for justice?

It was my daughter who snapped me out of my

119

indecision. She had decided, despite her youth, to whisper words of advice: 'To hell with them! Let them eat the stupid keys if they want.'

My friend the engine driver and admirer of Hamlet might have put it more subtly:

> *. . . Rightly to be great*
> *Is not to stir without great argument . . .*

We resist the One who, in various disguises, rules over us; we want to wrest from Her at least the right to the footprint we would leave behind, to an act we consider our own. Our struggle for the right to a life of dignity is with Her. Yet She and Her assistants attempt to reduce to nothing everything the struggle is about, to transform a conflict in which everything is at stake into a petty squabble in which resistance seems the act of a clown.

When I handed the keys over to the more polite of the two officers, I asked him if he could at least give me a receipt of some kind.

'Of course, that goes without saying!' He seemed relieved to put this embarrassing interlude behind him. He took his notepad from his case, then hesitated. He asked me to bear with him and walked over to his car. A few moments later he returned. 'I regret to say,' he announced, without even looking at me, 'that I cannot give you a receipt for your keys.' I could learn, he said, about the fate of my keys at my local police station.

We managed to flag down a taxi. The driver wondered how two women in evening gowns had managed to find themselves on an empty highway. We tried to explain it to him, but he didn't seem to understand, much less believe us. At the detention centre, where we went after we'd changed our clothes, they looked at me suspiciously when I asked them to take a sample of my blood. The nurse looked at my ID for a long time as though she hoped to find something there that would explain what had driven me to make such an unusual request.

I sat on a bench in a room with filthy walls covered with anti-alcohol slogans and waited for them to call me into the office. I could hear incoherent shouts, and then two men in white lab coats dragged a struggling drunk past me, while a third orderly walked along behind them, ready to help if necessary. The drunk was yelling obscenities. He reeked of stale beer.

Ten years before we had been guests of the Presbyterian Church in Midland, Texas. Our hosts asked us what sights we'd like to see. We had no idea what we should look at, until it occurred to me that I would like to see the local prison.

What surprised us about the prison was its hospital-like cleanliness. Most of the prisoners were black, men and women, and they were kept in large cells. They were dressed in normal clothes; some of them lay asleep on benches, others stared at us with obvious hostility. Our guide, like all prison guides, praised the orderliness of the prison. He claimed the prisoners were prostitutes or people arrested for being drunk and disorderly. Most of them, he said, would be released the following day.

We were living near the Canadian border; the journey to this spot had taken us three days, and the return trip took a day and a night longer. We covered about five thousand miles, staying at various hotels; we took a small boat over to Mexico, where we spent a day. When we finally returned home to the peninsula between Lake Michigan and Lake Huron, we realized something unbelievable: the whole time, no one had asked to see any identification. Not even when we visited the prison did anyone suspect that we might not be who we said we were.

They took a sample of my blood and told me that they would send me the bill, and the results of the test, by mail.

When we returned by the night tram, which was full of drunks, the streets were empty. Not a single yellow and white car was in sight, not a single uniform. The green day had ended.

Our car was where we had left it. My wife unlocked it with her keys, got in behind the wheel, and drove us home. No one followed us. Our street was dark—they'd turned off the electricity. Inside, we undressed for bed by candlelight. My first ball had surpassed all my expectations.

The following afternoon, when I left for the local police station, I was surprised to see a small crowd in front of the building where Mr Novák lived. They were gathered around the open hood of his shiny Mercedes.

'Come and look at this!' Novák called out as soon as he caught sight of me. 'I'll bet you've never seen anything like it.'

When he had got into his car that morning, the starter was dead. As soon as he lifted up the hood, he saw why: in the darkness of the night, someone had stolen his engine.

Why would thieves risk being seen or heard driving off with a stolen car? They would sell the engine for parts and no one could prove anything. 'They must have come here with a mobile workshop,' shouted Novák. 'And explain to me how they could have known that the lights would be off in our street all night?'

I asked if the police from the criminal investigation branch, or at least the local police, had been here to look for clues. I was naïve, he said. When he called them, they said they'd drop around during the day, if they had the time. After all, last night they were out on a big campaign. Wouldn't I grant them even a day off to rest?

Even when they do come, said people in the crowd, they'll only record the theft for their statistics. A single stolen engine was not worth starting a formal search over.

As a matter of principle we never confiscate the keys to anyone's car, I was told at the police station. Was I aware that I was committing a crime by falsely accusing an officer?

I returned home without my driver's licence.

My experience over the years had led me to two more contradictory conclusions. One said: what the strong take from the weak they will never voluntarily return. The second one comforted me: bureaucracy always has to take a case to its ultimate conclusion, so it can close the file.

My keys had to be lying around somewhere and soon they would be getting in someone's way. I decided not to think about them. I went out to prepare the garden for spring planting.

Not long ago I read that ten per cent of Americans believe that the car is the greatest invention of all time, and another twelve per cent chose the wheel as the greatest invention, presumably thinking of car wheels.

I don't think I'd be a good American; I could get along very well without a car. I prefer to walk. I realize, of course, that a car is not just a means of transportation. What we value about a car, sometimes even more than the fact that it goes, is the fact that it can be driven. In a world that is less and less driven by people, the car provides man with an opportunity to express himself more personally than he can in the rest of his life. As a driver, he can escape his everyday roles and responsibilities—or at least he can tell himself that this is so. Sitting behind the wheel, he is no longer a clerk, a deluded husband, an unsuccessful and insignificant city dweller; he is a driver. By driving, he becomes what he imagines himself to be. Instead of running in dull and monotonous circles, he flies down roads to the unknown, in pursuit of ancient longings and phantoms. He flies down roads and becomes dangerous— through his dreams as much as his driving. That is why he must be stopped by the ever-watchful guardians of road safety.

When Martin, the engine driver, returned my books, he talked about crime on the railway. Trains would arrive at their destinations, he said, with only a part of their freight. It was understandable and even forgivable. When oranges disappear from a freight car, they may be the only oranges people in that part of the country will ever see. But of course oranges are only the beginning. Once, fifteen cars loaded with Wartburg automobiles were left on a siding, and several days later, just before they were dispatched, it was discovered that on the side facing away from the station, all the wheels had been stolen.

Martin had applied for a hard currency voucher for a trip to Denmark. As expected, he'd been turned down.

That evening Pavel stopped by to see me, his head still wrapped in bandages. He told me that several of our friends had been arrested on the way home from the ball, and no one knew what had happened to them. As usual, there was no mention of this in the media.

We tried to tune in to some foreign radio station, but

124

jammers drowned out the announcers' voices.

Jammers are the sound of a life that She—the one in disguise—directs according to Her notions. She knows that man has a different notion of his fate and good fortune, that he wants to win, through his defiance, his right to his own footprint, action, sentence, to a truthful thought that he could declare out loud or at least hear expressed. But She is convinced that She and She alone can decide our fate; say what is good and what is evil. She desires that the sentences she passes stay with us from morning till night, from the cradle to the grave, where one day She will lay us low. All voices other than Her own she brands false; they are banned and cannot be heard even from beyond the borders that She has ordered closely guarded. She has had recorded the creaking of Her joints and the howling of the wind in Her empty skull. She orders that they be broadcast, amplified a thousand times, to drown all sounds of life.

Three weeks later the authorities sent me a message. I went to the local police station where the same young officer who not long ago had explained to me that my request for my keys amounted to the false accusation of a public officer now asked me impatiently why I wasn't taking an interest in getting them back. Did I think that the police were some kind of baggage depository? I was to report at once to the commander of the special operations team.

The barracks of the special operations team was next to the street where I spent my childhood, so I found it with no difficulty. The commander of special operations was small and stocky, almost bald, and he wore glasses. His tunic was undone and underneath it I could see striped braces. He had a fatherly expression.

Yes indeed, he had seen my driver's licence, and yes, he even remembered that there were some keys with it. Three, wasn't it? Two? It was possible. One was bigger than the other. However, since I hadn't requested them for so long . . . it was now being dealt with at Vinohrady. On Peace Square. Did I know where the station was? Perhaps he'd better give me exact directions.

He backed up to a large map of Prague that hung on the wall behind him.

I said that I had driven around the square almost every day for fifteen years, and I was last there when the railway workers had held their ball.

Yes, that was right: the railway workers' ball, that would have been three weeks ago, wouldn't it? Well, the ballroom dancing season was just about over, and if I was going to go dancing—and he circumspectly let the word that again had forced its way on to his tongue, slip from his lips—I would have to hurry. He shook my hand. When I was already walking through the door, he asked again, with concern in his voice, whether I was sure I'd find the station on the square.

The station was where it was supposed to be, but of course they had neither my keys, nor my driver's licence.

Crime was on the increase, even though the ballroom-dancing season was coming to an end. The paedophile—whom no one, evidently, was looking for—was still at large in our area. A young medical student was raped and strangled on an international express train. And there were stories going round that the director of the automobile factory had given away to influential comrades or, at least, sold for the price of scrap a wagon-load of cars, which naturally did not belong to him.

I paid a visit to a friend of mine, a playwright who alone among my colleagues can publish what he writes and therefore has access to the comrades. He claimed that they had transferred the director to a less responsible position, and that things were beginning to get better. During my visit, a car stopped outside the house and a woman in gardening clothes jumped out.

As I understood it, the woman taught my friend's daughter. The clothes in which she arrived were 'emergency' clothes. She had been wearing them when she returned from her cottage the previous evening—and now they were all she had to wear. Over the weekend, thieves had burgled her flat. What they hadn't taken they had destroyed, systematically. They had pulled the drawers out of the cupboards and dressers and smashed them. They had torn up her fabrics or poured varnish over them; they had burned her passport and bank-books and the parquet flooring, broken her china, slashed her pictures. They had drunk her spirits, and what they didn't drink, they poured over her Persian rug.

It was as though they were taking revenge on her for something, as though they enjoyed the act of destruction more than theft. The police guessed that there was a whole gang of them at work. The noise of the destruction must have been heard in the building, and her neighbours immediately beneath her and on each side of her were home all weekend, and didn't even come out of their flats to see who was making such a racket. What kind of people were they? The things the thieves carried off must have half filled a large truck. The tears in her eyes as she told the story were not only for the vandalism, but for the indifference of her neighbours, who did nothing to protect her property, and for the apathy of the investigators, who were unmoved by the wasteland her flat had become.

It occurred to me to ask what she taught.

She taught Marxism.

It didn't feel as though I missed being able to drive but oddly enough, at night, highways worked their way into my dreams with increasing frequency. I could read the names of exotic places on the road signs, or sometimes only the number of the roads that stretched through the prairies and clambered up mountainsides. The car was utterly unlike any I had ever driven; I was giving a lift to a girl utterly unlike any girl I had ever given a lift to, and I knew that we would make love as soon as I found an appropriate place. But could such a place be found on the highway? I turned on to a road that led into a wood, but that didn't seem deserted enough either; the trees were tall and widely spaced and offered no shelter, no real hiding place. I drove out of the wood and on to an empty plateau of sand. There was not a living soul in sight, and even the road vanished. I was still driving, and as the sand crunched under the wheels I felt the girl's naked body pressing against me. She had taken off her clothes. I stopped the car, hastily reclined the seats and transformed the interior into a perfect bed.

As we were lying in an embrace I realized that the car, now driven by no one, had begun to move forwards. I raised myself up, and through the window I saw the edge of a precipice. We were moving towards it. I wanted to grab the wheel and slam on the brakes, but the seats were in my way. There was nothing I could do. The car moved right to the edge of the precipice and I could see the depths below me. I screamed in terror, but no one heard me. I reached out for the girl, but felt only emptiness. She was no longer in the car, and I was alone as I plunged into the abyss.

When I told the dream to my non-existent psychoanalyst, he persuaded me that it was not about how I longed to drive a car again, nor about how I desired to make passionate love to a strange woman. My dream was about the state of disinheritance I found myself in. The girl symbolized the world beyond my family, my craving for the intimacy of other people. At the moment when real danger appeared and the abyss opened up before me, the girl, the symbol of that distant community, vanished—what remained was an overwhelming solitude.

Two weeks later, I was invited to the Traffic Inspectorate where a short, slightly built major was sitting behind his desk. 'Ah, it's you,' he said when he had studied my summons. He leaned over and pretended that he was looking for something before opening a file that he had on his desk. 'Now I wonder how these got here?' he said, taking out my keys. He held them between his thumb and forefinger, raised them up with a look of bemused curiosity, and jingled them. 'I believe these are the keys to your car.'

He handed them to me and then began to study the documents in the file. 'My goodness, the things I'm reading about you here,' he said. 'On the evening of 20 February, one of our squad cars followed you along the embankment for a while, and between the Charles Bridge and the Iron Bridge you committed five serious breaches of the Traffic Act. At the National Theatre you even ran a red light.' He looked at me disapprovingly; perhaps he actually believed what he was saying. 'Our comrades also administered a breathalyser test,' and he pulled the familiar tube out of the file, held it between finger and thumb and observed, as I had, its colourless state. 'The results, as you know, were negative.' He put the tube back in the file. 'Even so, the comrades justifiably held your driver's licence. Five offences—that's too many. Was something upsetting you?'

He fell silent, as if awaiting a meaningful answer to his meaningless question. 'It happens,' he said. 'The driver may be sober, but because he's upset he can't concentrate, and instead of stopping and getting out of the car, he goes on driving and becomes a threat to other road users.' Once again he fell silent. When I still had nothing to say, he asked if I were willing to be re-tested.

I said I was, not to make his role too easy, and he gave me a form with questions printed on it.

'You've passed,' he said, when he'd scanned my answers. He took my almost brand-new driver's licence from the file, grasped it and held it up as though it were something distasteful, then opened it up, closed it again, opened it, looked at the photograph and then at me, and put it back in the file.

He said he couldn't possibly give my licence back to me in that state. Why the photograph didn't even look like me. I would have to apply for another one.

I asked him if, considering that the only thing at issue now was a new photograph, he could issue me with a temporary licence. But he was obviously so upset that he couldn't concentrate, and he didn't even appear to register my question. He stood up to indicate that our conversation was over.

When I got home, I found Martin the engine driver waiting for me. He had heard about my difficulties, and it occurred to him that the time had come for me to try driving a train. It couldn't be put off; at the end of the spring he was leaving the railway. They were offering him a place on a farm where he was to raise mink.

I told him that they were still hanging on to my driver's licence. He laughed. Wasn't that why he was here? I didn't need a licence to drive a train.

We left together, and got off the train in a small town in the foothills of the Ore Mountains.

We also long to drive so we can escape from Her. We step up to the driver's seat as though it were a royal (or presidential or secretarial) throne. It seems that we have dominion over the living and the dead. Dumbfounded by our own power, we succumb to the delusion that we have dominion over Her as well, since She could not possibly creep up to us and take us into Her embrace without our consent.

Once, far in the past, people believed those who ruled to be gods; later, it became clear that even they were controlled by a superior force; the same force that controlled everyone. It was also believed that the force, whatever it was called, had the power of judgement and the knowledge of good and evil. Those who ruled must have known that they could only do so imperfectly; that they were stand-ins and that everything they judged would be judged in a higher court. But of course this didn't stop many from giving themselves over to the self-delusion and the intoxication that goes with power. But this is nothing compared to the self-delusion and intoxication of those who rule oblivious of the power above them.

We talked for a long time, and it wasn't until midnight that I finally got to bed, in a bunk that was lined on three sides with books. I knew that we would be getting up at four and that then I would be entrusted with driving an engine I had never seen. I couldn't sleep. I listened intently to see if I couldn't hear, from somewhere, the whistle of the trains of my childhood, but there was only the silence of a house in the country.

Next morning the darkness was so deep that it was still black when we got on to a commuter train that would take us to the station where our engine was waiting for us. The passenger car was crammed with sleepy men and women driven from their beds by duty. We had to stand in the aisle. Did I understand the signals, at least a little, my host asked.

The language of lights, semaphors, grade indicators, detectors, markers, fishtails, order boards, wig-wags and targets was something I had learned as a child. I trusted that an institution as conservative as the railways had not changed its language.

Very well, but he would test me all the same.

At the station we walked over to an engine that, now the possibility of actually driving it loomed, overwhelmed me with its size. My friend had to go to the office for his working orders. He said it would be best if I kept out of sight. He would let me in from the other side.

The station seemed deserted. The train we'd arrived on had gone, and the passengers had dispersed. A lone old man in a blue uniform with an oil can walked along, oiling the wheels of the freight train. The tracks gave off an oily sheen in the light of the station lamps. The diesel engine smelled of kerosene. I walked around the train. Beyond the last set of tracks there was a steep embankment overgrown with shrubs. I sat down on an overturned stone bollard and waited. I was neither excited nor impatient; I had, after all, advanced well beyond the age when a man wishes to experience everything that excites him, just as he wants to make love to every woman he finds attractive.

Why, then, had I come here?

At that moment, the window of the engine lit up, then the headlights went on. A door high up opened. 'Come up, quick. We leave soon.'

I clambered up the steep steps and entered the cabin.

'Do you want to change your clothes?' he said, and opened up a small locker. On the inside of the door I caught sight of some pornographic pictures accompanied by the dry commentary: 'Stop! Warning signal! Then all clear, all clear!'

I said that I didn't think I would get changed; I'd rather he showed me what everything was for.

On the outside of the locker door, a blonde smiled on the shore of some lake, and next to her was a picture of Kronborg, Hamlet's castle:

> *The time is out of joint: o cursed spite,*
> *That ever I was born to set it right!*

There isn't much to show you, he said. It's easier to drive than a bicycle. But he showed me how to start the engine, and warned me that the half-wheel in the middle of the control panel wasn't a steering wheel, but an accelerator. It had eight positions and I would be controlling the speed with it. This was the emergency brake. The button next to the accelerator was called an 'alert button' and it would be my responsibility to push it once every ten seconds. It would probably bother me until I got used to it. Here was the speedometer. I would have to keep an eye on it all the time because the speed was recorded on a tape and the

133

tape was handed in after the trip. If we had gone over the limit anywhere, we'd be fined.

He also told me that initially we'd only be hauling 320 tonnes, and would be picking up another eighty on the way. It wasn't a lot, but it was enough for those hills, especially if we had to get underway on a slope. Starting was the only thing that needed a little practice, so that the couplings wouldn't pull loose, or the wheels begin to spin. The first time, he would start himself. I would also have to realize that I was not sitting in a car, that 400 tonnes was a substantial weight and when I was going downhill I should be careful not to go too quickly and fly off the rails. And when going uphill I had to make sure I didn't lose speed. If I did, I would find myself standing still before I knew it.

At that moment, I noticed the signal ahead had turned from red to green. Despite myself I felt a twinge of excitement. 'Keep your head down for now,' Martin said, and leaning out of the side window he waved his hand to the dispatcher, turned the half-wheel slightly and, while I obediently crouched in a corner, we pulled out of the station.

The awakening countryside began to flow past us, but I paid little attention; I was looking at the speed signs: the speed limit here was low, and the whistle signals came one after another.

'You can take over now,' he said, turning to me and making room on the seat. 'Don't forget the alert button. If you want, I'll push it for you, for now.'

I said that I would try to press it myself. I sat down in front of the control panel, but the machine was not aware of this change. It was going by itself, as it was meant to do. The little light above the alert button came on at regular intervals, but I always managed to deactivate it in time, so that the machine didn't honk at me. The track began to rise gently and, mindful of my mentor's advice, I turned the accelerator a little. Thus we went through several stations, at least twenty level crossings, some with gates, some without, the engine rumbling regularly and the needle on the speedometer steady. The speed limit varied from thirty to fifty kilometres an hour, and on the whole, I managed to accelerate or decelerate that enormous mass of metal smoothly. It was only after a while that I saw what an unusual view I had of the track unwinding in front of me, and heard the regular sound of the wheels clacking over the joints in the rails.

After an hour my instructor, who until now had kept a keen eye on the track, the engine, and my actions, took out his lunch, leaned up against the wall by the locker, and poured himself a cup of tea. More than any words could have done, his actions expressed his confidence in my capacities as an engine driver.

At one of the stations the guard came into the cabin and, paying no attention whatsoever to me, as though having a guest driver were absolutely normal, he began to talk about people I couldn't have known, one of whom was a colleague who got so drunk on duty that he couldn't even stand up, and was in that state when an inspector found him.

The story interested me, but at the same time I couldn't really listen, though I gathered that nothing happened to the drunken engine driver; he had faked an acute attack of lower back pain, and who would be so cruel as to compel a colleague suffering from excruciating pain to submit to a breathalyser test?

It seemed to me that the two of them were enjoying themselves and not paying any attention to the track, but suddenly my friend called out, 'D'you see them? Now you can blow your horn at them.'

It was then that I noticed, at the level crossing we were approaching, a yellow and white automobile with the widely ridiculed letters on it.

'If only they could see you like this,' he laughed, 'those brothers of theirs, the ones who hung all that nonsense on you.'

I gave a blast on the horn. Perhaps I actually caught a glimpse of Her at that moment. At least I thought I saw Her sitting there: all bone, her favourite disguise, grinning and showing her teeth at me, while I flashed past. Now I was aware of the massive weight I was controlling, and I saw the wagons behind me in a bend in the tracks and I surrendered to the illusion that I was pulling them along with my own enormous power. I had crossed Her path.

'Can you brake a little? We're going downhill anyway,' he reminded me.

I understood why he had invited me, offered me the opportunity, for a moment at least, to cross paths with Her, so that I would know I was not battling Her alone.

'You forgot the alert button,' he said immediately afterwards, reproachfully.

In an instant I returned to my place and pressed the button, as a sign that I was still alive.

The Courier's Story

ONE

I DIDN'T GET to the institute until nine; they almost never had anything to deliver before then anyway. They seldom had much after nine either. It was summer and most of the employees were on holiday. Besides that, the mainframe computer in Strašnice was down, so there weren't even the usual reams of print-outs to deliver. I took the stairs to the office on the fourth floor. I don't trust the elevator; I see no reason why elevators should be exempt from the general state of disrepair that holds everywhere and, in any case, I like going under my own steam.

The office was usually occupied by the secretary and the manager. Both were young and sweet, and each was pretty in her own way and liked to chat. The mail, if there was any, would be laid out for me on the table beside the door. Today only the manager was in and my table was empty or, to be more precise, it held only a vase full of gladioli. I said hello, and the manager looked up. 'You needn't have come at all today,' she said by way of welcome.

'But I love coming here,' I replied. 'I look forward to seeing you.'

She laughed. 'Have you heard the latest definition of socialism?' And she told me one of the many merciless jokes against the system we live under, and against which we are forbidden to grumble, for it is allegedly the best, the most just and the most humane way of organizing human affairs. In return, I told her another definition.

The telephone interrupted our illicit diversion. When the manager hung up, she asked, 'Do you know how Julinka is doing?'

I didn't.

Julinka Vandasová was the wife of one of the programmers. I had never met her, but I knew what she looked like from the photographs her husband kept under a sheet of glass on his desk. She looked delicate and gentle. Yesterday she was operated on for a cyst that was supposed to be benign. She had two little girls and all the women in the institute were wondering how Mr Vandas would cope by himself. 'I called Chodov this morning,' the manager announced, 'but Peter hadn't come in yet. Are you going over there today?'

'If they have anything for me.'

'They don't,' she said. 'I've already asked. They've finished work now in Strašnice, and they say there's a terrible jam at the the mainframe in Vrsovice.'

'Anyway,' I said, 'maybe something will show up there during the day.'

'Whatever you think. If I were in your place, I could . . .' and she began daydreaming about all the things she could do if all she had to do was run errands. 'If you're going there anyway, take this with you. Nobody reads it, of course, but it's just arrived.' She took several copies of the in-house journal from her drawer. 'And,' she said, getting up and walking over to the table, 'if you could give Vandas these and say they're for Julinka.' She took three gladioli from the vase, wrapped them in a damp tea-towel and handed them to me. I slipped them, along with the bundle of magazines, into my pushcart.

'Oh, and Engineer Kosinová wants to give this to someone.' She handed me a three-year-old mail-order catalogue from Neckermann's.

Outside, I was enveloped in a wave of hot air. I hurried across to the shady side of the street and walked towards the Old Town Square. I was wearing light cotton trousers, a short-sleeved shirt and a pair of deer-skin moccasins I'd purchased years ago in Chicago. I'd forgotten all about them until recently, when I started this job, which involves a lot of walking, and I loved them because they were so light and soft. I was in no hurry: no one was expecting the magazines, the three-year-old Neckermann catalogue could certainly wait as well, though the flowers would soon need water.

Two days before I had brought Mr Vandas several boxes of tape from Letna. He was sitting in his cubicle, but instead of looking at the monitor, he was staring into the forlorn, bulldozed meadow outside the window. There was a half-empty glass of wine in front of him. He asked me if I'd sit and have a drink with him. He'd taken his wife to the hospital that morning. 'You know, I felt strange when we said goodbye,' he confided. 'It didn't feel right, leaving her to the mercy of a stranger who would put her on a table and slice her open. I know,' he added quickly, 'it's what's best, but I think you should have the right to lie down and be cut open for someone else. I was afraid for her, too,' he admitted. 'Still am. For her, for the children—and I'm afraid for myself too. Know what I mean? You hear of someone dying of cancer and the first thing you know you're checking to see if you've got the same symptoms. I wish things were fairer. For instance, everyone should be allotted a minimum life-span. Forty years, at least. As it is . . . My cousin's little girl died late last winter. She wasn't even five. From the time she was three her days were numbered, and in the end, they were feeding her through tubes. We tried to find a healer at the last minute, but it was too late. The poor little thing was buried the first day of spring. The parents weep and what can you say? In the past, you could at least comfort them with the idea that they'd all meet again, but today? I told my cousin to be brave and she said: Why? I didn't know what to tell her. In fact I didn't know what she was really asking me. Not long ago we were driving along the highway to Hradec—Julinka was with me—and on one side of the road there was this brand new fence, a long wire fence, and do you know what was on the other side? Nothing. Weeds, an overgrown, empty field. No construction site, no military training ground, nothing. With this beautiful new fence around it. The fence was five kilometres long—I clocked it—and then suddenly it came to an end. All that nothing was only fenced in from one side. It was like a vision of what we are living through. Do you understand what I'm saying?'

I looked into a bookstore window, though I knew there'd be nothing interesting on display. Even if, miraculously, something good were to be published, they wouldn't put it in the window; they'd keep it under the counter for their friends. Several men, probably construction workers, were standing outside a pub with half-litre glasses of beer in their hands, spending their working hours in pleasant conversation. The repairs to the façades on the Old Town Square were almost finished, and the square gleamed with newness and colour like a grand Sacher cake; I liked it, and I got enormous pleasure out of just being able to wander about there. Before I found this job I came downtown twice a month at most, and then I was in a hurry to get back home and back to work. But now this job brought me here every day, and I could study the slow progress of repairs to the Týn Church, and peer into the exhibition room of the Town Hall. I could even have gone in, but felt reluctant to do so, for as long as I was moving through the streets with my pushcart in the general direction of my destination, I was working and no one could complain. But I had no business at an art show.

I stopped in front of the Town Hall tower. The first tourists of the morning were beginning to gather on the pavement below the astronomical clock. Tourists from the West were still asleep or perhaps having breakfast, whereas those standing beside me, already burdened with parcels and waiting for the Twelve Apostles to appear when the clock struck the hour, were a group from the empire of our eastern neighbours. I listened to their soft speech, a language that had seduced some of our reckless and gullible ancestors into dreaming dreams of a brotherhood of the strong and the weak. But the conversation didn't seem to be about anything that made sense.

The clock struck, the apostles paraded one by one past the tiny portals, but as always, they remained silent, telling us nothing and then vanishing into their darkness again.

I walked along Ironmonger's Street to Mustek where, in an antique store, I saw a Renaissance armoire costing 180,000 crowns. Doing the work I was doing now, this was the accumulated salary of ten years. I began to plan the story of a courier who decided not to eat, drink, live anywhere or even read so he could save all his money to buy this antique armoire. Several endings suggested themselves. The courier, who all that time had slept in a cellar and lived on the leftovers he picked off plates in the stand-up buffets, could die of exhaustion. Or he survives but meanwhile—and this was the most plausible outcome—the armoire is sold to someone else. Or, and this was my favourite: he finally drags himself to the shop, where he finds the armoire still waiting for him, but in the meantime the price has doubled.

Just outside the entrance to the subway, a small poster announced in a brief, pointed verse: 'Hey, hey, hey, our pizza's okay kay kay!' I wasn't hungry, but the pizza was surprisingly cheap and there were only about twenty people in the queue, so I decided to indulge in a snack.

In fact, I have no great desire to own a Renaissance armoire, and I make my living as a courier only during the summer months. I have no complaints about the pay; I understand that in the age of long-distance electronic data transfer, interlocking information systems and telecommunications satellites, my job is as archaic, or as folkloric, as a bagpiper, a Buckingham Palace guardsman or a writer. But I have always had a weakness for archaic jobs, even in times when I could, on the whole, choose freely what I wanted to do. I refused to become an engineer or a physician, although my professors tried to persuade me to do so, and although I had inherited a capacity for mathematical thinking from my father. Some time later I committed my first political transgression (I had written an article in praise of Karel Čapek) and when they threw me out of the editorial department of an illustrated weekly, I was offered a job as editor in a factory that manufactured aircraft engines. I turned it down, not because I felt it was demeaning to be editing an in-house magazine, but because I didn't trust aircraft engines. Had they offered me a similar position in a factory that made hats or mustard, I would have accepted.

As far as I can, I choose occupations that don't trap me within four walls. When I was an editor, I refused to sit in the office, but instead went out on assignments. Even as a hospital orderly, I spent most of my time rushing between the wards, the pharmacy, the morgue and the labs. Sitting behind a desk, there are no surprises. Outside, there is the possibility of a chance encounter.

I would have liked to work for the post office. People look forward to the postman, since most people, unreasonably, expect good news rather than bad. I used to long to bring people a message of great import. Now I'm more modest, and I'd be satisfied with bringing good news. But the post office didn't want me, so instead I took the job of courier in an institute that tests and evaluates air and water pollution across the country. The thing that interested me most about the institute was that a large number of computer programmers worked for it. I had heard a lot about computers but knew little about them and the people who serve them. I understood enough, however, that I could imagine the future belonging to them.

What will that future be like? I recently read an article, purporting to demonstrate that the interpersonal relationships of computer programmers suffer because of their constant contact with the computer. It used to be, the author went on to say, that a person could carry on a conversation only with another person. There was no other choice if he wanted to talk or to make love, even though that other person might, at times, have seemed dull and stupid, or even deceitful.

But now you can have a conversation with a computer; a computer not only understands, but replies. Moreover, you know the computer will not deceive you, or leave you; it will always be there, and may even outlive you. Soon, the article argued, you will be able to sit down in front of a friend of the sixth generation or so and converse with it wisely, as you could do with no human being. Can you love a computer, too? If the operator asks that question at all, the author suspects that yes, he will love it and, moreover, the computer will love him back. Who else could they love without being unfaithful?

It was a variation on the theme of robots, our future masters. It was neither inspiring nor, fortunately, very believable.

Because the results of the institute's work, important though they were, produced nothing but public concern, it did not enjoy official favour. It did not even have its own building. Its employees worked at two sites at opposite ends of the city. And, though a quarter of its employees were programmers, the institute had had its only mainframe computer confiscated, so the programmers had to travel to three other locations where they could get an hour or two of computer time to process their information on the state of our environment.

Because data transmission was something you can only read about in this country, the need for a courier became obvious. His—my—job was to deliver from one workplace to another everything that needed delivering. Sometimes it was just the newsletter, at other times a box of diskettes, bundles of punch cards or reams of computer print-outs.

Often there was nothing at all or, like today, flowers. In such cases, I would sit for a while in the modern hall of the institute in the Southern City—an enormous complex of high-rise apartments—and read a book, or study the WordPerfect manual that Engineer Klíma pressed upon me with the injunction that I must not leave the institute without some useful insight into the things a computer can do. In any case, he claimed, this knowledge would certainly be useful in my own profession.

I finally got my slice of Okay Pizza and left the gloomy passageway. A circular bench was occupied by tourists also eating pizza. A dark-haired woman, perhaps Italian or Spanish, was sitting on the lap of her Italian or Spanish boyfriend, feeding him. She had a very short skirt, short legs, and a firm left breast. Her boyfriend's hand covered the right one. I have never been to Italy or Spain, though I have always felt drawn to those countries, not so much by their famous historical attractions as by my theory that the people there are of a passionate nature, with whole, integrated characters and thus with interesting stories to tell. But perhaps I'm wrong; this beautiful young woman probably worked in a department store, and her story wouldn't be much different than the stories of our Czech girls who work in Kotva or Máj here in Prague. She noticed that I was observing her and stuck her tongue out at me. I looked away, above her. For the first time in my life I noticed an enormous clock which, not surprisingly, displayed some unreal time.

I started up Wenceslas Square towards the subway station. I don't find walking through the city distracting. In no time I'm alone, composing a story, a speech or a letter in my head. I don't enjoy writing letters, but sometimes I like to imagine writing to women I have loved, or even to authors who've drawn me to them with a sentence, an image or an idea. I also write imaginary letters to important personages—but such letters tend to be brief, and questioning rather than reproachful. I actually wrote some of the love letters, but so far, not a single one of the other kind.

In the subway train there was a group of young girls, probably students, or apprentices from one of the department stores. They were not wearing uniforms, yet they all seemed alike, as though they were all from the hand of a single uninspired and untalented artist. I took one of the newsletters out of my bag and opened it:

INTERNAL DIRECTIVES AND INSTITUTIONAL PRINCIPLES FOR THE USE OF THE F.C.S.N. FOR THE PURPOSES ESTABLISHED BY THE DECLARATION OF THE F.M.F., M.F., CSR, SSR, AND THE U.R.O. # 21/1986 SB., ON THE F.S.C.P.

Deciphering the headlines immediately absorbed all my attention, and while I read the details about the Fund for Cultural and Social Needs, the train rushed through the dark tunnel, carrying me to my next destination.

It was a six and a half minute walk from the subway station to the institute. The horizon on all sides was punctuated by blocks of grey, mostly unfinished pre-fab high-rise apartments with enormous broad-shouldered cranes towering above them; inspiration for poets who did not have to live there. But the walk itself was pleasant. There was a meadow on one side, and the pavement was separated from the road on the other side by a thick hedge of wild rose. With a little imagination, you could pretend you were walking down to the beach on the Baltic coast.

A fat guitarist was sitting in the porter's office. Students from the conservatory took turns working shifts on the door: the guitarist, a violinist and a clarinet player. All of them had the same peculiarity: they took no notice whatever of what went on outside the porter's booth. The guitarist had a girl-friend with him, and she was sitting on the table with her back to the new arrivals, symbolically emphasizing the wall between the world of the conservatory students and that of the computer programmers. Unobserved, I walked past the porter's lodge, then down several corridors before I came to the door to the main hall of the institute.

The building was new, clean, and full of light. What I liked most about it was a small atrium where, thanks to the efforts of the female programmers, dragon trees, dieffenbachia, plectranthus and even a tiny palm tree I was unable to classify flourished.

There was no one in the hall except a little girl sitting at a table drinking milk from a carton. I thought she must be Engineer Vandas' daughter, and I asked her where her father was.

She shrugged her shoulders and handed me a piece of coloured paper. 'Look what I drawed.'

The picture showed a bed, and on the bed was a figure sliced in two, with flowers laid on her breast.

'Who's that?' I asked.

'It's Mama, of course,' she said.

There was a fresh item on the notice board, a clipping from *Lidová demokracie.*

MYSTERY UNRAVELLED

Suva: After a sixty-five-year investigation, the Fiji police recently detained an eighty-two-year-old confidence man, R. Tama, who, according to police spokesmen, had 'dishonoured a hundred and thirty-two women and girls.' The police had long known about the octogenarian Romeo but lacked evidence. They later discovered that all of the women had subsequently perished in a coconut grove not far from Tama's place of residence. Another remarkable circumstance, however, was the fact that all of them had died when a coconut had fallen on their heads. The mystery was solved when Constable Ratilau discovered a personal computer and a large number of programmes under a mattress stuffed with palm leaves in Tama's air-conditioned apartment. Tama had used the computer to calculate when a coconut from a particular tree would fall. Then he would send his 'wives' to lie under the tree. Sources close to the investigation said that an unnamed Japanese electronics firm had, not without profit, helped to produce Tama's computer programmes.

Mr Bauer was just walking past and, noticing my look of disbelief, explained that Mr Vandas had send this report to the papers as part of a bet he'd made with someone that people would believe almost any nonsense about computers. He wrote this story, sent it off—and won.

Computer programmers love practical jokes. Once Mr Klíma added some built-in commands to the master programme used by Mrs Rybová. Suddenly, her terminal emitted a bubbling sound and a message flashed on the screen: *Water is entering your computer! Shut off mains water at once!* Rybová ran out of her office, yelling for someone to turn off the water. In addition to playing jokes on each other, the programmers play tennis, go on long weekend hikes, and occasionally get together, drink wine and tell stories, all so they won't go crazy from constant conversation with their computers.

I walked through the offices, but they were all empty. I put the catalogue on Miss Kosinová's desk; the gaudy cover looked out of place among the test reports and specialist magazines. Miss Kosinová was a group leader at this site, and I wasn't surprised that the catalogue was for someone else; she was always finding things for someone else. I couldn't imagine her wasting her time leafing through a catalogue. She had never married, they said, because a family would interfere with her work. But the real reason, it seemed to me, was her kindness. She was so kind, so concerned for others, that she could not serve two masters; the feeling that she was neglecting one of them would have been unbearable.

The next hall contained only a small desk-top computer, and it was there that I found them all, including Miss Kosinová and the only member of the Communist Party in the institute, Mrs Rybová. In the middle of the room, seated at the computer, was Mr Vandas with his younger daughter on his knee. His good-natured, bearded face showed tension or more likely pain. The coloured monitor displayed a two-lane highway with cars flashing by in opposite directions. Mr Vandas directed his car with subtle movements of his joystick, passing on the left, rejoining the flow while adroitly avoiding the cars that were hurtling towards him. Brightly lit cities, petrol pumps, bridges and side-roads flashed by, and silhouetted on the horizon were high mountains, perhaps the Rockies themselves, where the driver was heading.

The others in the room were so intent on the game that

they didn't notice me come in. I was somewhat surprised, for I was used to finding the programmers in their own cubicles or, when they managed to get some time on the mainframe computer in Strašnice, on Letni or in Vrsovice, they were scarcely here at all. Mr Vandas had just successfully cut in on three cars in a row while the onlookers breathed sighs of relief, and it was then I understood that they'd all gathered here to show him their support, since his wife had just had an operation.

The moment I stepped into the room, I was aware of an unusual atmosphere full of kindness and compassion. As a matter of fact, whenever these people asked me to deliver something that it was part of my job to deliver anyway, they always asked first whether they weren't putting me to too much trouble, then hastened to assure me they were in no hurry and if it was inconvenient now, I could bring them the tapes tomorrow. The kindly Miss Kosinová was certainly one of the reasons for this exceptional atmosphere. Several times, when I saw her dispirited by the sheer number of impediments she and her colleagues faced, I wanted to tell her that she was creating something far greater than a bunch of programmes. Moreover, the work they were doing here was important. To make light of the impediments was to make light of the work.

At last Mr Klíma noticed me and asked if I wanted to sit down at his computer and practise WordPerfect for a while, now that his terminal was free. So as not to offend him, I agreed and he led me away to his office. Usually Mr Klíma didn't talk much, but on the way he told me they'd operated on Mrs Vandas the night before. Everything had turned out well, she was in intensive care now but they expected to transfer her to a regular ward the next day. He switched on his computer, stepped back and with a smile of encouragement, said, 'It's all yours.'

The first time he sat me down at his computer, he had complained that they only had two terminals here, and that this was one of them. Two computers for twenty programmers! 'In the West, anyone who wants can buy something like this for a month's wages. But they can't import them because of the embargo. And for my monthly wages, the most I could buy over there would be a box of diskettes. This computer,' he informed me, 'was smuggled here all the way from Taiwan.'

If that were the case, I asked, why couldn't we manufacture computers here ourselves?

He explained to me that we could probably manage the electronics, but we'd still have to import hard disks. They aren't embargoed, but no company can get the currency to buy them. And Mr Klíma waved his hand dismissively, as though he were driving away an oppressive dream. I had only a vague notion of what he meant by a hard disk, but I understood that the programmers' work was not proceeding according to plan. In that, at least, it was not unlike the work of most of us have to do.

I sat down at the keyboard, slipped a system disk into the upper drive and a file disk into the lower. Messages began appearing on the screen, following one another so rapidly that I had no time to read them. When I got the A> sign, I wrote, as I had been instructed several days before, A:WP, and then I sent this strange code into the machine's innards by pressing the key marked 'Return'. The diabolical machine immediately announced, in English: 'Bad Command or File Name!' But it offered no advice about what to do. I repeated my command, and the machine, with astonishing speed, repeated its message. I stared helplessly at the screen and waited, afraid to turn around because I was certain I'd forgotten something quite basic and, in asking Mr Klíma's advice, would somehow betray the kind effort he had exerted on my behalf. 'You forgot to replace the system disk with the programme disk,' he said finally, behind me. 'How is it supposed to call up WordPerfect if it doesn't have it?'

I changed the disks and sent my commands to the computer, which now whirred and clicked, reminded me that it was from Utah (where, unlike Spain and Italy, I had once been) and then presented me with a blank screen, an invitation to write.

So I wrote: *Dear Mr President*

I looked around. A satisfied smile appeared on Mr Klíma's round, clean-shaven face. 'Go ahead and write whatever you feel like,' he said. 'We can wipe it out later.' And he sat down at his desk and began to leaf through some computer print-outs.

You are probably used to getting a lot of requests and complaints, I continued. I didn't like this introductory sentence, so I gave the computer instructions to wipe it out and it did so with a speed that still astonished me. Then I wrote:

I know that you are very busy, but I am not writing with a request or a complaint. I would only like to express the sympathy, or rather the regret, that you cause me to feel. I remember your inauguration ceremony, when you took your oath of office and were evidently moved to tears. At the time, I thought how hopelessly isolated you must be if you had no one around you to point out how inappropriate your tears were. After all, you accepted your position at a time so full of sorrow and despair that it brought shame rather than glory to your name. I have tried, several times, to listen to your speeches, for I was curious about the message you wanted to convey to us. After all, I am a citizen of this country and I also try (though I am forbidden to do so) to convey something to the people who live here. So I listened to you and shared with you the horror, the despair of a man who accedes to the throne and surveys his invisible subjects, to whom he may, indeed to whom he must, convey something, and at the same time does not know what to say because he has nothing to say.

I remembered the flowers that by now must have been wilting in my bag. I quickly commanded the computer to wipe out the text, and I went to look for Mr Vandas. I found him in the hall with Miss Kosinová, who, perhaps because she doesn't have children of her own, behaves all the more maternally to those around her. They were giving food to his two little girls.

'Do you know what?' he asked, rinsing out the milk bottle. 'They've just registered the eight millionth chemical. Wait a minute, I'll show it to you.'

What he brought was not the chemical itself, just a piece of paper on which he had written: 2-(4-chloro-5-etocy-2fluorophenyl)-4,5,6,7,-tetrahydro-3methyl-2 H-indazol.

'How long can they go on getting away with this?' he asked.

As if summoned to answer that gloomy question, the youthful Mr Bauer appeared in the hall. I knew him as a quiet man whose glum, rather dreamy expression reminded

155

me of that of a poet, but now he announced loudly: 'I've just finished my calculations. In five years, the Jeseníky Mountains will be kaput, and in seven, the Beskyds and the Šumava.'

Mr Vandas put the flowers next to a picture of his wife. 'How about the Tatras?' he asked.

'I don't have the Tatras, the Slovaks are doing them. If it wouldn't be too much trouble,' he said, turning to me, 'I have some print-outs here that should go to Dr Myslivec in Komořan. But there's no hurry; he'll be at lunch now anyway.'

'Of course,' I said.

His elder daughter handed me a piece of paper with a drawing on it. There were three green trees, with coloured birds flying among them, and several animals grazing on the grass, of which I could only safely identify a giraffe. There were no people.

'What's this you've drawn?'

'It's the Garden of Eden,' she said. 'It's for Mama, when she comes home.'

'Can't those forests be saved?' I asked Bauer.

'They could,' Bauer explained. 'But people would have to die out first. Of course, if this keeps up, they'll die out anyway, but not before they destroy everything.'

'The process could be slowed down,' Miss Kosinová explained to me, 'if we invested in conservation, but there's no money, and there's going to be less and less. It's enough to make you despair.'

'The only question,' said Bauer, 'is will the forests die out in five years or in ten. I recently ran the Krkonoše and the Jizerské Mountains through the computer. They write about all the reforestation going on, but nothing will ever grow there any more. And before some mutant species that thrives on sulphur establishes itself, there'll be nothing but rocks left.'

'I don't think it's so hopeless,' said Miss Kosinová. 'People will eventually come to understand that they're destroying the world they have to live in.'

'Sure, people will—maybe,' Bauer admitted. 'But the guys on top couldn't care less. They don't give a damn about our calculations.'

The younger girl began to cry.

'There, there now,' said Miss Kosinová. 'You see, you're only just scaring little children.'

I went with Bauer to get his papers. 'The forest situation doesn't seem so hopeless to her because she's not working on it,' he complained. 'But you should hear her when she's talking about her water full of salmonella. If it were up to me,' he went on, 'I'd devise a programme that would tell us how to take all the garbage that's destroying us and render it harmless before we throw it out—but no one would have it, not even if I gave it away.'

'Do you really think humanity won't survive?' I asked.

'Pretty much,' he said. 'This is how it is: our water is down the drain, the seas are full of oil and all kinds of poison, the air—well, you can see for yourself what kind of shape that's in, forests all over the world are dying or being cut down, soils are being eroded and degraded, the deserts are expanding and the gene pool is shrinking. Add in the degenerating ozone layer, plus a Chernobyl every once in a while, the awful waste products they're cramming down every big hole they can find, and—you just heard Vandas— the hideous new shit they're constantly creating . . . '

'How long do we have?' I asked.

'Well,' he said, thoughtfully, 'you could more or less calculate it.' He handed me a bundle of print-outs, I stuffed them into my bag and we parted.

At the bus stop, I discovered that the bus to Komořan had left a few minutes ahead of me, and the next one wouldn't be along for fifteen minutes. As I was taking a book out of my bag to read, I heard a tapping sound behind me, like the sound a blind person makes. And sure enough, when I turned around, there was an enormous old man with a white cane. I had seen him here several times before at this time of day; he was probably going somewhere for lunch. Usually, he had someone guiding him, but this time he was alone, so I asked him if I could be of any help. He thanked me and said that he'd be very grateful if I could take him through the underpass to the other side. He had a rather strange accent, perhaps from Ostrava, or even further east.

As I led him down into the underpass, he counted the steps. When he reached ten, he said, with regret in his voice, 'That's as far as I can count.'

His admission surprised me. 'Where are you from?' I asked.

'From Arobidzhan. In Asia.'

'Somewhere in Russia?'

'It's at ninety-one latitude and fifty-six longitude. Right where they cross.'

'There, you see, you can count to more than ten.'

'No, they told me, and I remembered it.' He started counting the stairs again up to ten. I continued for him to sixteen. By that time we were at the bottom.

'You know how to count?' He seemed astonished. 'How far? To a hundred?'

158

'About that.'

'Are you a legionnaire?'

'No, why did you think that?'

'There were legionnaires in Arobidzhan. They spoke Czech too.' He began to count the steps going up. When he got to ten, he didn't stop as he'd done before, but merely repeated, on each step, 'Ten, ten, ten.'

'I'm not from Arobidzhan,' I said. 'I've never even heard of it. Is it in Siberia?'

'Further than that.'

'I'll find it on the map.'

'Are you a geography teacher?'

'What makes you think that?'

'You have a map at home.' He stopped to catch his breath.

'I've got a lot of maps at home.'

'Aren't you afraid? Or are you from the cartographical institute?'

'No,' I said, 'I'm a courier.'

'Are you delivering letters?'

'No, other things.'

'Aha,' he said, 'Summonses, warrants, verdicts. Piff, paff, boom!'

'No,' I said. 'I've already said, I'm not from Arobidzhan.'

'That's too bad,' he said. 'You should see it in winter when the Northern Lights come out. Beautiful! And the snow! The harder the times, the more snow there was. And wolves. You'd be interested, because I'll bet you're not really a courier, I'll bet you're one of those artists.'

I was surprised. 'How did you know?' I said.

'Not a musician,' he said. 'You have no ear for music. Just for people. But that's important too.'

159

We were approaching the exit to the street. In a low voice he counted off the last stairs: 'Ten, ten, ten.'

'Which bus number are you taking?'

'The long bus,' he said. 'To Vrsovice. But you don't have to wait, I'll ask for help.'

In Komořan, I got out at the last stop and savoured the view of the wooded hilltop, but I had to go in the opposite direction, down to the river. The asphalt was sticky in the heat and there wasn't a cool spot to be had anywhere. I walked across a large, sun-baked area and came to a bar, toyed for a moment with the idea of going in, but continued on along a street lined with villas. In the middle of the road, an enormous crane was lifting a steel pipe. Two men in overalls were looking on, a third was sitting in the shade of the machine, drinking beer. Without removing the bottle from his mouth, he signalled to me with his free hand to wait until the gigantic pipe had been set in place in the ditch.

I was standing outside a villa with a cherry tree laden with fruit just inside the fence. Several branches were overhanging the street, but not a cherry was left on them.

I smelled the cherries, at least, and watched while the crane operator skilfully manoevred his unstable load into position. When it was situated properly in the ditch, he turned off the engine and got out. All four men now looked into the hole with approval, then wandered over to a wooden caravan trailer. I could see a case of beer in the shade underneath it.

The institute was at the top of a small hill in a one-storey wooden structure that reminded me of the buildings the Germans constructed during the war for various emergency contingencies; some were used as field hospitals. It was old and no longer smelled of wood inside, but rather of stale tobacco smoke and old paper, huge piles of which were stacked everywhere. Dr Myslivec's office was at the end of a long corridor lined with heaps of brochures, books and parcels. No one was in. The whole building seemed empty. After all, what would anyone be doing here in this heat? I took the parcel of print-outs from my bag, put it down next to the other bundles of paper in a place where, as far as I could determine, Dr Myslivec could not miss them. Then, one of the glass doors opened and a young woman in a light blouse and a denim skirt looked out.

I said hello.

'You're always smiling,' she said, 'even when you're dragging that heavy bag behind you.' She was rather pretty, though her hair was dyed several different colours.

'But my bag is on wheels,' I said. 'And why shouldn't I smile at you?'

'But you smile even when no one is looking at you.'

I couldn't understand how she could know what I did when no one was looking at me.

'I'll bet this heat is making you thirsty,' she said. 'Would you like me to make you a coffee?.'

'I can't put you to the trouble, not in this heat.'

'I'll have one too. Then you can tell me why you're always smiling.'

Her office looked like all the others. Three desks and a little table with a hotplate. She pointed to an empty chair. 'Won't you sit down?' On a cupboard among stacks of dusty papers there was a forgotten vase. Geraniums and cyclamens bloomed in the windows.

'Well, are you going to tell me?' She said, sitting down opposite me. 'Would it bother you if I smoked?'

'You're the one who's at home.'

'That'll be the day,' she said. 'I'm always surprised at anyone who can smile like that.'

'But you don't do yourself any good by looking glum.'

'Then why do most people look glum?' She stood up and began making the coffee.

'You didn't answer my question.'

'Maybe they don't like being in this world.'

'And do you?'

'Well, once you're here . . . '

She handed me the coffee. It was hot, but I swallowed it as quickly as I could to avoid this conversation.

'I would have said the same thing myself once, but since my first husband died, it's become harder and harder.'

'Did he die recently?'

'No, it was six years ago. But it was—awful.' She looked at me. Her eyes had the colour the sky above the city sometimes has. When I looked into them more closely, I realized that they shifted slightly back and forth, as though she couldn't keep them steady. 'He was dying for an awfully long time. It was Parkinson's Disease. They had a programme about it on TV not too long ago. Did you see it?'

'I don't have a television.'

'You don't have a television?' She was shocked at my poverty. How could someone who didn't even have a television smile?

I said, 'I don't want one. I've got a lot of books at home, and I'd rather read.'

'You're right about that. It does eat up your time. But what's a body to do all evening?' She finished her cigarette, pulled another out of the packet, then put it back. She had slender, pretty hands, but her fingers trembled slightly.

162

'Did you remarry?'

'Of course,' she said. 'And I'm not smiling any more.' She tried to smile. 'This certainly can't be your profession.'

'Why don't you think so?'

'If you did this all the time, you wouldn't smile.'

I said nothing.

'Also, you wouldn't be wearing shoes like that,' she said, pointing at my moccasins. 'You'd have tennis shoes.'

'Well,' I admitted, somewhat taken aback by this feminine logic, 'I have done other things in my life.'

'Yes, and so have I. And do you enjoy this work?'

'Why not? It's OK for a while.' I drank the coffee and stood up to go.

'Next time you come, stop by,' she suggested. 'Too bad you can't bring me something.'

'What would you like?'

She shrugged her shoulders. 'A body's always waiting for something. You know, some good news. Even though you know by now there's no point. I found that out when Karel died.' She took my coffee cup and went to rinse it out. She didn't offer me her hand to shake, but as she walked by me, she brushed me lightly with her hip.

There were three name-plates outside her door: Anna, Jiřina and Natasha something or other. The Russian name seemed to suit her best.

Outside the wooden caravan, the four workers were sitting in the sun, stripped to the waist and drinking beer. They seemed at least as content with their fate as I was. I walked across the gaping ditch they had dug on a tiny wooden bridge. My working day was over.

At home, I found the intersection of ninety-one east latitude and fifty-six north longitude. It was close to

Krasnojara, but there wasn't a trace of Arobidzhan, nor did it seem likely that there would be any Northern Lights. Summonses, warrants, sentences, perhaps. And snow. The harder the times, the more snow. You fall into a snowdrift and it's the last they hear of you.

Two

THE MAINFRAME COMPUTER in Strašnice is operating again. The Strašnice computer is located in the basement of a tall building belonging to an import–export company. I brought them three bags of blank tape and I'm supposed to pick up tapes with data for delivery. In an enormous subterranean vault, where the air-conditioning hums and smoking is strictly forbidden, the computer screens glow and men and women in white lab coats hurry to and fro. At one of the terminals I recognize the tall, gaunt figure of Mr Bauer. He doesn't see me; his dreamy eyes are fixed on the screen where numbers are marching up and down, aligning themselves into columns. Bauer is collating data on the atmospheric pollution above the Czech mountain ranges. I look over his shoulder. Aerosols and sulphur dioxide are recorded in micrograms; lead, cadmium, copper and zinc are in nanograms—but beyond that I can't make sense of the numbers.

The tapes are waiting for me on the small table beside the entrance. The top reel has a piece of white tape stuck to it with *Šumava* written across it with a ball-point pen. I stuff the destruction of the Šumava forest into my bag. Through the windows of the glass hallway I see that it's

165

begun raining heavily. I sit down in a soft chair and watch the traffic in the hall. At a small table next to me are two Arabs, gesticulating violently and talking to each other in loud voices, certain that no one can understand them.

During the war, and then in the 1950s, it was good news when we got a letter from father or the uncles. It meant they were still alive somewhere in the camps or in prison, and that there was still hope we'd meet again. Of course in the end, they killed both my uncles.

I also considered it good news when my wife, whom I loved, sent a message that she was looking forward to seeing me. Genuine good news always relates to encounters that take place in love or in freedom—and best of all, in both conditions: a loving encounter in a state of freedom. The best news of all told us about a free encounter with God's love, which is why I am wary of giving unconditional credence to it.

I delivered my first message when I was still a student. It was pouring with rain outside like this too, but it must have been sometime in early spring, because a couple of days before that they had come to arrest my father. Early in the morning someone rang the doorbell. At that time, every ring of the doorbell made my mother nervous, so I went to answer it. It wasn't them, however, but one of my former classmates from high school. I can still see him standing there, drenched, inadequately dressed in a worn anorak, his ginger hair wet and stringy, his face unshaven, his eyes hollow and red from smoke or lack of sleep. Before I'd had a chance to invite him in, he pushed his way into the flat and closed the door behind him.

'What's up?' I wanted to know.

He assured me I had nothing to be afraid of; he'd made

sure no one was following him.

'Why should anyone be following you?'

He explained that they were after him, but he'd managed to lose them.

I wanted to know what they were after him for.

It was better I didn't know, he said.

Very well, but what did he want of me?

I had to hide him. At least until tomorrow. And to deliver one message.

'Me? Why me?'

'Who else have I got to turn to?' he asked. 'They won't look for me here, you have a national hero in your family. And I know you won't turn me in, because you've been in prison yourself.'

'That was during the war.' I felt myself becoming afraid.

'Makes no difference,' he assured me. 'A prisoner won't betray a fellow.'

'They were here a week ago and took my father away.' I was convinced they'd made a mistake, but I didn't say so out loud.

This made him uneasy. 'Is your place being watched?'

'No. At least I don't think so.' It had never occurred to me that we might still be under surveillance. After all, they'd searched our flat so thoroughly. And the rest of us? Surely they had nothing to suspect us of.

My mother appeared and asked why I didn't invite my friend in.

Then we sat in the living-room, drinking tea and pretending to reminisce about things we'd done together. The second my mother left the room he asked me for a piece of paper and an envelope and hastily scribbled something down. He put the paper into an envelope and stuck it shut. 'Could you deliver this for me?' he asked.

'What's in it?'

'You saw—a letter.'

'What's it say?'

'That's irrelevant. But it mustn't fall into their hands. If . . . if they go after you, you have to destroy it.'

'Wouldn't it be better if you delivered it yourself?'

Hadn't he told me they were after him, and that it was a miracle he escaped?

Very well, why didn't he stay until dark when he could deliver it himself.

'It's worse at night than in broad daylight.'

This letter would change everything. He promised. As soon as I brought him a reply, he would disappear, because he would know where to go, and how.

I had to bring him back a reply as well?

'You're not going to leave me in this alone, are you?' he said. 'Surely you understand, now that they've arrested your father.' He gave me a name and address and told me to memorize it. He told me how to get there as well: I had to take the tram and trolley-bus and then walk the rest of the way. And I had to be constantly on the lookout. If I saw them coming after me . . .

Yes, he told me that already. But how should I destroy the letter?

'You could eat it.'

I went to explain to my mother that my friend would be staying until evening, but I had to go to a lecture. I got dressed to go out. I was afraid, and angry. He could at least have told me why they were chasing him, why I should have taken this risk for him, and what was in the letter. What if they caught me before I had a chance to swallow

168

it? Besides, I had never had any burning desire to deliver spy messages.

He came into my room one more time. He was very nervous. 'If you're thinking of turning me in,' he said, 'they won't believe you anyway, not when they find me here.'

I wasn't hurt by his insinuation because the possibility had occurred to me. But despite his threats I could never have brought myself to turn someone over to the police who probably hadn't done anything.

I set off in the rain, which had at least emptied the streets. In those days, there were so few cars that I would certainly have noticed if I were being followed. My errand took me all the way to Jinonice on the outskirts of Prague, a village with narrow streets and low country houses. Occasionally a dog barked at me, and I would start with fright. Here, on the hilltop, the rain had changed to sleet that slid down my forehead and into my eyes.

Who was I was going to see? What if he were an agent for some spy service? Or head of an entire network they had just uncovered, and I stepped into his house as they were arresting him?

I couldn't drive out the scarecrows they had put out in my mind at the many political schooling sessions I'd had to attend. They, the secret police, were still fresh in my memory. Grey faces, grey suits. I didn't want to admit it, but they reminded me of the men who had turned over our flat at the beginning of the war, except that those men had spoken German.

I was twenty-two, I wanted to paint pictures and write love poetry, not visit houses I might never leave.

The person I was taking the message to lived in a cottage with a well-kept garden. The tree trunks were painted with lime, the flower-beds were protected with evergreen branches and the leaves had been carefully raked from the grass. The curtains were drawn. I checked several times to make sure I'd got the right house. There was no name on the door. I rang the bell.

For a long time nothing moved. I seemed to be able to discern the outline of a face behind the curtains. I remained still; so did the face. I longed to tear up the letter, throw it off a bridge and never come here again.

However, my uninvited guest was waiting for me back home and if I didn't deliver the letter, he wouldn't leave. He would stay with us until they caught him or I drove him out, and then they would arrest him. He, of course, would tell them where he had hidden.

I rang the bell again. At last the door opened. There stood a man with a wreath of white hair around a bald head. His face was sickly yellow, he had a sharply protruding nose and on it, a pair of spectacles with thick lenses. 'What do you want?'

I asked him if he was —— , the man I was looking for.

He said he was. 'And what do you want?'

'I have a letter for you.'

He nodded and invited me in.

I stepped into a small entrance hall with a floor of well-scrubbed boards. A few pairs of shoes stood beside a painted wooden box, along with a sweet-smelling basket of apples. A cross hung over the doorway. Through another half-open door I could see shelves full of books. I handed him the letter. He took it carefully, scarcely touching it. He put it on the box, took a penknife out of his pocket and slit the envelope open. He stared for a while at the paper with the message on it, then he folded it and put it back in the envelope and handed it to me. 'I don't know what this is about. I don't know this person. I don't understand what he wants from me.'

This took me by surprise. 'But he . . . I mean you . . . he knows you,' I stammered. 'He sent me here with this note. He's expecting a reply.'

'So I see,' he said. 'My reply is that I don't know him and I don't understand what he wants from me.'

He spoke with such emphasis, with such exaggerated certainty, that it occurred to me he was lying. He was afraid of me. He didn't know me and was therefore afraid that I was part of a trap.

I didn't know what to do. I refused to take the letter back home. I asked him to destroy it. Then I suggested that he come with me because the writer of the letter was waiting at my place and desperately needed to speak to him.

He took the envelope from me and went into the next room. I heard a stove door snap shut. Then silence. Nothing moved; from somewhere high up, a cat miaowed.

If he came with me, what would my mother say? She was already frightened enough without me bringing a stranger into our flat. The neighbours might notice. Or was this a trap to catch both of us? What if all of this had to do with my father's arrest? What if they simply wanted to test me to see how I would behave, and, for some reason, they wanted to test this man as well. Or perhaps he really did not know what any of this was about, and I was behaving like a fool.

He appeared at last, wearing a black, threadbare winter coat. 'Well, let's be off,' he said.

We arrived at our flat just after mid-day. I didn't think anyone had seen us. Most people were at work.

The two of them did know each other. I left them alone

171

in the next room, but even though they lowered their voices, I could tell that they were arguing. Half an hour later they announced that they were both going. As he was leaving, the old man said, 'God bless you, and forgive me. These days you just don't know who's the good messenger and who's the evil one.'

It wasn't until years later that I fully realized just how oppressive and destructive a state is in which people are afraid to accept messages brought to them by a stranger. I never heard from either man again and so I never found out what the message I delivered said.

Outside it had stopped raining. The Arabs had long ago disappeared somewhere.

The guitarist was on duty in the porter's lodge again, and because his girl-friend wasn't with him today, he was playing. It was a wild Spanish melody, and he played with such passion and concentration that if a gang of masked bandits had carried the director of the institute out bound and gagged he would certainly not have let it interrupt him. I listened for a while, but my sense of duty did not permit me to stay until the piece was over. I had already spent too long in Strašnice because of the rain.

It was noon, and from a small kitchen adjacent to the hall I could smell soup, as Miss Kosinová made lunch for everyone who didn't eat in the works canteen. 'Did you read,' Mr Klíma was saying to the only member of the Party in the institute, Mrs Rybová, 'that they've set up a special prize for scientists in America?'

'What are you trying to tell me? That we have no prizes here?'

'Three hundred and fifty thousand dollars!' said Klíma gleefully.

'You could really do something with that,' remarked Vandas, his good-natured, bearded face radiating contentment. He was expecting his wife home the following week; she was doing well.

'Certainly, if money is what it takes to get some people thinking,' Rybová shot back. She turned to me. 'Are you going to Komořan this afternoon?'

'If you need me to.'

'I'll leave it here,' she said, pointing to the table.

Klíma called me over, and I knew he wanted to torment me with WordPerfect again.

This time I remembered to change diskettes, and when the computer told me it was ready, I began to write:

Ladies and gentlemen,
Permit me to take advantage of this extraordinary opportunity to address the representatives of all nations and express some of my concerns at least to you—

In the days when I was still working for a literary magazine, an experienced colleague told me always to cut the first paragraph of any article, regardless of who wrote it. It is always expendable, he said.

I erased my paragraph, and then wrote:

I know that many wise words have been spoken in this forum, and I fear there is not a lot I can add. Yet I know as well as you do that we are rushing headlong towards a catastrophe that we refuse to see, that we are hoping to postpone, though know too that each day we choose postponement over change, we make the catastrophe all the more inevitable. This assembly is like a boat attempting to rescue the drowning while it itself is sinking. I know you must be quite deaf to the cries for help, to the voices of the sick, the hungry, the innocently imprisoned, the voices of the tortured and the powerless. I know that when you look at our planet, you see below you a sea of flammable liquid waiting for a spark to ignite it. This is our tragedy: we are on the lookout for sparks, while we keep on filling that flammable sea with rubbish, tanker ships full of crude oil, cubic kilometers of gas, the last living forests. We cannot prevent a spark from flying. We must realize at last that it is not just nations that are in danger, it is not just freedom and rights that are threatened, but life itself, as long as we do not stop our insane, headlong race after the mirage of prosperity, the lazy consumption of . . .

I felt excited and agitated, as I always am when I feel the desire to communicate too much at once and, at the same time, realize how fruitless my efforts are. You can't change things with words. With what, then? And besides, the telephone had been ringing for about half a minute and no one was answering it. I got up to do so, though I knew it wouldn't be for me. Miss Kosinová got there first. 'Yes, he is,' she said. 'No—oh, that can't be true! . . . But just yesterday . . .' She laid the receiver down beside the telephone. 'Peter,' she called. 'Peter—the phone.'

The parcel of print-outs was ready for me beside the telephone.

Vandas emerged from his cubicle.

'It's the hospital,' Miss Kosinová said, as though she were wondering whether or not to give him the receiver. 'But it's not good news.' She looked at me and I saw tears running down her cheeks.

Vandas held the receiver to his ear and listened to what

they were telling him. 'Yes,' he said. 'I'm still here.' Then he hung up. He turned to us and said: 'And they told us it wasn't malignant! It wasn't malignant—that's what they said. Everything is malignant.' He sat down and put his head in his hands. Miss Kosinová stood over him and stroked his hair. Others came up to comfort him, while I stood back; I felt out of place, as though I were a parasite on someone else's pain. I was an outsider here. I went back into Mr Klíma's cubicle and destroyed another of my pointless, incomplete and undelivered speeches. Then I took the parcel of print-outs, stuffed them into my bag and slipped out of the hall without anyone noticing.

At the subway station I bought three irises.

The door to Natasha's office opened before I had a chance to knock.

'You've brought something again?' she asked.

'Something for you, too.'

She took the flowers. 'Thank you. They're beautiful. They look like orchids. But you needn't have done that. That's not what I meant last time.' She took the vase from the cupboard, dusted it off and filled it with water. 'I'll make some coffee. Or would you rather have some wine? Yesterday was payday,' she explained. 'Otherwise I couldn't afford it. In any case, I'll be short by the end of the week.'

'Do they pay you badly?'

'When I pay the rent, I have a hundred left from the advance. And when I get the rest at the end of the month, I try to send something to my boy—he's in the army.'

'You have a son that old?'

'I was eighteen when I got married.'

'And your second husband?'

She waved her hand dismissively.

'I'm sorry. I didn't mean to pry.'

'Why not? He's in prison. Over in Ostrava.'

I didn't ask further, but she continued. 'He had an enterprising spirit—nothing more. In a normal world, he'd have opened a shop, and that would be it. He understood videos and tape recorders, even though he was a chemist. Just like my first husband—and like me.'

'You studied chemistry?'

'I taught it. Ten years. But then when my husband was arrested—well, they investigated me too. They had nothing on me; I wasn't involved. They were his deals, but they told me I couldn't teach any more.'

'Didn't you fight back?'

'What's the difference? They do whatever they want with you anyway. I was lucky to get this job. The people here are decent—but there's not much money, nor much work either, as you can see. Especially not now. And what about you? Are you going to be coming around for much longer?'

'That doesn't depend on me.'

'And if it did?'

'Another two weeks.'

'See what I mean? And what then?'

I shrugged my shoulders. 'Something will turn up.'

'Well, I don't want to pry. Will you have another drink?'

I said I'd had enough, but she poured herself another glass. 'If you hear of anything half decent, would you let me know?'

'But I have nothing to do with chemistry—not a thing.'

'Neither do I—any more, and I wouldn't want to, either.'

'What would you like?'

She stretched, and then attempted a smile. 'Right now I'd like to go swimming. How about it?'

176

'I'm not too fond of swimming.'

'Just my luck,' she said. 'My first husband didn't like swimming either. He was born under a fire sign. That was why he started doing what he did, and it was probably why he burnt himself out so soon, too. By the end, he was almost totally paralysed.'

'How old was he?'

'Thirty-one. We went to university together. He was a real athletic type—basketball, tennis, cross-country.' She filled her glass again. 'Am I annoying you with all this talk? But you don't like swimming. And it's hot in here. Aren't you hot?'

I was hot, but I didn't like the idea of swimming in the river, especially one as filthy as the Vltava. So I invited her to a pub near the bus stop, where we could sit in a small garden in the shade.

'Do you think I could leave now?' She was already taking a white handbag out of the cupboard. 'I'll leave the flowers here till tomorrow,' she decided. 'I spend more time here than at home anyway.' She locked the office.

Outside, they were laying another length of pipe with the crane. We had to wait for them to finish, and she put her arm in mine. 'My head's spinning a little,' she said. 'It's the sun. And I haven't had lunch.'

'Why didn't you have lunch?'

'I can't afford it.'

We found an empty table in the garden in the shade of a chestnut tree. The waiter offered us beer and a menu.

'Do you think I could have something to eat? I'll pick something cheap.'

'Order anything you'd like.'

'You haven't told me anything about you yet.'

177

'That's not important, after all.'

'All right, if it's not important, I'll have the wiener-schnitzel.'

'I was a teacher once myself,' I said. 'But only for half a year.'

'What did you teach?'

'Literature.'

'At university?'

'Yes.'

'Can you tell me something about literature?'

'What do you want to know?'

'What does it mean?'

'It's an encounter.'

'Who with?'

'With another person. The one who wrote the book.'

'I prefer live people.'

'So do I, mostly.'

The waiter brought her food.

'Thank you,' she said. 'You're very kind to me. That's what I thought when I first saw you: maybe that's what he'd have looked like if . . .'

'Do you still think about him?'

'I'm sorry, I know it's not—polite.' For a while she ate in silence. Then she said, 'You know, they say that when you have that illness, it's really important how the sick person feels—his mental health. But I did look after him all that time, really well. And then, he couldn't even move, or anything. And Libor came to visit him too.'

'Who?'

'Libor—the one I married afterwards. He and Karel were friends. They worked in the same place. When Karel's illness began, lots of people came to visit, but then there were fewer and fewer, you know how it is. In the end, only Libor came.'

'Because of you.'

'He helped me. It wasn't until . . . But by that time, we knew it was the end.'

'Did your husband know it too?'

'I'm not sure what you mean.'

'Did he know Libor was coming because of you?'

'I don't know. We didn't do anything in front of him that might have . . . But now sometimes I wonder . . . In those final weeks, I would sometimes get ready and go out in the evening . . . I was awfully tired . . . No, not tired, really, but overwhelmed, and so I went out with Libor while my poor husband just lay there. He couldn't even move, or look out of the window to see where I was going.'

'Didn't he ask you?'

'No, he never did. He'd say: go out somewhere, go out and have some fun. You don't want to be cooped up with me all the time. He also asked me to put him in the hospital, but I knew he didn't really want that, that he was terrified of dying surrounded by strangers.'

'So you didn't put him in the hospital?'

'No!'

'That probably meant a lot to him.'

'Do you think so? Those final days keep coming back to me. The horror of it, and at the same time, the relief when it was all over. I was relieved. Don't you think that's awful? Someone I loved dies, and I feel relieved.'

'It's understandable.'

'I sometimes think that what happened afterwards was a punishment. Because I couldn't wait.'

'No, you mustn't think that way.'

179

'Forgive me. Here you are, treating me to a meal, and I'm carrying on like this.' She drained her glass. 'I only wanted you to know why I never smile. But now I can, now that I've told you all this. Now that you know what I'm capable of.'

Under the table, I could feel her shifting her leg to touch mine. Perhaps she hadn't made love to anyone for ages and was longing to be embraced and therefore offering herself to me. I only had to go with her, or invite her for a stroll in the wood that was just a short walk from here. Then again, perhaps this was just me, a man, imagining her longing. Perhaps she didn't really need to make love, perhaps she merely longed to hear words of absolution. Or she needed both, but felt that if she wanted absolution, she had to offer herself first. So I said something about how I thought she was more capable of good than of bad, then I paid the bill. We parted, saying that we'd certainly run into each other again.

When I went back to the office, the only one left was Miss Kosinová, her eyes red from crying. She told me that Mr Vandas's wife had died from an embolism. The funeral would probably be next Tuesday. Tomorrow they would take up a collection for a wreath. 'But you don't have to contribute,' Miss Kosinová said. 'You didn't know her, after all.'

THREE

IN THE FOURTH-FLOOR office only the pretty manager was left. She was reading the satirical weekly *Dikobraz* and taking great pleasure from the fact that there was even greater chaos elsewhere in the economy than here. 'There's nothing today, again,' she said, welcoming me, 'but they say you should stop by in Vrsovice about nine. The labels have arrived. About twenty packages of them. That is, if you still feel like hauling them around on your last day.'

'I'm actually looking forward to it,' I said. 'I've had nothing to do this week.'

'I wouldn't worry—not for the money you're getting.'

It seemed to me that they were giving me quite enough money for carrying a few extra bags along with the mail, but I said nothing.

'I heard you're going to be cooking something interesting at Chodov today. Is it true?' asked the manager.

'It's a farewell party.' I had let it slip that cooking used to be a hobby of mine.

'And what's on the menu, if I may ask?'

'Chicken à la Rawalpindi,' I said, off the top of my head, because if I like anything about cooking, its the possibility of inventing new and apparently nonsensical taste

181

combinations.

'Sounds exotic.'

'You're coming to try it out, aren't you?'

'I don't know,' she said. 'The end of the month, one deadline after another, and reports to fill out. And the deputy-director wants the plan for the next six months ready.'

I said I'd be delighted if she could come, and then, as usual, the telephone rang, and I had nothing else to do here anyway.

It was only seven-fifteen—I had a lot of time left before nine. When it's your last day as a courier, you should have something more important to deliver than a bundle of perforated labels. But my letters to the President of the Republic were still not ready to send.

The trolley-bus to Jinonice had long ago been taken out of service and replaced with a regular bus. I went to the last stop and looked around me, feeling perplexed. I hadn't been here in all that time. It was childish to expect nothing to have changed.

I wandered about the housing project for a while in the hope that somewhere at the end of it, I'd find the narrow street with the little country cottages.

This early in the morning, the empty spaces between the high-rises were deserted. The grass was covered with rubbish. Every time there was a gust of wind, large sheets of plastic would rise off the ground and flap in the air like the wings of great doleful birds.

I couldn't remember the name of the street—only the name of the man, which was of no use to me. I would probably only find it in the cemetery.

I had delivered many letters and many messages since

that first one. But I still think that message was the most important of all—at least for me.

In Vrsovice, the mainframe computer was on the second floor; it occupied a huge hall, while the programmers sat in their cubicles in front of their terminals. Miss Kosinová was watching rows of coloured numbers dancing across her screen. The figures stopped and the screen became still. Kosinová looked at it for a while longer, then she turned to me and said, 'You came at a bad time.'

'Is the system down?' I asked.

'No, just overloaded.' She explained that this type of American computer normally has ten times the memory, but the Americans aren't allowed to export computers with that kind of capacity to Czechoslovakia. They had warned our buyer not to attach more than ten terminals, but they'd gone ahead and connected three times that many anyway, hoping they could get the extra memory capacity from somewhere else. They hadn't. 'It's like everything else; we wait in line and hope we can scrounge a few extra minutes. And if we're lucky they let us stay here a couple of extra hours. When there's a greater demand, we always get bumped completely. But it doesn't really matter,' she added. 'We work ourselves to a frazzle and then the results just sit upstairs on somebody's desk. And even if someone does read them, no one does anything about it. Never mind about those labels,' she said, realizing why I had come. 'We'll manage to deliver them somehow.'

The boxes with the labels in them had piled up in the little entrance hall. I stuffed them into my bag, and into the rucksack I brought with me. Altogether, they must have weighed about thirty kilos.

As I finished, the numbers on Kosinová's screen began to

move again. 'Hurrah!' she cried, and ran to her little chair to continue working at a task whose outcome no one was waiting for.

In the porter's lodge, the violinist was on duty today. He stood, legs apart, behind his counter, his violin under his chin and played from memory the solo from the finale of Dvořák's Concerto in A Minor.

I would have loved to listen to him for a while, but I still wanted to get out to Komořan before I began cooking, so I didn't have much time left.

I put the box with the labels down in the hall. Mr Bauer emerged from his cubicle, and when he saw me, he remarked dryly: 'Well, I've worked it out for you.'

'What have you worked out?'

'Don't you remember? Wait, I'll bring it to you. You'll only be interested in the results anyway.'

I went into the kitchen once more to make sure nothing was missing. The spices stood neatly on the shelf—I'd prepared the curry myself. There weren't many utensils here—two frying pans and two pots, one large and one small. Not a single lid.

'Here it is,' said Engineer Bauer, handing me a sheaf of paper.

I skimmed a column of figures and symbols. At the bottom, the computer had remarked:

LIFE IMPROBABLE IN 2069

LIFE COMPLETELY IMPOSSIBLE FROM 2084 ON

'That leaves us ninety-seven years,' said Mr Klíma, who was looking over his shoulder. 'I'll be exactly a hundred and thirty years old. I'd never have thought it—just think of all the things I won't live to see.'

Mr Vandas, who had come out as well, still had rings of sadness under his eyes. 'You'll be lucky to live to thirty,' he said darkly. 'If by any chance you should prove too disease-resistant, our health system will make good and sure you won't go on haunting us here for too much longer.'

Many people had come to the crematorium for the funeral ceremony last week. Both the little girls were dressed in coloured dresses and they stood out among the mourners like bright flowers on a black meadow. Vandas did not want a eulogy. It's too late to say what we haven't already said, he explained. So they just played music the whole time. When the curtain was drawn and the coffin began to move towards the fire, the elder of the girls jumped up, leaped over that long fence and ran into the dead area behind it to hold her mother back, since they had all told her she'd only gone out there for a while.

They pulled the girl back, whispering something in her ear, most probably to be brave.

'I did what I could,' Bauer explained. 'I calculated that by 2025, more than half the budget would be spent on saving the environment. In actual fact, people will never be that determined. Also, I didn't factor in a single nuclear catastrophe, not to mention war, although when you take the number of nuclear generating plants in operation today, and their probable number in 2025, there should be at least three more Chernobyls.'

'Well, thank you very much,' I said.

'Don't mention it,' said Bauer. 'I was interested in this myself.'

'So, are you going to write something for us by way of farewell?' asked Klíma.

'I wanted to nip out to Komořan first. And I have to cook that lunch.'

'As you wish,' said Klíma, somewhat miffed. 'But it's not even half past ten.'

I sat down at the computer. I should have written a few words of farewell. But all I could think of was a quatrain:

> *All around the city's towers*
> *Fall the wildest little showers;*
> *But now we're in the mood*
> *We'll surely stop a flood!*

Still moved by the fresh prognosis of Mr Bauer, I put another quatrain together. Klíma, though he normally did not do so, read the fruits of my labour. 'Did you just write this now?'

'I told you, I was in a hurry,' I said apologetically.

'It's not bad,' he said, delighted. 'Do you want me to print it out?'

He printed both my poems, I stuck the page into my rucksack (I no longer needed my bag) and hurried out of the hall.

Dvořák was still emanating from the porter's lodge, and could be heard from outside the building. In the flower shop they had a single, wilting orchid. I looked around to see if I could see my blind man, but it was too early. Several days ago we'd come back on the same bus. I heard him explaining loudly to someone that in Arobidzhan—which lies on the ninety-first meridian and the fifty-sixth parallel—blind people don't go to school.

'What did you do, then?' a fat man sitting beside him had asked.

'I played the violin,' said the blind man. He lifted his

white cane, put it under his chin and pretended to coax a few plaintive tones out of it. 'I used to play in bars on winter evenings,' he said later. 'While I played, the guests talked, drank vodka and took bites of bread. Sometimes there'd be a blizzard, or the temperature would drop so low that no one could go outside. Then we drank a lot of vodka, and ate a lot of bread.'

'Did you have any bacon to go with the bread?'

'You think too much about bacon!' shouted the blind man. 'Are you a cook, by any chance?'

'What would be wrong with that?'

People around them burst into laughter.

'You haven't got an ear for music, or for people, only for something to fill your face. When there was bacon,' replied the blind man, 'people ate. When there was no bacon, there was salt, and when the salt ran out, there were tears.'

In the corridor of the wooden building I knocked on the familiar door and then entered without waiting for an answer. An unfamiliar woman sat behind one of the desks.

'Are you looking for someone?'

'For Natasha,' I said, someone thrown off balance.

'That's me.'

'Excuse me . . . I mean, I was thinking the woman who sits at the other desk,' I said, pointing.

'Unfortunately, Anička has the day off today. She had to go to Ostrava.'

'Ah.' I felt strangely put out. 'Can I leave something here for her?' I took out the flower. 'You'll probably have to put this in some water.'

'I'll look after it.'

I gave her the flower. I felt I should write her a message to go with it. Something like: I'm sending you a smile and I wish you . . . Or: Thanks for the trust. Or simply: Goodbye. And my signature. I took out the piece of paper with the print-out of my quatrain. The second one went this way:

> *In far-off Dubai you do or you die,*
> *In the Yukon you ken what you can,*
> *In Wooloomooloo there's no one but you—*
> *Oh, the end of the world is at hand!*

There was no point in signing it; we'd talked but never introduced ourselves.

I folded the paper into a small square and handed it to the real Natasha. 'And would you be kind enough to give her this too, please?' My message was probably bad news, but it could also be understood as good news, if only because it existed at all.

She took the paper from me and promised to pass it on. I thanked her and hurried back to catch the bus so I could get back in time to prepare the Chicken à la Rawalpindi to celebrate my parting with the kind-hearted programmers, and my own career as a courier.

THE SURVEYOR'S STORY

THE HOUSE

I KNEW ONLY the name of the street and the number; that was all my friend the surveyor, who got me the job, could tell me, since he'd never been there. I'd have no trouble finding the house, he said, because it was right next to the town square. But I wasn't to expect any luxury. Surveyors tend to be frugal; much of their income comes in expenses—living allowances, remuneration for being separated from spouses and children and so on, and if they actually had to spend it on room and board, the work would quickly lose its appeal. So they try to find cheap accommodation.

In addition to bedding and a pillow, therefore, I took some dishes, a wash-basin, an immersion heater for coffee, and a lamp with a set of jaws that allowed me to attach it to anything solid.

I had taken a job as a surveyor's assistant after receiving a letter from the office dealing with my social insurance. The letter was only five lines long:

> We are returning the documents you submitted to us in support of your application for artists' social insurance. It is impossible to ascertain from these documents with any degree of certainty whether your earnings did, in

191

fact, derive from artistic activity.

When I asked the kindly woman at the office, whom I had known for years, for an explanation, she assured me I was not alone. A new director had taken charge and decided to cut insurance to people like me.

Was that legal? I asked. And who were these people like me anyway?

The woman told me that the new director's name was Mr Král and that I had best ask him.

I didn't feel like dealing with the director. This was hardly a disaster, after all. In two years and a few weeks I'd be eligible for a pension—if I survived with my health intact, that is. Surely forty years of insurance contributions would be enough to guarantee that.

A lawyer friend put me straight. If, he explained, I did not hold some documentable job for at least a single day during those two years, I would have the same right to a pension as someone who had never done a day's work—which is to say, none at all.

So those forty years would be simply wiped away?

Just work for a single day, he assured me, and I can save your pension.

Both of us knew that no one would ever put me on a payroll for a single day.

To put off, even briefly, the moment when I would officially start my new job, I had a look around the square. Its spaciousness was a credit to the generosity of the lords of Mrdice, who had founded the town 700 years ago. From where I stood, the square broadened to a point about two-thirds down its length where a baroque church emerged from a screen of century-old lime-trees. Even from a distance, I could see that the church was as shabby as all the other buildings on the square. In front of it, in an area where they had probably held markets in the past—since the town, as I had read at home, had once been renowned for its grand horse markets—they had placed, with an aesthetic sensitivity typical of the present town fathers, an open-air bus station. Beyond a row of houses at the far end of the square rose a baroque roof with turrets, a small château, perhaps. I was delighted, because when I'd accepted this job, I had thought of Kafka's *Castle* and K. the surveyor.

I looked in through the glass door of a shop. Behind the counter stacked with stationery supplies a long-haired, bespectacled creature was staring back at me. I averted my eyes. Above the filthy windows, I could recognize the remains of a laurel-leaf festoon, betraying the building's origins in the Napoleonic era.

The girl in the stationery shop kept watching me, so I moved along to the main entrance to the building. Someone had fastened a piece of wrapping-paper to the door with three tacks. On it, written with a magic marker, was a sign indicating that the surveying office was on the third floor. I entered, walked down a dark corridor, then up an even darker staircase that led to a glassed-in balcony overlooking a courtyard. Various doors opened on to the balcony. Everything was big, dirty and decrepit. Outside one of the doors, an old kitchen stove was gathering rust, and beside it there was a bucket full of water.

I knocked on the door, opened it and went inside to find myself in a large, gloomily lit room. There was nothing in it but a new kitchen stove, a bag of cement and two flags twisted around poles leaning against a brightly coloured washbasin. The air had an acrid smell to it, like the air in a pub urinal. A grimy film covered the window, making the light that came through it seem grey. The ancient floorboards were covered in cement dust. Two halves of a French-window were leaning against the wall to my left. And suspended from the ceiling in the dead centre of the room hung a single strand of electrical wire with part of the insulation burnt away. It brought to mind another room where I had been compelled to spend a part of my childhood during the war. The similarity horrified me.

I stepped into the next room through an opening in the side wall. There, seated at a table that was missing one leg, was a young man with short cropped hair. Behind him, I could see a camp-bed, some chairs, several crates of various sizes, a green metal container shaped like a bomb, a pair of rubber boots, a suitcase, and an electrical cable nailed to the wall.

The young man got up to greet me. He was about as tall as me, but thinner. I introduced myself.

He offered me his hand and said that his name was Kos. He hoped we'd get along. Had I done this kind of work before? he asked.

I told him the truth, that I hadn't, but that I came from a family of engineers, and that perhaps surveying wouldn't be completely alien to me. I had experience working in the garden, I said, adding quickly that I realized the work he was expecting me to do was different.

We returned to the first room together, and I opened a window that had not been washed, and possibly not even opened, for many years.

Was the room all right? he asked.

I replied, evasively, that it was certainly what you'd expect in a building like this, but that I didn't know what

194

I'd be sleeping on; I hadn't brought a mattress with me.

He assured me he'd look after everything. He'd already arranged for a bed from the old-people's home, and across the street, in an empty building earmarked for demolition, he had seen several pieces of fairly decent furniture.

I hadn't exaggerated about the engineers in my family. My father, my grandfather, my uncles and my aunts were all engineers. According to family lore, one of my aunts had been the first woman in the country to get a degree in chemical engineering. My brother is a physicist. And my son has already decided to continue the tradition—and in a completely new field, which made my father happy. I was the only defector. Not because I was afraid of theory—my mathematics professor found it incredible that I decided to study the humanities—but I couldn't relate to technology, and most of its creations scared me.

We went down to the square and, pushing our way past dustbins and empty orange crates, entered one of the buildings that, from the outside at least, looked no worse for wear than those around it. Its former inhabitants had obviously moved out some time ago. The floor was strewn with old magazines and letters, shards of glass, odd socks and torn underwear. There was a pair of ragged slippers lying beside a small cupboard with its door ripped off to reveal shelves with a few small cups and cheap plates covered in dust. My eye was immediately caught by two kitchen chairs. One had a broken back rest, but the other seemed in good repair. We set both of them aside, then emptied the useless dishes out of the cupboard—and thus I acquired the furniture I needed.

'We'll be out every day anyway,' said the surveyor. We packed our booty into the four-wheel drive, a station wagon manufactured in Romania with the name of my new employer in fresh paint on its grey-green doors. It looked as though it could self-destruct at any moment. We got in and drove off to fetch my bed.

The old people's home was located in the old château; its long corridors swarmed not with courtiers, lackeys, princes and princesses, but old men and women wearing the same kind of slippers I had just seen in the abandoned flat.

My new boss asked me to wait while he went to the office and signed for the bed. I leaned against a parapet and looked out into the courtyard, where red and butter-coloured roses were blooming beside a pathway of yellow sand. Several old women were sunning themselves on a bench against the wall.

Kafka had certainly never tried to be a surveyor; and his novel, of course, was neither about surveying nor about a castle. It was a story about his own vain longing to go behind closed doors. We all have different doors through which we may not pass. The greatness of an artist consists in constructing his door so that in it, we can also see the door that blocks our own way.

An old man with a large, angular head was approaching me along the hallway. A pair of prominent ears poked out from under his curly grey hair. He stopped. I could feel him measuring me with his eyes. 'Looking for someone, comrade?'

The word 'comrade' grated on me and I replied, reluctantly, that I wasn't. Then, afraid that I had been too brusque with the old man, I added, 'I'm here to arrange something.'

'Ah,' he said. 'If you want to get your parents in here,

196

you haven't got a chance.'

'No, that's not what I'm here for.'

'Unless you can fork out over ten thousand—like that.' He struck his thigh with a big, ruddy fist. 'Everyone here goes around with their hand out. If you don't shell out, they won't even sweep under your bed. And you'll get a piece of rotten meat for lunch. Complain and you'll never see a decent piece of meat again. That's what we've come to.'

Fortunately, the surveyor arrived and took me into a store-room where a congenial-looking housekeeper gave us a metal hospital bed and a mattress.

When we returned with it to the square, the surveyor remarked that our faded Napoleonic palace was soon to be demolished. That was why we were getting it rent free, he said. There was a flush toilet on the balcony, and although they'd cut the water off, it didn't matter because I had running water in my room. They'd disconnected the electricity as well, but fortunately Mr Wolf, who moved out last week, still kept a garage in the courtyard, which meant he had his own meter. For a fee, said the surveyor, he's allowed us to tap into his circuit. The stationer's store was all that was left, and Mrs Pokorná, the former owner, who lived in a flat on the ground floor.

When I'd swept the worst of the mess off the floor and brought my things in from the car, the surveyor looked at his watch as if to say it was time to go. But before we set off to work he pulled a well-thumbed book out from his desk and asked me if I'd like to read the safety regulations. I replied that I didn't think it would be necessary, and he agreed that they were mostly hot air. He did recommend, however, that I always wear the gloves he would issue me with now. He handed me a pair of yellow work gloves made of rough pig-skin, and I signed a paper saying I'd been informed about safety on the job.

In the courtyard there were several sheds in varying states of collapse. One had a waterproof roof and a door with a lock. This housed the instruments and items worth stealing: tripods, an axe, a machete, a hoe, shovels, a pick-axe, paintbrushes, stakes, paint, solvents and a sack of coal. A shed that leaked contained poles and stone plates, while cement markers were piled untidily in a shed missing its entire front wall. Between the sheds and the entrance to the courtyard was a pile of rubbish so old that it no longer smelled.

We loaded the tools and equipment we needed into the car—I rather carefully, anxious not to spill or break or misplace anything. We took three colours of paint with us: red, white and black. Had we felt like painting national flags on walls, we couldn't have done much—the colours of Bohemia, the Polish, the Danish, the Swiss and the Canadian flags—these were the only ones I could think of. The paintbrushes, Kos told me, should always be kept in plastic bags, securely tied so they wouldn't dry out. Japan and Laos also had red and white flags, I remembered. But we wouldn't have been able to do Laos unless we could paint elephants.

It was already eleven-thirty. Expecting the worst, I got in beside the surveyor and we drove off. My new boss asked me if I could understand maps.

I did understand maps; in fact, I used to collect them.

He handed me a brand new ordnance survey map, stamped with a warning that it was a secret document. The trigonometric points were marked with orange circles.

We had five maps, with a total of almost two hundred points, each of which we were to locate and re-survey; if necessary, we would also have to relocate or replace the stone or set in a new one and paint the stake. Our first point that morning was number twenty-three outside the hamlet of Tribucha. It wouldn't be easy to find, Kos said. He'd already driven out that way, and the stake was missing and the stone had vanished under the alluvium. Then, having said all there was to say, he fell silent and concentrated on driving.

Although it was early September, the sun was still hot. I studied the countryside, constantly referring back to the map, bringing us nearer to the invisible point number twenty-three.

EVENING

WHEN WE RETURNED to our residence that evening, I rinsed myself off and changed my clothes, then connected my lamp to the cable we used to bring in the borrowed current. I had planned to wash at least one of the windows, but I was too tired.

That afternoon we had dug six holes into which we set concrete markers; we had painted nine stakes and cut a twenty-metre sight-line through the vegetation with our machetes. I had helped with the actual surveying, which, compared with the digging, had seemed like a rest. I wasn't used to the pick and, after digging the third hole, I didn't think I could go on. Yet I did, and my young boss took turns with me, doing his share and, as the day progressed, taking on more and and more without making it look as though he were doing me a favour. Now he retired to his room and I saw him sit down at his wretched little table, take out his calculator and start working up the figures we'd gathered that afternoon.

I wasn't surprised to find him working at night. I was used to it from my childhood. Engineering is a monastic discipline to which you must sacrifice everything. To its disciples the only time well spent is time spent working.

Early in life I recognized that while fantasists, prophets and politicians struggle among themselves about how better to organize and articulate the world, it is scientists and engineers who silently and tirelessly put their notions of the world and life into practice. They measure everything they can touch. They calculate the bearing capacity of bridges and causeways; they wrap the world in a network of pathways on water, on land and in the air. They raise buildings higher than the pyramids; they drive tunnels under the Alps. They build factories and hospitals, and are constantly inventing new machines and instruments to use inside them. They draw up plans for rapid-firing weapons, body scanners, explosives, gas-chambers—and assembly-lines to produce them. They invent thousands of new drugs, chemical weapons, herbicides and fungicides. They build rockets, feeder farms, enormous generators and nuclear reactors. And when the world is slowly suffocating under the waste products of these labours, where do we turn for help? To the scientists, of course. They will decide which of the waste products can be easily and cheaply disposed of. They will invent antidotes to the toxins. And antidotes to the antidotes.

The idea of a countable, measurable and precisely expressible world is a seductive one. It has seduced even those who, by the very nature of their activity, ought to resist it. Not only have painters, poets, composers, literary critics and philosophers fallen in love with the dazzle of electric lights and fast cars, they have begun, in their work and research, to adapt to the scientist's world. They paint geometric images, compose concrete music and poetry, transform verse into diagrams and the mystery of Being into mathematical formulae.

When I was still young, I understood that, despite what I was taught in school, the age I lived in was probably called the age of engineering.

I disconnected my lamp and put my immersion heater in a cup of water. While I was waiting for it to boil, I spread a serviette over the chair that had no back, and unwrapped a piece of cake my wife had baked; then, so I wouldn't entirely lose touch with the world, I turned on one of the portable products of the technological age and, from the airwaves, tried to collect news from different corners of the planet.

The night air flowed through the open window, cool and pleasant. Carefully, so as not to get dirty, I approached the window ledge and looked down the square. It was empty. Prime time was just beginning on another revolutionary achievement of our civilization. Two drunks staggered about in front of the pub across from the church. Occasionally a car roared past. There was not a single woman in sight. Before me stretched an evening promising neither joy nor guilt: I didn't have to write or study. I could enjoy my freedom the way a worker does, freshly showered and freshly dressed after work; and moreover, hidden away in a town where no one knows him, expects him, or limits his movements.

I drank my tea and its aroma helped to cover the stench that still lingered in the room. I ate the cake, switched off the radio and walked out of my inhospitable bedroom.

There was light in the hallway of my building and, sitting on a kitchen chair, a rather plump woman of around sixty. She was stretching her short, fat legs in front of her; her hair, crudely bleached, was fluffed up in a messy bouffant. She had been reading an illustrated weekly for young people. Beside her on a small pile of bricks sat a birdcage with a canary inside.

I greeted her and was about to go on when she called to me, 'Are you the new surveyor?'

I admitted that I was.

She stood up and offered me a chubby hand. 'Welcome to my house. I used to have five tenants,' she said. 'There was Mr Wolf, an army captain, and Dr Tereba—do you know him? He was a great prophet. He knew the stars and could cast people's horoscopes and tell their fortunes, but he'd only give them the rough outlines and keep the bad stuff, and the worse stuff, to himself. Now there's only Julka and me,' she nodded towards the cage. 'I hear they're going to build a railway station on this spot.'

'That can't be true,' I said. 'The line doesn't run anywhere near here.'

'That kind of detail never bothers them.'

Her objection had a logic of its own, and so I merely shrugged my shoulders, meaning that I knew nothing about a new station.

'My great-grandfather built this house, sir. And it was declared an historical building. They used to print diaries, almanacs and poetry here.'

'Was he a printer—your great-grandfather?'

'He was the district and episcopalian printer. He was born in eighteen hundred odd, but this is where he got his start, and when he died he left the building to my grandfather. And you know how long he lived? An even one hundred years. Back then, in Chrudim, there was a woman called Kroupova—she was Turkish. A soldier brought her back from Belgrade when she was just a little girl. He had her christened and he brought her up himself.

Then she lived in the same street as my great-grandfather, and she lived till she was a hundred and six—such are the ways of the Lord. At her funeral, my great-grandfather promised that if the Lord was willing, he'd live to be a hundred as well and enter the new century. If he'd had any idea what this one'd be like, he'd have thought twice about it. Grandfather lived to be ninety-six, but my father was killed in a concentration camp before he'd even turned forty. It was the Lord's will. At least he didn't have to look at this destruction,' and she waved her hands at the wall behind her, where bare brick and the broken windows of empty flats stared back at us. 'He should have had a memorial plaque here but they wouldn't allow it because he was a private businessman and a member of Sokol.'

'Was he a printer too?'

'No, he sold books—and mainly stationery. You should have seen our sign. "Antonín Pokorný," it said, and underneath that, in gold lettering: "Purveyor of Books, Lithographs and Stationery Supplies." Everyone knew my father, and he knew all his customers by name; he'd always give the children a free picture or a decal. You could buy whatever you wanted—even if it was paper with a special snake-grain finish. And if, by some miracle, it wasn't in stock, Dad would try to get it for you, would go all the way to Prague for it if he had to. Today? Just try going into the store now and asking for ordinary writing-paper. The girl will laugh in your face. Have you seen her?' she lowered her voice. 'The little tramp they've got looking after the stationery goods? Just try going in there to buy something and what do you see on the door? She's got a sign up saying: "Deliveries." "Gone to the post office." "Inventory Day." "I'm at the doctor's." And you know where she is all the time? Back here in the stock-room,' she jerked a fat thumb behind her, where I could see only a barred window with opaque glass in it. 'She brings in soldiers and boys from the cement plant. She makes more on her back than she does standing behind the counter. So you haven't heard about the station?' she said, returning to her main preoccupation. 'Maybe they meant a bus station. The chaplain's been complaining that he can't say mass with the buses making all that noise just outside his door.'

To them, that would have been a reason for leaving the bus station where it was, but I didn't argue with her and, taking advantage of the pause in the flow of talk, I left the courtyard.

Even though he never said as much, I know my father was disappointed that I hadn't become an engineer. I had never known his father—he had died twelve years before I was born—but not long ago, I came across an article he had written. He'd learned that an American colleague of his had discovered a cheap way to produce acetylene. 'The ancient dreams of chemists of creating organic compounds from mineral substances have been resurrected. To get not only kerosene or alcohol, but to create, on the way, purely chemical substances necessary for the nourishment of man. Thus far, such dreams have been vain indeed, but recalling the enormous achievements of chemistry in our time, there is no reason to doubt that they might one day become true.' His article ended with a vision that seemed to him joyous and full of hope.

A few fluorescent lights flickered on the square, and a small group of people had gathered to wait for a late bus in front of the church. The shops were shuttered and dark, and the only light came from a pub called The Blackbird. The din of many voices floated out through the open window.

I walked as far as the château. The gate was now shut and only a single window in a whole row was lit. An ambulance was parked in front of the gate.

Kafka had lived at the end of an era when a castle was still a good symbol of mystery and inaccessibility. People associated castles with nobility and sophistication. Today, our castle gates are open wide. Some have been turned into tourist attractions, but most have become warehouses for things or people. The fine furniture and valuable porcelain has been stolen or destroyed, rare books have been taken to waste-paper depots, and the princesses who didn't manage to make their escape were asked to work behind counters, on assembly lines or in offices. In our era, party secretariats have replaced the castles. They are the new symbols of inaccessibility, but they don't evoke notions of nobility; no one would associate them with ideas of gentle birth, bravery, wisdom or chivalry.

A hero who tries to pry open the gate of a secretariat will scarcely gain anyone's approval.

Back home I took off my clothes and threw them over the back of a chair. (Tomorrow I would have to hammer a few nails, at least, into the wall to hang them on.) It was only nine-thirty, but I fell asleep at once.

I was awakened by a rumbling clatter. The windows were shaking as though an air-raid was going on. I opened my eyes and looked around a room empty of people and things.

Where had everyone gone?

They'd been transported to Poland. Only I remained behind, forgotten, waiting for the man bearing my death sentence to enter.

The rumbling kept up, and I became fully awake. Through the open window I saw one of the enormous transport trucks disappearing around a corner. A bell in the tower struck twice. It might have been two in the morning, but when I looked at my watch, it was only half-past eleven.

With a sense of relief, I realized that the transportations had long since departed and it was unlikely that someone would come through the door to inform me that my presence was a burden to be removed from the world without delay. Those to whom I was a nuisance at present were certainly satisfied that I was now precisely where I was.

Another truck roared by outside. I got up and closed the window. One of the ancient panes of glass in it cracked with a high, rasping sound. Midnight struck.

I looked into the darkness in front of me. Now that I had closed the window, the air was filled with the room's own foul exhalations. My body felt broken and I was aware of a slight pain near my heart. I desperately wanted to fall asleep again, but instead, I kept hearing the sounds from the street and a silent rumbling in the bowels of the old building.

We all have our own castle whose gates we long to pass through. Most of the time, when we find them closed, we go off in another direction and enter doors that someone else has opened for us or through which we have no wish to pass.

STONE

WE WERE DIGGING a hole for a stone pillar in a clearing near the logging road. From the first blow of the pick, the ground had resisted. It was close to noon and a light breeze made the air tremble in the heat of the sun. After an hour's hard work we had only managed to make a shallow depression in the earth. We had hoped that once we'd made it through the tangle of tree roots in the top layer of soil the work would get easier. Instead, we had hit hardened clay full of chunks of solid rock.

My young boss, understandably, was stronger than I was, and more skillful, so he took the pick out of my hands and, with regular, rhythmic blows, tried to subdue the rock bit by bit. But a dull pick is no substitute for a pneumatic drill.

Do we have to put our stone pillar exactly here? I wondered. Perhaps the ground a little to one side would be softer.

'This is the best place for it.'

My knowledge of the work I was doing was so slight that I couldn't judge whether the location he chose was really the best of several possibilities, or whether he was simply revealing more of the stubbornness he had demonstrated several times over the past few days.

Our stone pillar was still lying on the floor of the station wagon. Perhaps anticipating the bedrock, the surveyor had selected the smallest of the stone makers we had, but even so it was just a little under three-quarters of a metre long. And we had to lay the mark-stone tablet underneath it. And between the mark-stone and the stone pillar there had to be a layer of soil at least twenty centimetres thick. Though it lay buried under a metre of earth, the mark-stone was the most important part of the trigonometrical station. While the stone pillar above it was often damaged, the mark-stone usually remained unmoved. There were crosses on both the mark-stone and the pillar, and they had to be aligned. Thus the position of the pillar could always be re-set with reference to the mark-stone beneath it.

In the past, they used to build tall wooden constructions over the stone pillar. I remember towers so high it made me dizzy to look up at them. They don't build those towers any more; there aren't the carpenters to make them. Adjacent to the stone pillar, at a distance indicated by a notch on the handle of my pick, a concrete base had to be set in the ground to which a pole was fixed; at the trigonometrical point, the pole was red and white; at the intermediate points, black and white. Wherever there was a threat of damage, we put up two poles. There was always the threat of damage, even though it was an offence to tamper with the poles. In woods, seldom had surveyors bothered to erect markers; they would simply paint arrows on the nearest tree, one pointing left, the other right. And because over the years the stone pillar would become buried in earth or overgrown with grass or bushes, we would have to poke around in the undergrowth with a metal probe until we found it. When we had uncovered the top of it, Kos would pull out the spirit-level while I would anxiously try to determine if the pillar had been moved.

If the bubble deviated from its circular centre-point so much as a millimetre in any direction, the pillar would have to be dug up, realigned with the mark-stone, and relaid.

Once, when the stone was out to a barely perceptible degree, I suggested we might simply dig around it to make it level. From the expression on the surveyor's face, however, I realized that my idea was sacrilegious.

It was my turn to take the pick again. Trying to emulate the surveyor's technique I threw myself at the rock as though deranged, but I managed only to chip away a few tiny fragments. Drops of my sweat fell on the ground and were quickly soaked up by the dry dust.

I crawled out of the trench and went to the car, where I had left some warmish water in a bottle. I took a drink and then pulled a hammer and chisel from under the car seat.

If only we had decent tools.

The surveyor now took his turn. The rock sang like a stone bell.

I sat down on the fresh pile of broken rock. I didn't have the energy to walk the short distance into the shade.

The bell rang insistently, summoning the prisoners.

I had tried to position myself in one of the back ranks, but the others had pushed me into the front row. From the right, where they were ringing the bell, a group of supervisors and overseers in yellowish uniforms and red arm-bands approached. The officer leading the group, turned to me. Don't like the look of this one, he said. Two weeks of special treatment.

They grabbed me and led back to the wooden barracks. I was not surprised; not even frightened. I knew that,

eventually, I would meet everyone I loved in those special
treatment barracks. They were merely leading me off to
meet my fate, my story. I even looked forward to new
encounters.

The surveyor jumped out of the trench, peeled off the
rust-coloured sweater which he almost never removed, and
measured the results of our work so far with a folding ruler.
We were two-thirds finished. He handed me the hammer
and the chisel: it was my turn to make the bell ring. When I
had prised away an especially large chunk of rock and
tossed it out of the pit, I discovered nothing underneath it
but a layer of earth mixed with small stones.

After half an hour, we had set the mark-stone in the
bottom of the hole and jockeyed it into position so that the
bubble stood motionless in the centre of the level. The
surveyor set up a tripod over the pit and dropped a plumb-
line from it. Then he balanced himself over the hole like an
acrobat and I helped him shift the tripod until the plumb-
line pointed to the centre of the crossed lines. We
measured the depth of the mark-stone below ground level
and then very carefully, so as not to knock over the tripod,
we filled earth in over the plate, packed it down and
measured the height again. Only now could the stone pillar
be set over it.

The upper part of the stone had been properly shaped,
while the lower part looked like an undignified, ridiculous
leg. We carried it from the car and carefully lowered it into
the hole. Kos then sat on the edge of the hole, held the
stone in place with his knees and, armed only with the
spirit-level, the plumb-line and his patience, he began his
duel with a piece of rock that I could scarcely lift.

I was now sitting a little way off, watching him work

with the precision of a clock-maker on a 150 pound chunk of granite. Just when it seemed that the plumb-line was properly centred at last, the surveyor would set his level and the stone, with its ridiculous, misshapen leg, would refuse to sit true. He would then try to straighten it with gentle, almost invisible movements, but now the plumb-line was off-centre and the whole annoying operation would start all over again.

Finally, in a whisper, as though he were afraid his breath might unbalance the stone, he said: 'That's it!' The stone stood true in all its axes. So I took some earth, and carefully, so as not to move either the tripod or the stone, which Kos was still holding firmly clamped between his knees, I tipped it into the hole. At the same time, I felt a sense of relief, even satisfaction, as though I had just placed a word in a sentence so firmly and precisely that no one could question it, and the sentence would sound exactly as I had meant it to.

Mr K
Director
The Office of Social Security
Prague

Dear Mr K.

By casting doubt on the nature of my work, an activity that, until now, I and several other people considered artistic, you have played a role in my becoming, for a time at least, a surveyor's assistant. I consider it proper, therefore, to report to you on my progress so that, among other reasons, you may lack no opportunity to cast doubt on this work also.

In evidence of my work as a surveyor's assistant, may I provide you with the following information: during the month of September, I have cleaned and painted seventy-nine stakes, dug out approximately eight cubic metres of earth, set thirty concrete bases and five mark-stones in the ground. In various walls, mostly church and cemetery walls, I have chiselled holes for five bolts. I have also assisted in most of the surveying and related work.

I am aware that it is only with the approval of your office or rather of those who have been summoned to its head (I am employing the Russian turn of phrase favoured in your circles) that reality becomes genuine reality and work becomes genuine work, and I am not succumbing to any false or inflated notions about what I have accomplished in the field of surveying. It is entirely possible that I am living in a state of complete and utter illusion. I am truly curious about what conclusions you will come to.

Yours sincerely

K. (Surveyor's Assistant)

HOME

ON FRIDAYS WE would return to town around noon and, having removed the tools from the car and swept out the week's debris so that the car looked almost clean, I'd hurry inside to change in time to catch the afternoon train.

The station was neat and full of flowers, and I was usually the only passenger there. The train stopped here, it seemed, out of nostalgia, as a gesture to the old days, which I could scarcely remember, days when there had been farmers' markets, fairs and isolated farm cottages in the countryside with women who would take the train into town to do the shopping.

When the train arrived—a single, red locomotive with a driver and perhaps three or four passengers, usually Vietnamese men—I would get on, dust off a seat, and sit down. Then I would look out of the window and watch as autumn settled on the now familiar countryside, as the last fields of sugar beet were harvested, as the reeds in the marshlands turned ochre and grey, as the tamaracks yellowed and the dogwood and sumacs burned an ever more brilliant red.

I have a home, of course, but have always lived in a city. So there is no country landscape to which I can properly return. Yet I've always enjoyed walking in the countryside with my wife. Because I am, by nature, introverted, I liked to absorb silently the multitude of shapes, sounds, colours and odours, the fragments of accidental conversations and scenes. My wife, on the other hand, would always look for analogies to what we saw. Everything was transformed in her mind into a cluster of images mingling dream and reality. That was her way of leaving the narrow pathways which we, like all walkers, had to keep to.

But we didn't have a landscape of our own outside the city, and we never found it.

The local train took me to a station where I would transfer to a train going to Prague. Here, the platform was crowded with people who, like me, were going home from work: men with leather tool-bags hanging on their shoulders, often wearing only dirty overalls; and young factory girls from the gramophone plants, looking as alike as the products they made.

The windows of this train were so filthy that the countryside seemed to have vanished in a fog. I'd find a seat that was free and, if possible, not broken, and fall asleep immediately from exhaustion.

At home, my wife would be expecting me, glad that we were together again, and already annoyed that I had to leave again on Monday. Why didn't I quit? What sense did it make, wasting my time painting dumb stakes, digging rocks out of the ground and straining my heart, my back or whatever it was that hurt that weekend?

I'd tell her I'd stick with it until we finished the work to be done outside. I didn't tell her I actually enjoyed leaving those pathways that, as an ordinary walker, I would have to follow; that I got pleasure from coming into close touch with the landscape.

My wife would accuse me angrily of being pig-headed. There's so much work to be done here at home. Our son is redecorating his room, and if I was so keen to work with my hands, why didn't I help him out?

So I would change into my blue overalls and go to chip the plaster off a few bricks.

There is a Greek fable about a giant, Antaeus, the son of Poseidon and Gaia, goddess of the earth. Antaeus would challenge anyone at all to a duel because he knew he was invincible, for whenever he sank to the ground, his mother would renew his strength. He never once lost, until one day he encountered Heracles, who held him up in the air and so was able to strangle him to death. The Greeks, of course, were on Heracles's side; he was, I suppose, their favourite hero. Nevertheless, the unconscious wisdom of this myth warns us not to let any contemporary Heracles hold us away from the earth for too long.

When the bricks were clean, I'd take a pile of letters that had come for me during the week and read them.

From her home in Sweden, my translator sent me this letter:

We have had a magnificent hot summer and after a few lean years we can be delighted with the enormous harvest of fruits, vegetables and mushrooms. But how can we enjoy them when there is radioactivity still lurking in the cultivated parts of Sweden, especially in the most fertile lands? People are ignoring the warnings, and I'm terrified of what the results of their indifference might be. We have a good monitoring system for our air, water and land, and that's why we know that the catastrophe is a fact. Thousands of seals

216

have died from a virus we have not yet been able to identify. Even our water fowl are affected, and it isn't known whether that was caused by the same virus that struck the seals. The fish population is decreasing. Hunters in the north have been shocked to learn that deer contain more than 45,000 bequerelles, despite all the time that has passed since Chernobyl. Every day there's a new warning, or new facts about the catastrophe. They find, for instance, that they've added thirty chemicals that are harmful to human health, especially children's health, to ice cream in order to make it last in storage. Red peppers imported from Spain are treated with a poison, and their skins are as tough as orange peel. Another panic: tampons contain such a high percentage of dioxin that they are carcinogenic. The news about the decay of the ozone layer, especially around the poles, is terrifying. And nothing is being done to lower the number of cars on the road. This spring we had an excellent exhibition on the destruction of nature and historical buildings, which are almost all damaged beyond recovery. When I come to Prague, I'll bring you a catalogue . . .

That evening my wife and I put on our best clothes and went to a reception for an American writer at the US embassy. I was invited as a fellow writer, not as a surveyor's assistant. My new job was too fresh and I'd done it for too short a time to be able to make anything more than small talk out of it. What would my life be like now, I wondered, if I'd been driven into this substitute profession twenty or even forty years ago, like so many others? Who remembers any more that those stokers, window-washers, ditch-diggers or warehouse workers, exhausted by hard

217

work and monotony, once had other callings and professions: they studied Kant, St Augustine or Paret's theory of the élite; they lectured to students and led discussions on the radio.

We are sitting at a well-laid table tended by waiters in white gloves. My American colleague, having been asked about it, talks of his latest novel. It's about the son of a respectable family who falls in with drug addicts, runs away from home and lives on the street, in abandoned garages or drug dens. His mother goes looking for him, but in order to gain credibility in the drug underworld, she allows someone to shoot her up with heroin. She soon ends up like her son.

The American writer's wife was asked to help distribute aid to the starving children of Ethiopia, and she tells horrific stories about the long march those wretched people had to undertake, and how many of them dropped dead of exhaustion before they could ever reach the places where milk—and salvation—awaited them. The world is full of tragic human stories.

What do I write about?

I'm at a loss, for I'm not writing anything at the moment; I'm doing something else. But, I think, I would like to write about Mother Earth. I can see that my answer is neither complete enough, nor very understandable. The theme doesn't seem attractive enough. It would be more appropriate to write about terrorists, coprophilia and necrophilia, homicidal perverts or, even better, female killers or fugitives from justice or, at the very least, about the suffering of prisoners in the gulag; it would be hard to excite audiences, inured to bloodshed by television, with anything else.

218

Fortunately, no one asks me what I am writing. They want to know what I think about the idea of Central Europe. Do I expect some kind of intellectual and moral renewal to come from this region?

I reply that I didn't know of any place where people are willing to give up the advantages of technology, so what kind of renewal is possible?

Someone hastily corrects my rather gloomy answer by saying that he believes in the purifying power of a reborn Christianity, and he gives persuasive examples, while I— and I am surprised by this myself—find myself returning to an expansive beet field, moving slowly forward with my little box of paints and brushes. From a thicket of enormous leaves, two slender furry bodies emerge, then disappear, emerge and disappear again, two apparitions that seem to be swimming straight for me through the beet field ocean. I can already hear their wheezing, eager breath. Obedient to a long forgotten reflex, I bend down, tear a clump of soil from the earth, and heave it at the creatures.

And what do I think about my own position and the position of my friends?

I don't want to complain: complete favour from the authorities is as dangerous for an artist as complete disfavour. In the former case, the artist's spirit usually perishes; in the latter, the artist himself.

And what would I say about the state we find ourselves in now?

We find ourselves up in the air, lifted high above the head of an invisible hero, on whom we bestow our favours. Intoxicated by the altitude, we think we are approaching the stars; we are conquering the heavens. We

219

don't even try to disengage ourselves and touch the earth to renew our strength. In any case, the earth is, by our own hand, radioactive.

The dogs run away with swimming leaps and I bend down to pick up a handful of dirt, knead it with my fingers, and feel relief.

THE SHOP GIRL

WHEN I RETURNED to Meštec one Monday morning, I found the door of our residence locked and a note stuck in a crack in the door jamb. The note was from my boss. He'd left the ownership papers for his car at home and had gone to fetch them. He apologized, and said he'd be back in the afternoon. The keys were in the stationer's shop.

It was exactly eleven o'clock, and the shop was already closed. Recalling what the former owner of the building had told me, I went through the dark passageway to the inner courtyard and knocked on the door of the stock-room. When no one answered, I turned the handle. The door opened and the smell of paper, mould and mustiness greeted me. Looking around, all I could see were a lot of shelves. Through an arched opening in the wall where a door had probably been came the dim glow of artificial light. I waited, and when no one appeared I walked through the opening.

In the next room, sitting on a couch made of empty crates and two or three rugs, was the familiar long-haired, bespectacled creature wearing a white sweater and a denim skirt. A kettle of water was boiling on an electric hot-plate next to the couch.

221

I said hello.

She looked up in alarm and jumped to her feet. 'Oh, it's you,' she said, obviously relieved. She reached into her pocket and rummaged around in it for a moment before finding the key. 'Will you have a coffee with me?'

I sat down in the only chair in the room.

'He was really steamed up about forgetting his papers,' she said, referring to my boss. Her voice sounded veiled. She took a cup from a shelf containing kitchen utensils. 'This is probably not such a hot place to live,' she said, putting a little ground coffee into the cup, 'but I'd enjoy driving around like you do. I'm stuck inside here all day long.'

I took a piece of cake out of my bag, unwrapped it, and placed it on the small table.

'I won't have to go for lunch,' she said, delighted. 'Actually, it's not so bad here,' she admitted. 'When I was working in the Tesla plant, I was soldering all day long like an idiot, and when I came home at night I was seeing double.'

She took out a lighter and a pack of cigarettes and offered me one. I refused, but lit hers for her. Her face was impassive; I had trouble guessing her age. If her features had anything quirky or individual about them, she'd wiped it out with make-up.

'But it can be a drag here sometimes too,' she remarked.

'What would you rather do?'

'Oh, well,' she said, frowning at my simplistic question. 'I'd travel, wouldn't I? Isn't that what everyone wants to do?'

'Where would you go?'

'Who cares? Just get out. But I'd steer clear of the south; they say the men down there are a pain. I'd go north. I hear

222

they still have nice forests up there, and lakes and rare birds. They showed it on TV a while ago. Did you see it?'

'Do you ever go travelling?'

'Oh, sure! Happen to know where I could get a currency voucher?' She frowned again. 'And even if I did manage to get one, do you think a woman can go anywhere alone? And who'd look after the kid? Granny's only willing to do it during the day; she likes the evening to herself.'

'Are you from Meštec?'

She shook her head. 'Can I have some?' She reached for a piece of cake. Little paper chimney-sweeps, the kind they sold at Christmas for good luck, looked down at us from the opposite shelf. There were also new year's pigs for the same purpose.

'My family's in Pardubice, I mean my mother and brother,' she said. 'Mom's in the hospital now, been there two months already.'

'What's wrong with her?'

'She was working with aniline, right?' she said, as though that explained it. 'I ran away from home the minute I turned fifteen. I married a guy from Usti and now I'm living with my grandma out in the country, two stops away by train. They've built a cement plant right bang on the other side of her fence. It's fabulous. If you leave your coffee on the table, it'll turn white by evening without adding cream.' She gathered up the cups and went to rinse them out.

Her figure was boyish, and she had dark hair on her legs. She didn't seem like the type of woman men go crazy over, and even less did she seem the type to go crazy over men.

'I'm probably quitting my job here soon,' she announced when she came back.

'What then?'

'If I'm going to sell things, I want to get something out of it.' She frowned. 'The father sends four hundred a month for the kid, and the rest is down to me. You know how long I had to save up for this stupid skirt?' She took another piece of cake, remarking on how good it was. 'They'd take me on in the canteen at the cement plant, but I'm through with places where you have to punch a clock. They're also not going to get me working anywhere I have to be with guys. And I shouldn't be having to stand up a lot. My hip joints are a mess and sometimes they hurt so much at night I cry. But maybe I'll find something,' she said with sudden hopefulness. 'Or maybe something will happen.'

'What could happen?' I said, not understanding her remark.

'Oh, I don't know. Maybe some U.F.O.s will land, or something. Like E.T. Did you see that?'

'Yes, I did.' The film hadn't appealed to me much, but I had a faithful representation of the loveable little monster at home. Someone brought it into the country as a present for my children, not realizing that they were too old for dolls.

'I saw it nine times. When they showed it in Prague, I took time off work to go and see it even though it was always sold out. I slipped the woman taking tickets forty crowns and she let me sit on an extra chair for all the showings that day.'

'Would you like to have an E.T. at home?'

My question was so obviously foolish that she decided not to answer it. 'He was kind of—you know, like really from another world.'

'Would you like to go there?'

She sighed, frowned, and then said, 'Even if you could go somewhere like that, they wouldn't take me.'

THE ATTIC

WE RETURNED FROM work earlier than usual today, while it was still light. The surveyor had to deal with damages incurred by the company when several of our stone markers were knocked over by tractors. Before I went into my room, I noticed that the door to the attic was ajar. I couldn't resist and went up the creaking, dusty stairs.

The attic was large and full of old junk. Everything was still except for some flies buzzing under the dormer. The beams were huge and ancient, though the tiles covering the roof seemed almost new. Old dresses were draped among the swallows' nests on the beams. In some doorless cupboards there were stacks of battered shoes, and between a mound of straw and a pile of old handbags I found some rusty stove pipes and several empty boxes and fruit crates.

Clearly nothing of value was left, but I wasn't looking for gold candlesticks. I was always more interested in printed paper—and sure enough, in one of the boxes I found a century-old book, a 'Reader for Schools of Farming and Winter Economics'. Just then I heard something creak behind me. I looked round and saw Mrs Pokorná's head emerging from the stairwell.

225

Aware that I had been caught trespassing, I greeted her with a guilty look. But she seemed glad to have found me. She started right in by telling me that many interesting things had once been stored up here, before people had carried them all away. The museum had even expressed an interest in the cavalry officer's uniform worn by her great-grandfather, and her grandfather's drum had been here too, though the skin was broken. Her grandfather had served with Count Haugwitz's infantry regiment. It wasn't nearly as bad in those days: they only had tallow candles for light, of course, but on the other hand there was less lying and no stealing. When her grandfather was transferred to the cavalry, he played on a harp so big they had to transport it on a cart pulled by ponies. In 1866 he had fought in the battle near Hradec, and he had proud memories of it, even though he'd been on the losing end.

'We were occupied then, too,' she winked at me conspiratorially, 'but it was a Prussian occupation. And the Prussians,' she added at once, 'put a notice on the wall here saying they hadn't come as conquerors, and would fully respect our national rights. Sir, this building has memories. During the last war, when they shot Heydrich, the Germans pasted on our wall a list of people they'd executed. Father ordered a special shipment of black-bordered envelopes, but then they locked him up, and six months later my mother was sending them out herself with letters of condolence.

'After that, by God's will, the blows came one after the other. Our building was confiscated by our own people and they were worse than the foreigners, and on top of that there was no one to drive them out. Last thing, right over there,' and she pointed to the corner of the attic where there was a new mansard, 'Doctor Tereba had his observatory. He didn't have a family, and he'd spend all his nights up here. Venus was his wife, he'd say, and the moon and the planets were his children. You'll understand that, sir, because I know you measure by the stars, too; that young man who drives you around explained it to me. But you just figure out where things are on the earth. Doctor Tereba, he could figure out what would happen on the earth. Even before it happened, he told us about the disaster of the communist take-over in 'forty-eight. He had his telescope right here,' she walked over to the mansard and pointed to a pile of handbags on the floor, 'when the Americans flew to the moon; I invited everyone in the building up here so we could be a little closer to such a momentous event. And would you believe it? With my own eyes I saw how a cloud of dust was raised up there on the moon when that rocket landed. That's when I realized the moon wasn't what it used to be, if people can go walking about on it. Well, Doctor Tereba's gone too, and now they want to tear the place down. I tell you, that'll be the end of me. I don't think I could survive that.' She looked at me imploringly, as though it were within my power to save the building from destruction.

As I looked into her eyes, I could suddenly see, despite the vast distance in time, a line of Hussars in snow-white greatcoats, silvered by the light of the moon. The ominous sound of drumming reached the attic, and among the drummers a lone soldier was riding on a wagon, playing a harp. But no one could hear it over the drumming, not even when the soldier plucked the strings with all his might.

227

THE SURVEYOR

WE DROVE OUR Romanian car to the top of a hill outside Chrudim and stopped a short distance from the new water tower. A road led up here, made of concrete slabs laid end to end. The point we had to re-survey should have been right beside the road, but someone had moved the marker stake, along with the cement base and the warning plate saying that anyone who moved the state's triangulation point was liable to prosecution.

The surveyor studied his map for a while. We then ran the tape-measure over the ground until we found, right by the edge of one of the concrete slabs, the spot where the triangulation point was supposed to be. I fetched the probe, a long iron bar with a point at one end, and for a few minutes we stabbed it into the earth without result. I expressed doubts that the mark-stone could have survived all the changes that had obviously taken place. The bulldozer, after all, would have hollowed out a roadbed wider than the concrete slabs. The stone must have been dug up.

'But then where is it?' the surveyor asked. 'They could have dug it up and then covered it with fill,' he admitted, 'but maybe they raised the level of the terrain when they made the road. In that case, the stone would have remained in its proper spot, but buried even deeper.' He took the pick and began to dig. The earth I shovelled out of the hole—mainly gravel—was obviously fill. I couldn't imagine finding our stone underneath it, but the surveyor worked tirelessly and, as though aware of the folly of his effort, refused to let me dissuade him. When the trench he'd dug was deep enough to accommodate a kneeling sniper, he took the iron probe again and rammed it repeatedly into the ground right up to the grip. He struck nothing. 'It's always possible,' he said, 'that we've measured the distances imprecisely, or that some inaccuracies crept into the map we inherited. We ought to measure the position of the point again.'

The next day we brought a theodolite along. The surveyor levelled the instrument, tightened it on its pedestal, and began to focus in on the church tower while I, happy not to have either to dig or paint stakes, wrote down the angles he called out.

That evening the surveyor sat at his crippled table doing his calculations. The precision he worked to astonished me, especially since I know that slapdash work on our part would either never be discovered at all, or found out only after many years had gone by. Undoubtedly the knowledge that our measurements were as accurate as he could make them gave him satisfaction.

He was a rural man. He lived in a hamlet somewhere in the borderland between Bohemia and Moravia and he travelled about as far to Meštec as I did. His train arrived on Monday around ten; my bus from Prague got there an hour later. From that moment until Friday afternoon, we couldn't escape from each other; we even sat down to lunch

229

together. But both of us were silent types, and besides, there wasn't much time for conversation when we were working. I knew he was building an extension to his parents' house, in which he and his wife would live; that he was fattening up a bull he'd been given as a wedding present; that he ran for the fun of it, and played hockey and chess when he had the time.

He was my son's age; they both had finished their studies at the same time. And both had married only a few months before. He reminded me of my son, too, in his closed nature, and his kindly smile. These similarities inspired me to try to communicate with him on more than just a superficial level. But when people have no shared inheritance of work or songs or rituals or holy books or even heroes—when the bridges between us are fewer— what can bring them together?

Both of us were looking for a dining-room table.

Above the furniture store we occasionally drove past, a large red banner with yellow lettering on it declared that the aim of our ruling party was prosperity for all humanity. The surveyor would occasionally drop in to ask if they had a table. They never did. The bombastic claim over the doorway ridiculed us and we knew it, just as everyone who lived under this government of sloganeers knew it. Collectively humiliated, we shared contempt for those who humiliated us. But contempt and humiliation cannot uplift people and therefore cannot bring them closer together.

Sometimes I could see us as others saw us. Two figures of unequal age and position who moved through the countryside, across wet meadows and beet fields, carrying worn-out instruments and coloured stakes.

The older man would like to know what the younger

one thought about the world and whether he perhaps blamed his older companion for the state of the country. The older man has even prepared a defence should the question come up in conversation. He would explain what the war had done to him and his peers, how much anxiety and how many wrong-headed utopian visions it had inspired in them. And he would explain the blindness that every vision produces.

He is apprehensive about the moment the younger man will begin this conversation, but he is even more apprehensive that the younger man will not start the conversation at all because the questions have never crossed his mind. Perhaps the old lies, the *coup d'états,* the wrongs, the controversies, the illusions, the torturing, the artifice and the crimes no longer interest him, just like the war, even further in the past. Perhaps the younger man thinks the grey cloud that has hung over his head all his life is the natural colour of the sky, if he ever looks up at it at all.

One day, the two men lose their way in the woods and start walking back down a hill in the wrong direction. The younger man, of course, has his spirit-level and his stop-watch, the older man his wire-brush, his machete and his box of paints and brushes, but none of these is any use in finding their way.

The younger man becomes upset. He is responsible for the work they are doing and for the car they have left in a field. He suggests they retrace their steps, but the older man is not enthusiastic about the idea. He doesn't feel like going back up the hill. Wandering through the woods makes far more sense to him than digging holes in the ground and burying slabs of concrete. He suggests they keep on

231

walking; they will certainly get somewhere eventually.

But what if that takes us further from the car? the younger man objects.

Don't think about the car.

This answer surprises the younger man, but then he says: I understand, but what do you expect to find?

He has a point. What is there to expect? What surprises? What unsurveyed countryside? What hope?

The younger man is waiting for an answer. He has not met many people in his life from whom he might expect a meaningful answer. He has been educated, of course: they handed him a lot of formulae, practical information and also many superstitions and half-truths about the world he lives in. At home, they raised him to be honest and diligent. One must work to live. But why he should live, that they didn't tell him, or didn't know.

Perhaps the older man has experience or knowledge that he could relate to his young friend—perhaps this is the reason for his being here.

But the younger man does not receive an answer; so he shrugs his shoulders and says, 'Whatever you think.'

So they continue on their way, not knowing where it will lead. The woods thin out, the air begins to smell strangely of cinders, smoke, even of sulphur, as though they were not walking through a wood, but the scene of some conflagration.

It's a good sign that he's come this way with me, the older man thinks. He says: 'Don't you think it's interesting that the act of measuring inevitably leads to a descent?'

The younger man does not understand what he means.

'We are constantly becoming more precise,' the older man explains, 'as we try to describe the Earth or the organization of matter. We are forever finding smaller particles, but we can't seem to shift in the other direction.'

'But,' the younger man objects. 'We're always discovering new galaxies.'

'I'm not thinking of galaxies, I'm thinking of what's above us, I mean above man.'

The younger man nods.

'I was brought up to believe there was nothing above me,' says the older man. 'When the war came, they locked us up, and they murdered almost everyone in our family. Back then, the killing was going on all over the world. My father saw in that a confirmation of his beliefs: if God existed, he would never have allowed such cruel, unjust and pointless bloodshed. But others saw it as God's punishment for the sins of men. After all, the slaughter of children is presented in the Bible as one of the punishments for denying God.'

They are coming to a crossroads; it's not the right time to get involved in a discussion of abstract ideas. The younger man silently chooses one of the paths and continues walking.

'After the war,' the older man recalls, 'I knew other people who were locked up just as absurdly and arbitrarily as we were. This happened to our landlord's daughter, who was seventeen at the time.' The older man doesn't say out loud that in his imagination he had longed to make love to the girl. He only says that when she came back many years later and told him about her miserable internment in the camp, she mentioned that one thing had become clear to her there: it was simply not possible that man was the highest form of life in the universe.

'That's an interesting idea,' the younger man says.

'Sometimes people really can be worse than animals. Not long ago, I don't know if you read about it, some guy in England murdered a woman, a total stranger, right in front of her kids, then he went home, shot his mother and then went on the rampage and killed fourteen more people—just for fun. '

For a while they talk about insane gunmen, both the kind that wear stocking masks over their faces and the kind that wear a uniform. The younger man, it seems, is interested in this problem of gunmen. He plays chess, and finds it pleasant to talk about distant violence. The older man, for his part, is sorry that their conversation is losing its point.

They finally emerge from the woods. Below them a dirty river winds through the countryside. The bank is riddled with ditches full of stagnant rainbow-tinged water. The earth here is bare; only the steep piles of rubble are overgrown with weeds. There are no murderers lying in wait, but across the river tall, ash-covered smokestacks vomit thick billowy grey smoke into the air. The smoke kills slowly and invisibly.

The younger man asks: 'Don't you think that what you were talking about—some higher wisdom or whatever it was—moves in a completely different space or in different dimensions from ours?'

The older man admits it is possible.

The path leads down to the river. A tug-boat is approaching, drawing a barge loaded with coal. The boat is black, the coal is dark brown, and the clay banks of the river are ochre, like the muddy river water. There is no colour here, except for some bright clothes drying on a rope strung across the stern of the tug.

Both men look at this unexpected display, and as the tug

234

draws level with them, a girl in a colourful dress emerges from below, her long hair cascading over her bare shoulders. The younger man waves. The girl leans back against the wall of the wheelhouse and she stares at both men, motionless.

The younger man puts his hands to his mouth and calls out: 'Take us with you!'

'Come aboard!' the young woman replies. They can distinguish a smile on her face.

'But what about the water between us?' the younger man shouts. The river is wide here and the boat is almost on the other side.

'So, get a little wet!' The girl disappears below.

'Let's go and meet her when the boat docks. After all, she's invited us,' suggests the younger man. The older man wonders if, hidden in this encounter, in the few words he has heard, there isn't some deeper meaning, or even something like a sign.

As we were driving around, we talked mostly about work, sometimes about sports. I also tried to understand something of what we were doing, and the surveyor willingly gave me lectures on azimuths, geodetic lines and the co-ordinates of terminal points.

To get his degree, he'd had to live away from home since he was fourteen. He had been taught how to adapt to the conditions of the surveyor's life in the field. During the day, his teachers were strict and demanded precision. In the evenings, they played cards, drank beer and told stories from their bachelor days, and thus helped prepare the students for the isolation to come. A real surveyor spends most of his life far from the home he has often had no time to establish.

When he started working, then, there were no surprises. As the youngest in the firm, he was sent to the most desolate places. When there was work to do, time went by quickly, but when it rained, he didn't know how to kill time. He read a little, but the available books could not, for the most part, hold his interest. Sometimes, even when it was raining, he would go out for a run, but he would always end up sitting with strangers in village pubs, drinking with them and having the kind of conversations he'd have had in the same place back home. After his fifth or sixth beer, he no longer needed to drink or talk, or even listen too carefully. The world rolled itself into a cone in which he could exist quite comfortably until the time came to sleep. He would wake up with an aching head, overwhelmed by an emptiness that could not be dispelled.

A year ago, when he was twenty-seven, he had been sent to survey in the south of Moravia. He lived in a hamlet that was 156 metres above sea-level. The highest point of land was seven metres above that. Moaning winds blew across the flat expanses. Sometimes, when he climbed to the top of the church tower and looked across the river, he would catch glimpses of neat houses in Austrian villages and brightly coloured cars that flashed by on Austrian roads. In such moments, he was overcome by strange misgivings. Something was going on outside, in the world, and his time was standing still.

The people in the hamlet seemed nice enough. They drank wine and loved to talk and sing noisily. He drank beer and took no part in the singing. Once, when he was walking back to his dormitory, he left the road. For a while he wandered along in a ditch, until he finally collapsed under a thick blackthorn bush. The cold in the middle of the night awakened him. Above his head little drops of dew, illuminated by moonlight, glistened on the leaves and branches. He knew that he should get up and go back to the dormitory. His head was clear, clearer then it had ever been during the day, and for that reason he knew that it didn't matter where he was lying, or whether he caught a cold or even died of exposure. He closed his eyes again and fell asleep.

Next morning, he realized that things were beginning to go wrong in his life, and he was astonished at how little it bothered him. Nevertheless, when Friday came around and he was getting ready to go home, he changed into his good clothes as usual, because his parents were proudly expecting their son, the surveyor.

On the train he developed a thirst and when he got out, he stopped for a beer and missed the last bus. It was at least a two-hour walk home, and it was going to rain. Fortunately, he hadn't forgotten how to run. In a small park behind a school he noticed a girl sitting on a bench with her head in her hands. He ran past her, but he came back. The wind whipped up swirls of dust on the path and it began to rain. He didn't know why the girl was crying, or even how he could comfort her. But it didn't seem right to leave her there. He helped her up, and they ran into a kind of passageway for shelter. He know nothing about her, but he tried to cheer her up, or at least to get her mind off her troubles. When the rain slackened, he walked her home. He gave her his address; she wrote to him. But she never told him why she was crying in the park, and they never talked about it afterwards. He spent a whole evening composing a reply. He was unaccustomed to writing letters, particularly this kind, but the letter worked.

When they were married a few months ago, colleagues and school friends gathered from all over the country. Two came on horseback dressed in white and yellow leggings and long, dark blue overcoats, the kind the imperial military engineers used to wear. Afterwards they persuaded him and his bride to mount a horse and ride through a triumphal arch of red and white striped surveying stakes.

They were expecting a child just before Christmas. By the time the child was born, the surveyor would be living at home. This is, in fact, his last surveying job; as of next year, he was changing employers.

Had he found something more interesting?

No, not really. He'd be spending most of his time in an office, but he'd be able to go home every evening. That's the way his wife wanted it, and it would be better for the child as well.

I couldn't imagine my father ever showing any concern for my mother or me while he was working. He never doubted that work took precedence over everything else. My father believed, as his father did before him, in the unambiguous benefits of his work.

I asked the surveyor if he wanted a son or a daughter. He shrugged his shoulders. 'It makes no difference. Women have a hard life—and so do we, in different ways. My wife says she doesn't care either,' he added. 'But she'd prefer a girl. She thinks she'd get along better with a girl, and besides, a girl wouldn't have to do time in the army.'

He never mentioned his wife by name. Perhaps he was trying to preserve his privacy and her mystery.

We were on top of the hill by the water tower, looking for our lost triangulation point again.

By precise calculations, the surveyor had determined that

the point should be the same distance from the edge of the concrete slabs, but slightly above the place we'd first begun to dig. In fact, all we needed to do was lengthen our original hole.

I expressed admiration for a science that, by measuring from a distant church tower, could accurately locate any point on the earth's surface. But I still didn't believe we could find the missing stone.

The surveyor started digging down towards the hypothetical point. I shovelled the loose dirt out of the hole.

'They must have at least left the marker here somewhere,' he said as he doggedly stabbed the ground with the probe.

But they hadn't. All we could do was install a new one. Why wouldn't he do so? I preferred not to ask.

As usual, we returned as it was getting dark. I couldn't tell whether he felt badly about not finding the stone, or whether he was content to be able to report, with some certainty, that the point had been destroyed.

At home, he retired to his three-legged table, turned on his radio and began to work something out. Later he appeared in my room. 'I've just heard an interesting programme,' he announced. 'Have you heard of the "Big Bang"?'

I had.

'So listen to this,' he said excitedly. 'They apparently calculated the volume of the material from which everything else, the whole universe, was made.'

'Is that possible?'

He shrugged his shoulders to indicate that he took no responsibility for the information. 'They claim the volume can be expressed by the figure ten to the minus fifty cubic metres.'

'That's pretty small.'

'Small? It's less than nothing. The diameter of an atom is something on the order of ten to the minus eight cubic metres. Can you imagine that?'

I had to admit that I couldn't.

The Countryside

I BROUGHT the girl who worked in the stationery shop the plastic figurine representing the hideous-looking E.T., but I couldn't give it to her right away. That morning, we set out before the store opened, and by the time we returned she was already gone. I'd have to wait for a rainy day, when we'd stay at home. That wasn't the only thing I'd reserved for a rainy day. There was also a package of books I hoped to read.

But that autumn turned out to be the driest we'd ever had and I saw the girl only once. I'd lost a pencil that morning, and I went into the store to buy a new one.

There were no customers in the shop. The girl was sitting behind the counter reading. 'It's you?' she said, astonished. 'I thought you'd gone. I never see you around.' She stood up and groaned. 'Everything hurts today,' and she ran her hands over both hips. 'Somewhere over by Hlinsko they say they've found this really fantastic healer who works miracles. Have you heard of him?'

She walked unsteadily to the drawer where she kept the pencils, pulled it out and asked me to choose one. 'They say he takes one look at you and he can tell exactly what's wrong. And he cures you with the power that comes from

241

his fingers and his eyes.'

'That's what they say,' I admitted. I knew the priest in the village where the healer lived.

'Do you think he'd see me?'

'Certainly. He sees everyone.'

'There must be loads of people who want to see him.'

'Sometimes you have to wait all night.'

'They say he even cured people who couldn't walk. Do you believe that?'

'It depends on what was wrong with them,' I said. 'And what about your mother?' I asked. 'Is she still in hospital?'

'She won't be coming home,' she said matter-of-factly. 'I haven't been able to see her for at least two weeks. I'd go there with my little girl, but she's had an ear-ache. And if I go alone, there's nothing to talk about. All she can do is lie there.'

Her voice seemed unsteady. I paid for the pencil, and as I left I caught sight of her through the glass door sitting down, with some difficulty, to read her magazine.

If he is to check all the points in his network, a surveyor must criss-cross the countryside, not omitting a single field, and there is scarcely a village he will not have walked through many times, or at least driven through. Because his points are located on high land and in other prominent places, he must climb hills and church towers. He surveys a landscape bathed in sunlight and submerged in shadow. He sees its delectability and its distress.

One day, on a gentle slope near the Labe River, we were looking for a stone marker in a cornfield. The field was huge and the corn was so high that the surveyor had to jump on the bonnet of his car to scan the field with binoculars. When he saw the tip of the black and white stake in the distance, he sent me ahead to find it. I held a staff above my head so that he would not lose sight of me, and pushed my way through the thick corn following his shouted directions.

When I reached the stone, I saw that a third of it was sticking out of the ground. It was easy to dig up; the soil here was soft, viscid and black. You could feel the fecundity of Mother Earth in it. We set the stone back in the ground properly and added several shovels of topsoil to fill the hole.

'The water will just erode it again,' the surveyor remarked, speaking of the topsoil. 'You can see how much of it was washed away since the last survey.' This, I learned, had taken place seven years ago.

'Growing corn here,' the surveyor added, 'is a crime.'

A greedy farmer, not really a farmer at all, can destroy in a single seven-year period what it took thousands of years to create. And what he destroyed no one could ever restore.

While we were in the middle of the huge field, we were caught by a vehicle spewing dust from a line of nozzles. We couldn't pack our tools and escape in time, and suddenly found ourselves engulfed in a suffocating cloud. Tears streamed down our cheeks and we coughed, gasping for breath.

What would my wife have seen in this slowly dissipating cloud?

Perhaps from a distance it would have reminded her of a snowstorm, the floating clouds of milkweed seed on an Indian summer day, or mist rising from the bottom of a waterfall. But to me, in the middle of it, it was thick with memories of gas attacks and war.

There were fields that we passed every day. I observed

how the corn tassles turned grey and the kernels yellowed and hardened. When the corn in these fields was harvested, and all that remained of them was stubble, I saw bare patches previously hidden by the corn. Nothing grew there and nothing ever would. The next day tractors were turning over the soil with gigantic ploughs. Some time later, when we passed the same fields again, it was windy, and there were clouds of dust over the fields. The wind carried the earth away for ever. We were no longer looking at a field but at a desert. On these journeys we never saw a pheasant or a quail, or even a rabbit. Only mouse-holes and swarms of flies. These, I realized, were the life forms that would most probably survive.

At noon, depending on where we happened to be, we would either go somewhere for lunch or just sit down on the edge of a field, eat salami and a bun, and drink a bottle of mineral water. Most often we would stop at a roadside pub. Such places practiced strict segregation. A small taproom was set aside for workers, but entry into the dining-room in work clothes was forbidden. But that day, a smiling barwoman wouldn't even let us into the room set aside for us, because a wedding party had taken over the whole restaurant.

We left our quasi-military vehicle beside some colourful little cars decked out in streamers and went to buy something in the store around the corner. From the windows of the restaurant we were not allowed to enter because of our clothes, we could hear the shrieks of the wedding guests. Suddenly the door opened and three young men appeared, dragging the bride between them. She wore a garland of freesias in her hair and offered little resistance, merely holding the lacy hem of her long

244

wedding gown off the ground and occasionally making a show of trying to escape from her captors. When they pushed her into a decorated car that had squealed to a stop by the main entrance, she began to giggle in a high, joyous, seductive voice. As the car careered out on to the road, she managed to wave out of the window at us and at the other wedding guests who had meanwhile gathered in the doorway.

Before we knew it we were surrounded by a second group of young men in suits who, with the persistence of people who've been drinking, tried to persuade us that we had a duty—we were the only sober men around—to take them with us and give chase to the kidnappers. If we caught up with them we could have all the food we could eat and all the beer we could drink.

As usual, I couldn't read the surveyor's thoughts from the expression on his face, but he moved a bundle of stakes from the seat in the back of the car and nodded to the young man who was obviously the groom, and two other wedding guests, to climb aboard. We got in the front and drove off in pursuit.

In every village we came to, we stopped at the pub, or at least slowed down to look for the car decorated with streamers. We finally caught up with them at the fifth pub. The groom and his two guests jumped out while the car was still moving and I heard the loud laughter when they appeared inside. I saw the bride cautiously sipping from a mug of beer she'd been treated to.

One of the groom's companions quickly paid the bill for the kidnappers, the kidnapped and the rest of the people in the room, and then we got back in the car, this time with the bride. I offered her my seat beside the driver, but she preferred to squeeze in beside her newly acquired husband.

The surveyor suggested a short cut, and took off across the fields of stubble. I did not look around, but I could hear behind me the whispering of a happy female voice; the air was filled with the fragrance of flowers.

Perhaps the car itself felt the strangeness of the occasion. Certainly the driver must have realized that this was perhaps the last such opportunity in his surveying career. We bounced lightly over the ridge of a hill, and then we were practically flying above the reddish stubble in the fields. The surveyor's whole body was tensed; all he needed was a helmet and he was an aviator, gently and skilfully manoeuvring his machine so close to the ground that the onlookers gasped in wonder.

I glanced briefly over my shoulder into the back of the car. The bride was resting her head on the groom's shoulder. Her eyes were closed and her garland had slipped to one side. She was a country girl with a pert little nose and freckled cheeks. There were a few small beads of perspiration on her upper lip. It occurred to me that her gentleness, her mystery, was precisely what was missing from our work, from the whole age of engineering.

Only on one other occasion did our job bring us into the proximity of women. While we were surveying a narrow strip of meadow beside a stream, there were several young women just across the water, picking flowers from a field of asters that stretched as far as we could see. As we worked, the sound of their voices was constantly in our ears.

I was holding the tape and looking into the shallow brook. I noticed how tranquil the place and the moment were. Even the distant tower blocks, which usually made me feel crowded, seemed, in the haze of autumn mists and behind a screen of feminine laughter, more like a constructivist painting or a theatrical backdrop.

'When we finish the survey,' Kos suggested, 'let's go over and pick some flowers.'

Though I knew that the flowers would have wilted by tomorrow I didn't object: the slide from our monotonous routine into a field of flowers inhabited by young women meant more than just a short walk across a bridge.

So that we wouldn't forget which world we belong to and the god we serve, a roll of thunder sounded behind us. The noise grew quickly to a crescendo and became recognizable as the roar of a jet engine at full throttle.

Then we saw them. Not far from us, midway between where we were standing and the mist-shrouded apartment towers, contemptuous of all living things, jet fighters speeding towards an invisible but precisely surveyed concrete runway. I looked regretfully across the stream at the field of flowers, which seemed to tremble in alarm and then flee, fading from our sight like a dream vision.

At regular intervals, this same ceremony was repeated. And each time the languages of birds, animals, people, silence and even our inmost thoughts were sacrificed on enormous funeral pyres.

We finished the survey, got into the car and, adding some noise of our own to the ceremony, drove off to another place to continue our work, preparing fresh data for new and better runways.

THE FACTORY

WE SET OUT in a sticky autumn fog when it was still dark.

There were several triangulation points inside the grounds of a factory, and in the area around it, but the surveyor had put off checking them. We needed several letters of reference and permits from the department of special projects and, anyway, we assumed that the benchmarks inside the factory would be the least likely to be damaged.

The factory lay just off the main road in the most fertile part of the country's Golden Belt of arable land. A high wall surrounded the factory and only the foul odour of the fog warned us that we had arrived. We parked the car and walked over to the main entrance where a fat female guard asked us if we were carrying matches. When we assured her we were not, she let us into the waiting-room where we were to remain until the company surveyor came to get us.

The waiting-room was painted from floor to ceiling in a greyish-brown oil-based paint. The floor was covered with worn and dirty ochre-coloured linoleum. The only décor was a poster warning against the danger of naked flame, and a clumsy-looking metal telephone. Anyone finding himself here could have no illusions about what to expect inside.

All I could see of the interior of the factory was a concrete yard and a few grey buildings. Occasionally the door would open and someone would hurry through importantly. A young woman in a black dress with a sickly pale face ran in. Paying no attention to us, she lifted the receiver on the phone and dialled a three-digit number. She was having trouble getting a line and while she pleaded, nearly in tears, to be connected, to communicate what I had no doubt was some bad news, I could hear the shrieking laughter of women behind me. Turning round, I saw four women in the unattractive dark grey uniforms of the factory guards bent over a magazine which, I surmised from the tone of their laughter, was 'objectionable,' or even 'diversionist,' as our police terminology has it. But perhaps the magazine was not objectionable; perhaps they were only delighted that they had got the better of life, with their pistols on their hips.

Finally, the factory surveyor showed up. He was short, wearing a leather jacket, jeans, and high-heeled shoes to increase his stature. He carried a roll of paper under his arm. He and Kos stared at each other for a while, then realized they'd gone to school together, and at once began trading accounts of their recent lives and comparing incomes.

We returned to our car, where the factory surveyor looked at our letters of recommendation and our permits, cursed the local bureaucracy, then pulled a top-secret map out of his roll. Two of the triangulation points, it seemed, were easily accessible; the third and fourth lay in a highly restricted area. The factory surveyor would inform the guard of our presence to prevent our being shot as spies. He smiled and left us.

249

'I wish this thing were over with,' my boss said. 'You never know here what you'll get mixed up in. The last time this place blew up, it took about four hundred people with it. Some of them completely vanished, except for maybe a watch that they found two kilometres away.'

When the diminutive factory surveyor returned we asked him about this catastrophe.

'That's bullshit,' he said. 'The gunpowder section blew up two years ago; it happened during the lunch break. Five dead and a couple of wounded. Mostly cuts and bruises. There was glass flying around all over the place,' he said, warming to the memory. 'But no one lost an eye. That's the thing, my friends, when you see a flash of light around here—even if it's only a thunderstorm—cover your eyes.'

While we were waiting for a yard engine to shunt some cisterns out of the way that, as far as we know, might have been filled with dynamite, trinitrotoluene or even nitroglycerine, he explained to us how in the aniline department they only took women over the age of forty and, even then, they had to sign a statement saying they're aware of the dangers.

'What are the dangers?'

'A hundred and eighteen per cent increased chance of cancer of the bladder.'

'And they sign?'

'Of course they do. They get risk money every month—at least four hundred crowns.'

Although they were not marked with stakes, we found the first two points easily. I gave them a fresh coat of paint, and painted red arrows on the surrounding trees.

The third point was on a wooded knoll just inside a high barbed-wire fence. It was a double fence of the kind they

250

put around prison camps. There was even a watch-tower. The oak and birch trees in the woods had already turned yellow and brown and seemed to be exhaling a chemical stench. The surveyors were poring over the map again, arguing. Eventually they came to the conclusion that one of the stones lay outside the fence.

We set the tripod up over the accessible stone and returned to the car. We turned on to the road, passed a high cooling tower and an assembly of boilers and pipes in which something liquid I didn't want to know about was being created, drove through a side gate and came to a halt at the edge of the woods. We took another tripod out and very carefully, as though it were sacred, the surveyor brought out the case containing the spirit level. Even outside the factory, enormous pipes supported on low trestles snaked through the trees. In several places, a vapour of some sort was escaping from them.

We positioned the level over the stone with great effort and the surveyor tried to get a clear view of the tripod we'd left on the knoll inside the fence. All we could see was a thicket of tree trunks, large and small. Using the machete and the axe, we chopped a trail right to the fence where, with our combined strength, we felled a spruce tree. We returned to the stone pillar and even I could now see the yellow leg of the tripod on the small knoll across the way.

My young boss looked dissatisfied and widened the swathe to the fence with the machete. Then he ordered me to stay with the expensive equipment while he drove back around to the other side of the fence.

Left alone, I could hear the thud of distant explosions and the honking of yard engines, but otherwise it was silent. It was near the end of October and the birds, if any survived here, weren't singing. A watery sun was beginning to force its way through the mist above the treetops. Occasionally, with a quiet plop, a toxic drop of dew would slip off the edge of a leaf.

Mystery is a direct insult to our self-assurance. If there were no longer any mystery, we imagine that a beautiful and safe sense of certainty would inhabit the world (even though we don't know what it would be certainty about). We have thus become accustomed to celebrating as giants those who have worked hardest to rid us of mystery. After all, they have led us out of darkness where, at any moment, we might have been assaulted by the inexplicable, where pestilence and witches lie in wait. It never occurs to us that they have also set us down here in the middle of a bland superhighway planted with signs. We pass our lives rushing from sign to sign.

One day we will come up against the limit of the tolerable and the possible. It seems to me that this day is already drawing near. Man, it would seem, cannot remain in one place. The moment he finds himself at a border he cannot go beyond, he must give up. But where could he return to now?

In the distance, I caught sight of the surveyor's rust-coloured sweater. For a while, it flitted here and there, then I heard the familiar voice calling to me to throw the tools over the fence. More branches and trunks were felled; I was now able to make out the legs of the tripod. Still, however, my boss could not see the two discs on the ends of the apparatus on my side of the fence.

Again and again, following his instructions, I lopped off branches that seemed to block his view, until he discovered that the real impediment was the trunk of a stately birch.

He came down the hill with his fellow surveyor and, for a while, across the fence, we discussed what we should do. The two of them decided they would have to cut the birch down.

I objected. We couldn't chop down such a magnificent tree simply because we wanted to.

The factory surveyor looked at me with contemptuous astonishment. 'Here?' he said, pointing up at the diseased treetops.

Later, I thought of what I should have said: 'That's exactly why we shouldn't.' Meanwhile, they had thrown me a saw over the barbed wire.

As a student, I had cut down trees infested with bark-beetles, and I even felt proud of being able to do such manly work, bringing down a fifteen-metre spruce right where I wanted it to fall. I tried to remember whether I'd felt any regret for the tree.

I walked over to the birch, which as yet knew nothing of its fate, and looked up into its crown. The sky had cleared, and the yellow leaves seemed to be radiating their own light. I remembered that the captive spirits of innocent maidens lived in birch trees. I could not have put my arms around it. The tree was at least two metres in diameter. I took the axe and drove it into the white bark to make a notch in the side I wanted it to fall towards, then I grasped the saw and began to cut. The saw bit into the wood, the white sawdust spilled out and I breathed in its smell.

As the saw cut deeper into the wood, the trunk resisted more and more. It was its only defence—to squeeze the blade tightly and not let it go. I decided to pull the saw out and start cutting from the opposite side. Sweat was running down my forehead. I took off my jacket and went on working. The tree groaned and creaked silently. I could hear the terrified, astonished whispering of the leaves in the crown.

I pulled the saw out and rested a while. There were quiet footfalls, and when I looked in the direction they were coming from, I saw a soldier with a gun. He was approaching slowly along a path beside the fence. When he walked past, he looked at me without stopping or even slowing down.

The trunk, now full of desperate determination, was binding the saw blade on both sides.

I hated myself for getting forced into this job. What good is all our surveying? What was the use of us pounding through the corn? Why did I have to take the life of this pure, white tree? Those who obey contemptible orders are themselves contemptible.

But my regret, as often happens in life, had come too late. The tree was already dying.

They called over from the other side of the fence, wanting to know how far through I was, but I didn't answer. I pulled the saw out again, took the axe and began with a fury to widen the cut. Then I pushed against the tree to test its resistance. But the birch was still firm, as though its veins had not yet been cut.

Man has struggled with nature from the beginning, killing animals and clearing forests, but he took life so he himself could survive. We take life so we can erect the works of the age of engineering. We do not kill from an instinct to preserve life, but from an instinct that leads us to extinction.

Gradually, the desperate squeezing of the tree against the blade relaxed, and silently, desperately and for the last time, the spirit of the tree groaned—then cracked. Its branches clutched at the surrounding trees but could not hang on. The yellowing leaves rained to the ground.

On the opposite slope the surveyors cheered. Now nothing blocked their view. I sat down on my coat while they gathered their measurements.

The soldier returned along the path between the fences. He must have seen the fallen tree, the branches that reached out to the fence, but he was not interested. Like other soldiers, who ignored fallen men and women with arms outstretched to other fences.

When the surveyor reappeared on my side of the fence, it was twenty-five to two. We packed up all the instruments and carried them back to the car. Then the surveyor went to inform the department of special projects of our departure.

He came back, smiling. It seems the factory surveyor had forgotten to tell the guards what we were up to. They wanted to know if there had been any unpleasantness.

I mentioned the soldier pacing up and down inside his wire cage as though drugged, without noticing me, without even registering my existence.

'Can you blame him?' asked the surveyor. 'If I were him, the only thing I'd feel like shooting at would be that fence.'

Mr. K.
Director
Office of Social Security
Prague

Dear Mr K.

In talking to my fellow writers, I have discovered that it is not only my work you have doubted, but theirs as well. I understand that most of them have decided to appeal against your decision and prove that they are artists. In evidence, they are bringing you books, clippings to show that their plays have been presented on various world stages, and even documentation of their literary prizes.

Perhaps you have wondered why I haven't done the same. I could simply declare that such behaviour seems undignified, or proclaim that I would rather accept my fate than rebel against it, and there would undeniably be some truth in that. But I would be lying if I pretended that it is not my wish for people like you to disappear from the positions you occupy in the castles where you ply your contemptible trade. It still remains unclear, however, what to do to make you disappear.

No one, as perhaps even you know, is immortal or invulnerable. Even the most magnificent heroes and demigods, when you take away their impregnable shields, their magic swords and tireless muscles, have their Achilles' heel, their need to touch the earth. Your shield and your sword are your position, raised high not only above the earth, but above all of life, above everything human—not to mention everything just.

Anyone who joins in debate with you—I mean an honest debate—not only cannot win, but also, by acknowledging your arbitrary power, confirms the feeling of superiority that

256

power brings. What does a book or a play mean to you—or any work, no matter how brilliant? What does an artist who is debating with you mean? You have him exactly where you—and those who have nominated you—want him: at your feet, and you let him stay there as long as possible. You let him tremble, let him squirm, let him grovel, let him write requests which you are only too happy to fill your waste-basket with. You enjoy his humiliation. After all, you are beyond reach.

So where is your vulnerable spot?

Of course, your body, just as your entire being, can be replaced, traded in for another one at any time. But what cannot be traded in and replaced is the world that you and those who appointed you have created for yourselves. It is an artificial world that you declare to be the only real one, for in it the only laws that count are the laws that you have made, and truth is only what you declare it to be. You are vulnerable only to a power which can disrupt the unity of your world, and thus make you visible to people.

That power, Mr K., lies in stories. In stories from the real world. You may throw a hundred appeals for justice out with the garbage and no heart will tremble, but you cannot silence a hundred stories. These stories, no matter what they say, if they are carried by love, by suffering or by tenderness, will always throw into relief your contemptible and empty work. In the end, they will wound you and you will fall from your apparently unconquerable height back into the nothingness from which you emerged. I would only hope that, as you fall, at least you will understand that these stories will outlive you.

With regards

K. (Surveyor's Assistant)

257

CEMETERIES

THE GIRL from the stationers was wearing black.

Her mother's story was a simple one. She worked for twenty years in a factory, mostly in shipping. The work was badly paid, but it seemed safe. Her husband was a warehouse manager. With his job he got a two-room company flat in a housing estate. They had two children.

The girl didn't know what more she could say about her mother. Sometimes on Sundays after lunch, when time allowed, they would go together to visit Grandma. On the train, her mother would unwrap sweet buns or breaded pork cutlets. Sometimes, in the evening, they would watch television together. The television set was so old that the picture was always fading. The father was seldom home; he spent his evenings in bars and would come back drunk, but he was kind, never shouted at anyone, and never beat them.

They didn't go on holidays. The children spent part of their vacation at a young pioneers camp, and part of it with their grandmother near the cement factory.

But the mother had promised that one day they would all go to the seaside together. She reckoned that when she went over to work in the aniline department, she could save up enough in two years to take the whole family to

Bulgaria. The father did not object; he never objected to anything. But several weeks before they were to go, he packed his things and moved in with some slut. The girl in the stationery shop was fourteen when this happened, her brother was ten. Their mother took them to Bulgaria all the same. There was numbing heat on the Golden Sands and crowds of people. Mother didn't know how to swim, so she lay on the beach and the first day got so badly burned that she cried for two nights in pain. On the third day they all got a bowel infection, and when they began to feel better, the weather changed and the sea became so rough no one was allowed to go in.

So the mother went for a walk, at least, along the beach. She saw an enormous white bird she didn't know the name of. It hovered just above the waves, and it even landed on the crest of one wave as though it were the deck of a ship. The mother stared at it transfixed, then ran for the children. But by the time they had come back to the sea, the remarkable bird was gone.

The mother worked in the aniline department for another three years, then went back to shipping. Last year she had begun to pass blood, but she told no one about it, and was afraid to see a doctor. Just ten weeks ago they had taken her to the hospital, and by that time, it was too late for a cure.

The girl had been to visit her mother three times during that period. On the third visit, her mother didn't recognize her. She'd been given morphine. Her eyes were tightly closed, her breathing slow and laboured. But the girl thought that she was smiling, and perhaps she really was. Perhaps she felt herself slipping away from suffering, or perhaps she had already glimpsed something that none of us will see in this world. Perhaps it was some extraterrestrial being; perhaps it was that enormous white bird. The mother died that night and the hospital notified the girl by telegram. The funeral was tomorrow, at home and then in the cemetery just past the cement works. The dust doesn't bother the dead, though the flowers turn grey and have to be replaced frequently.

The village with the cement plant did not lie within the area we were surveying. We had, however, often been in cemeteries simply because they were usually next to churches where our benchmarks were.

The surveyor had to call on the priests or the vergers in their crumbling houses, to determine whether anything had been shifted or altered, particularly on the steeple or the dome, since the last survey. Sometimes I would see them in the doorway, old men with white collars, shaking their heads, confirming that no, the church had not been repaired. Sometimes they would invite him inside to complain about just that, that their church was deteriorating.

Meanwhile I would go to the cemetery, which was always open. Immediately I walked through the gate, I found myself in a different world. The graves seemed to be competing to see which could display the greatest variety and number of flowers, and if they were covered with grass, the green was not marred by a single weed. Something of the old values, customs and usages that have been forgotten everywhere else had survived here. Even in the most thinly populated villages, there would almost always be someone with a shovel or a rake or a watering can, tending a grave. And if they were not working, then they would stand in contemplation, or in silent prayer.

Just beyond the wall of one cemetery, there were two stone pillars and we worked on them until dusk. A cluster of children watched us from a distance. The moon came out over the low village roofs and when it appeared, so did the local priest. He had come to ask us if we'd like some refreshment.

He brought us out some coffee, and as we drank it he told us the story of an old farmer who had hidden in the mortuary in the 1950s. His friends had warned him that 'they' were coming to arrest him. The mortuary was locked, having been disused for years. People died in hospitals, after all, or they laid them out at home until the funeral. Only the sexton and the priest had the keys, and they brought the farmer food. The voluntary prisoner was given the third key so that he could leave this house of the dead whenever he had to. Fortunately, the lock worked both from inside and outside, although given the original purpose of the place, that should have been unnecessary. The cemetery was a good place to hide since, as we must have noticed, it was surrounded by a high wall and could only be seen from the steeple. It had its own water supply, and a compost heap in the corner right behind the mortuary.

The man lived there for almost a year. At night, when the moon was out, he did a little of the maintenance work in the churchyard. What did he do during the day? Perhaps he read, and apparently he also wrote something about his own life, but nothing of that survived. Then winter set in and things became more difficult. It was cold inside the mortuary, and outside there was snow, so the farmer left tracks when he went out. Both the priest and the sexton tried to persuade him to hide in their homes, but he

261

hesitated, perhaps because he didn't want to put them in any danger. In those days everything was treated as high treason or subversion and sabotage. One morning they found him dead inside the mortuary. He was given a quick, but Christian, burial, and they decided to destroy everything he left behind. It was too bad about the notebooks. In such isolation, a person may catch a glimpse of things we are not even aware of.

As I walked among the graves, it occurred to me that our obsession with measuring, counting, drawing and inventing comes not just from trying to expel mystery from the world, but also from the need to hold life itself at a distance, since otherwise it would terrify us by its brevity and its transience. In a digitalized world, not only does life vanish, death disappears as well. What remains, at the most, are citizens, populations, property and land registries.

One day, at another cemetery, I saw, bent over a grave, an oddly familiar angular head with prominent ears. For a moment I couldn't remember where I'd seen that head before, until the old man looked around and asked, 'Looking for someone's grave, comrade?' The word 'comrade' took me back to the corridor in the château that first day of my career as a surveyor's assistant. I answered as I had then: 'No, I'm not.'

'I have to come here once in a while,' he told me, as though apologizing, 'to look after my late wife's grave, to keep it from going to seed.'

The grave looked more neglected than the rest. The date on the stone indicated that his wife had passed away five years before. The grave had no cross and there were no flowers around it, only some desiccated heather.

'No one's even bothered to lay so much as a dry stick at

her grave,' he complained, 'and it's so close. And when she was alive they all greeted her, and whenever they needed something they came to her, even in the night.'

'Was your wife in the health service?' I asked, guessing.

'My wife made it further in life than I did. She was working for the district office,' he said proudly. 'And back in 1970, when we had to purge the party and society of anti-socialist elements, she was chairman of the screen-ing committee—higher than me again.'

I understood that I was standing face to face with the older brother of K., the director, the addressee of my letters.

'Why, she could still be with us,' the old man complained. 'She wasn't yet sixty.' His voice quavered. He pulled a large wallet from his breast pocket and fished around in it for something. As he did so, several photographs spilled out to the ground. I bent down to pick them up. I'd have done the same for K., the director, if he were so despondent, so surrounded by emptiness. In one of the photographs I saw a young man with an obviously angular head, in another a girl with thick long hair. I handed back the photographs and he quickly stuck them into his pocket. 'There she is,' he said, having found the snapshot he was looking for. 'Who would have thought it?'

The face of the older sister of that family of which Mr K., the director, was also a member, revealed nothing. The thin, tight, unsmiling lips perhaps spoke of rigidity or intolerance.

'And now I'm in the home,' he sobbed suddenly. 'And do you think anyone will talk to me there? I hear them talking to each other, but whenever I approach them, they stand up as though they were just going.'

'Were these your children in the snapshots?'

'Don't talk to me about them! I feel closer to children who aren't my own. The girl stayed in Austria, and I arranged for her to go on that trip myself. She didn't even come back for her mother's funeral. What did she want that she couldn't have had here? And I don't talk to the boy either. You know what he did?' He waved his hands as though trying to drive away a terrible vision. 'He joined up with the Adventists. He even tried to convert me. "Dad," he says, "the end of the world is coming. Repent while there's still time." So I said to him: "Repent yourself. I haven't betrayed my ideals, I don't need to repent!" And I told him not to even bother writing to me. Life, comrade, has taught me how to be tough.' And the cheeks of this wretched man burned with flames of rage.

The surveyor came through the gate, walking beside a priest. The man saw them as well, and suddenly became alert and guarded: 'Who are you anyway? What are you doing here?'

'We're surveying.'

'Surveying? What?'

'The earth.'

'Have you got a permit?'

For surveying, yes, but for simply walking upon the earth, we don't have the proper stamp. I walked away.

It is possible that this anxious stewardship of the cemeteries that sets them aside from the decay and neglect around them can be explained by something more than simple respect for past values. We avoid thinking about death, but death is all around us and impinges on us everywhere except here. In the cemetery lies lose their meaning, and without lies all the artificial world falls away.

And so this is where we, the living, retreat. We embellish the graves, adorn our asylum, build invisible but impenetrable walls to keep out the flags and banners, the slogans, the loudspeakers, the parades, the television screens.

The surveyor nodded to me. The priest was inviting us to climb the church tower to view the countryside.

I had a last look around. K.'s older brother was standing there alone, as though he himself had emerged from the grave. What was his past, and what lay ahead of him? What can a man who has lived in the grave have to look forward to? What could he be thinking about in his rigid isolation?

And suddenly, in a flash, it occurred to me: he was wondering whom he should report us to.

THE MOON

IF WE MANAGED to finish everything in time here, the surveyor wanted me to go with him to Moravia, which was not far from his home. When he'd been there on a surveying trip earlier in the year, he'd needed to measure two points by the North Star, but the nights had not been clear enough for him to do so.

Sometimes, when we would come back from work after dark, Kos would point to stars in the Little Dipper where the light of Polaris twinkled, and complain that all summer long the nights had never been this clear. Wouldn't this be a perfect time to survey?

If he felt like it, I would suggest, we could go first thing tomorrow. The weather looked stable.

'Do you think so?' I felt he was giving it serious thought, but next morning we would drive off to a field in the neighbourhood and, dripping with perspiration in the glaring sun, dig out a stone that had shifted position.

But as the autumn advanced and the number of underlined circles on the surveyor's map increased, the end of the work was in sight.

'Tomorrow, then,' he decided, 'if you agree, we could go.'

In fact it was a good idea to leave the night-time surveying until the end. Night makes every enterprise special and our work too, it seemed to me, ought to be concluded in a special way, at least. Besides that, I wanted to do something for my young boss when the work was over. I didn't know why, but I thought I might be more likely to find an opportunity on this trip.

There was no need to worry about accommodation, he added. He'd already told his wife I'd be staying over with them.

I was curious about his wife, but I said nothing, I only went to pack the best clothes I had with me.

Next morning we woke to a murky day. Under a cover of thick clouds, the smoke from a nearby chemical factory collected with no means of escape. We put our usual equipment in the car and drove off to a nearby village where there was still some work to do.

We set up our tripods and I sat down on a damp stone and wrote down the numbers the surveyor called out. I was sorry our trip had not materialized. Occasionally I would gaze up into the gloom, looking for signs of a change in the weather. Perhaps I saw a small opening in the clouds, but I suddenly found myself announcing, 'It's going to clear up this afternoon.'

The surveyor looked at me in astonishment. 'How do you know?'

I shrugged my shoulders.

'Do you think we ought to drop what we're doing here and go?'

I felt the way I once had in the woods when we'd lost our way. The responsibility was his; I was attracted by the journey itself. To be cautious, I suggested that we listen to the weather forecast.

The forecast was Pythian, as it always is when the meterologists don't know what to say. Slightly overcast to cloudy, with occasional showers.

But the sun was beginning to come through the clouds.

'Do you really think it will clear up?'

He wanted to shift at least some of the responsibility to me, so I accepted it.

We gathered up all the instruments, put a few more in the car at home, then changed our clothes and set off.

The road wound into the hills, and we passed through villages I was seeing for the first time in my life. As the sky began to turn blue, I felt it was partly my doing.

'I'm sorry we didn't leave first thing,' Kos said. 'We could have started straight away. You can see the North Star from four o'clock on.'

Eventually we stopped by a farm building that stood at the side of a pond. The surveyor sounded the horn, then jumped out of the car and unlocked the heavy wooden gates. As soon as they were opened wide enough, a black and white Newfoundland bounded out and greeted us noisily, followed by a slight young woman with a large belly, a freckled face and light-coloured hair, who flung herself into his arms. So this was the creature he had found in the park weeping, crushed by a secret grief.

I could tell that the surveyor would have preferred to load up the instruments we needed and leave at once, but his wife insisted that we rest a while and have something to eat. His mother and grandmother appeared as well, and they all tried to persuade us to stay. The surveyor said he would go and tend to the bull, and he left me to the mercies of the women.

Upstairs, where the young couple lived, the rooms smelled of whitewash, new wood and paint. The surveyor's wife set a small table. 'We haven't managed to get a proper dining-table yet,' she said. There wasn't much furniture of any kind, but the parquet flooring was recently laid and the window frames freshly painted. In the corner, by the door, the large lobe-shaped leaves of some foreign plant rose out of a flower-pot.

'It's a monstera,' she said. 'I brought it from home. We had a fig tree as well, and each year it produced a few little figs, at least.'

I felt she wanted to tell me something quite different, or ask about something more important—most probably what I thought of her husband—but she said nothing more, so I remarked on how nice I thought their place looked, and told her that I enjoyed working with her husband. She nodded, blushed and then ran out of the room.

I sat down in an armchair beside a bookshelf and looked at the books. Outside, I could hear the Newfoundland's deep bass bark, and the geese honking. Voices echoed through the house, someone arrived and then left again. There weren't many books, but most of the authors were American, oddly enough the same ones I had admired when I was young. But then as far as publishing went, time had stood still for seventeen years.

We had supper at a table for two. The surveyor's wife gave up her place to me and sat in an armchair. While we ate, she crocheted some tiny item of baby clothing.

I would have liked to have gone on sitting there, for I had suddenly lost interest in night-time surveying, and would have preferred to learn something, at least, about my quiet and gentle hostess. But the surveyor was in a hurry. What if the clouds were to move in?

So I went to put the instruments in the car, and then I opened the gate. His wife held the dog by the collar, and I realized why, back then in the park, my young boss had turned and gone back to this stranger, this weeping girl whose face he couldn't even see. He was drawn, through her, to the mystery that otherwise had no place in his strict and precisely measurable world.

'You see,' said Kos. 'It'll be dark in a little while.'

I replied that he had a nice home. That was all we said about his wife.

The shadows were lengthening across the countryside, and cool air was beginning to move in from the valley. We left the tripod with the disc by the woods and drove up a steep meadow to the top of a hill where a wooden pyramid stood intact, a relic of times past. There, over the stone pillar, we set up the theodolite. Then I got into the car and spread out sheets of paper with columns printed on them while the surveyor located the North Star in the still-light sky, and we were ready to begin.

So far, in our work I had uncovered nothing new or even exciting. I didn't care whether the surveyor's telescope was pointed at a star or a church steeple.

'Now we'll move to another hilltop,' said Kos when we had finished our measuring in the last bit of daylight. 'Then we'll have to use our flashlights.' As soon as he said it, he rushed over to the car and rummaged around in it furiously for a while until he was quite certain that he actually had forgotten the flashlights necessary to illuminate his instruments. So we packed everything into the car again and as we drove back as fast as our four-wheel drive could take us, he muttered over and over again: it had to happen just now, it's bound to cloud over while we waste valuable time because of his carelessness. It occurred to me that he had deliberately saved this bit of surveying until the last because he too wanted to end the job on a special note.

As far as the clouds were concerned, his worst fears were realized.

At nine-thirty that evening, when we were climbing through a ploughed field with a set of flashlights to the dark hilltop, opaque ridges of altocumulus were reaching out across the sky.

We still had to go down into the valley to place our levelling staff with its lamps. By the time everything was set up, it was close to ten o'clock and not a star was visible in the sky. We both got into the car to wait. It was becoming cold.

At eleven o'clock, the surveyor got out of the car again and scanned the heavens with his binoculars But once more, he could see nothing but cloud cover. He suggested we leave.

I got out of the car too, and felt a light, cool breeze on my face. 'I think it's going to clear up,' I said.

'Do you really think so? Take a look for yourself.' He handed me the binoculars.

Down in the valley, I could see a few lights in a distant village. Then I found an isolated point of light, our will o' the wisp, which we had set up on an abandoned track through the fields. Yet above us, all was darkness, and a dank coldness descended on us from the sky.

'Well, if you say so,' said the surveyor. We returned to the car and listened to some cheerless music on the radio.

At eleven-thirty the surveyor got out of the car, then shouted: 'I must be dreaming!'

The clouds had been swept away and the autumn stars shone so clearly that they almost seemed within reach.

We had to wait until midnight, when the surveyor set his stopwatch to the exact time. Meanwhile, I stuck a candle to the dashboard and prepared the sheets so that I could see them as clearly as possible.

The grass around the car was glistening. It could have been moonlight reflected in drops of dew, or perhaps a thin layer of hoarfrost. The temperature was now below freezing. Hard times were coming for birds, animals and outlaws, who had to find a place to hide. I wrapped my coat tightly about me, and at that moment I seemed to hear a muffled whispering that came from the frozen distances. As I looked down into the valley bathed in moonlight, I could see a small church spire beyond the grey of a cemetery wall. Now I could hear the words. It was a question: is the mortuary my whole world, or has the whole world become a mortuary?

It occurred to me, in fact I was certain, that this was probably the last sentence the old farmer hidden away in the mortuary had written in his notebook. The priest who had found him dead had read the sentence and the gloomy question, a question from the present world, not from the gospel of Christ, had not seemed worth taking a risk for, so he had thrown the notebook into the fire.

I would have liked to have heard more of that message, but the surveyor had begun calling out the first set of numbers and I had to concentrate; a mistake would render our efforts useless. I also had to announce the angle at which he should look for the North Star.

We filled in the last column of figures a few minutes before three in the morning. The surveyor, having stood hunched over his instrument all that time, was numb with cold, but he seemed contented, even moved, by his achievement.

'You once said,' he recalled, 'that you'd like to look at the stars, or the moon,' and he pointed to the almost completely round lunar sphere in the sky.

So I climbed out of the car, stood behind the theodolite, put my eye to the eyepiece and then pointed the lens in the direction I thought the moon would be.

At any time during the fifty years of my life, I undoubtedly could have gone to an observatory and studied the night sky through a telescope far bigger than this theodolite, but I was glad I hadn't. There are things a person should see at the best possible moment—and perhaps I sensed that one day I would stand here freezing on a cold, windy hilltop at three o'clock in the morning on the last day of our survey and be given a view of the moon, not as an opportunity to be grasped but as a reward.

And so I saw it: the moon as I had known it from books, films and television shots—the craters of Tycho, Copernicus, and Theophilos, the Mare Nubium, the Sea of Darkness and the Sea of Tranquillity, and all those other names, and everything I had known only from grey snapshots—was real and glowing and solid.

Surprised as I was at how this sight transported me, it seemed to me that the longer I looked, the more the lunar landscape resembled a face, a knowing face, a face of reconciliation. Suddenly, I recognized it as the face of my father, and he, from the distance of another world, asked me what I thought.

I had to admit that I liked it, that it was a miracle to look at the Earth's satellite in close-up.

Do you realize that people have already stood here? he asked.

And I agreed that too was miraculous, just as it was miraculous that people could fly above the earth, look into the heart of matter or say: let there be light, and light will indeed appear. The world you created is a miracle, I thought, just as the consequences of what you have created are so threatening. And even though I fear this world and rebel against it, I do so because I still hope that something of that miracle will survive, although I have no grounds for such hope other than the wish that so much of your effort, so much desire, so many fond and magnanimous dreams would not be utterly in vain.

Afterwards, we put the theodolite back in its case, then we carried all our things back to the car and drove down for the tripod, the light on it still twinkling, vainly luring insects that had long since gone to sleep for the winter.

We reached the farm towards four o'clock. Everyone had gone to bed. The surveyor took me to the room his wife had prepared for me and, before he wished me good night, he said, almost ceremonially: 'I want to thank you for your exemplary assistance.'

He didn't say whether he meant by that my diligent recording of his data, my capacity to stay with him to the end despite frequent exhaustion, or my mysterious ability to look into an overcast sky and predict the weather.

FLAGS

ON OUR FINAL morning in Meštec I was awakened by a tapping sound over my head. Something was falling on the ceiling, as though someone were pouring gravel on to the attic floor.

'Maybe they've started dismantling the roof,' I thought.

The surveyor rejected my suggestion: the stationery store was still open, and he'd seen Mrs Pokorná relaxing with her canary in the courtyard.

While I was having breakfast, the surveyor, in a suit and tie, went off to the National Committee office to announce that we were leaving, to thank them for providing excellent accommodation free of charge, and to beg them for the almost new stove that still brightened my room and which, Kos was convinced, they would scrap anyway.

From my trunk, I took the figure of the hideous extraterrestrial creature, wrapped it in a newspaper, and went out in front of the building.

Through the glass door of the stationery shop, I could see several customers inside, so I decided to wait. Stepping back a little way into the square, I had a good view of the roof of our building. A large hole had appeared in it from which a man was emerging.

The last old lady finally came out of the store and I went in.

'Your friend said you were all done,' the girl said.

'We are.'

'I haven't had a minute to sit down today,' she complained. 'There's been a constant stream of customers all morning.'

'I'm surprised you're still here,' I said. 'They're taking apart the roof over your head.'

'No one told me anything about it,' she said, shrugging.

'We're all packed,' I said. 'And I'd like to leave something for you.'

'Me?' She took the parcel from me. 'Can I look?'

I unwrapped the figure.

'No!' she shouted. 'No!'

'It's a souvenir.'

'No, it's impossible. I mean, why would you give this to me? You can't be serious—giving it to me just like that. Jesus, he's beautiful, he's real! It's him!'

Two young girls and a Vietnamese man with a suitcase came into the store, but she didn't even notice them. 'It must have been terribly expensive. And I—what could I give you for it?'

She began to rummage frantically in one of the drawers, and I took the opportunity to wish her good health, then left the store.

Even in that brief time, the hole in the roof had grown. The surveyor was walking back from the National Committee building, looking extremely pleased. They'd given him permission to take away the stove, and all we had to do was put the old stove outside the door in its place. 'They also want us to put flags out for the twenty-eighth of October,' he announced. 'But to hell with that, we're leaving anyway. Do you think the two of us can carry the stove down by ourselves?'

I doubted it. Fortunately, the roofers were in the building. They'd certainly help us. So while the surveyor went up to bargain with them, I unfurled both the flags, something I'd never done in the two months I'd shared my room with them. I was excited by the idea. They were almost brand new; only their edges were covered in cement dust. I rolled them up again and carried them down to the main entrance. Then I brought a ladder from the shed and put the flags in the rusty holders affixed, for that purpose, on either side of the door. Once again, I felt I had chosen the right place and the right time.

We still had to return the things we'd borrowed. The surveyor insisted that even the chair without a back belonged over the road. The last thing we did was take our borrowed beds back to the château.

I waited in the same corridor I'd waited in the first day, while the surveyor went to the office to get the formalities over with. Now, as then, I leaned against the parapet. The roses in the flowerbed had flowered, then faded, and only a few dried blooms remained on the bushes. The lawn was hidden under fallen leaves. The courtyard was full of shadows, but on a bench by the wall several old women were still trying to capture some of the sun's warmth, while in front of them a tall old man with thick, completely white hair was sketching something in the sand. I could make out circles and ellipses, and it suddenly occurred to me that the old man was telling the women's fortunes. Was he trying to tell them about the future that seems mysterious until the very last minute, or was he revealing the future that stretches beyond that last minute?

One of the women seemed familiar and indeed when I looked around I saw, sitting on a low stone wall, the cage with a canary inside.

My first impulse was to go down and say goodbye to Mrs Pokorná and her memories, but then I thought she might not approve, might perhaps feel ashamed at having abandoned her ancient family seat after swearing to remain to the end. And anyway, all the old women suddenly got up and started walking away, the white-haired seer rubbed out his circles with a foot shod in a checkered slipper and, by the time another old man, whose angular head I already knew well, arrived, they had all vanished.

My acquaintance came right up to the vacated bench and, examining the ground intently, he tried to discern meaning among what was left of the diagram. Finding nothing that might offer understanding, he continued in his wandering. When he came within earshot of me, he called out, 'I've already found out who you are. It's all right.' Then he frowned and said bitterly, 'Did you see them, comrade? That's how they treat a person here. Is this what we've worked so hard to achieve?'

Yes, that's what we've worked so hard to achieve. And we, who with all our strength have worked to achieve it, should not be scandalized. My dear sir, you see that I'm not placing myself above you, but I agree with your prodigal son. We should complain less and repent more.

We carried the beds into the store-room and returned to our quarters. With the help of the two roofers, we carried out the new stove and put it in the back of the car. Then we gradually filled the rest of the car up with all the surveying gear: the theodolite and the broom, the tapes and measuring chains and the buckets, the bags of unused coal and the brushes, the shovels, the briefcase full of forms, the axes, the machete and the half-empty cans of paint.

The surveyor and I said goodbye. I asked him to give my regards to his wife and wished them both a healthy daughter. Then, as I had done every day, I opened the iron gate, and the surveyor drove out. I followed in my car. Then I stopped and got out to close the gates for the last time. I looked up at the two flags snapping above the entrance in the autumn wind, and then a little higher to where the roof used to be, where I caught a glimpse of the roofers.

I got into my car again; the shop girl ran out of the stationery store with the doll in her arms to wave goodbye.

I drove off, but looked around a last time. The girl was still standing there, squeezing the ugly little rubber extraterrestrial in one arm, and in her other hand she waved a coloured handkerchief, as if I too were some extraterrestrial departing her desolate planet for ever.

AFTERWORD

THE TITLE OF this book, *My Golden Trades,* is meant somewhat ironically. There is a proverb in Czech that runs: 'A trade is a handful of gold,' suggesting that a skilled craftsman will never be poor. But there are other proverbs as well: 'For him with nine trades, the tenth is poverty,' meaning that if you never learn any trade properly, you'll never get rich.

The hero of my book, mostly involuntarily, tries his hand at a number of jobs, none of which he is really suited for. There is no gold in any of them, unless you count the unexpected gains experience brings. The book is autobiographical to the extent that I actually did most of the jobs mentioned in the stories. I took part in archaeological digs, I worked as a messenger and as a surveyor's assistant. I smuggled books and manuscripts. I even drove a train without derailing it (although, as readers who have driven a locomotive can attest, it's hard to have a head-on collision on the railway!).

Nevertheless, these experiences only provided the impulse or the occasion for me to say something I felt I had to say. Surveying, for example, is interesting work, but in and of itself, no job can ever be the subject for a story.

However, as an unskilled surveyor's assistant I got into places I would not normally have seen. I visited the Semtex factory where plastic explosives are manufactured. I saw the country from many church steeples, walked into the middle of vast fields and orchards, climbed at night to the top of lonely, terrifying hilltops and touched the earth countless times. I saw that the earth was suffering, and I decided to write something about it. And so 'The Surveyor's Story' came into being.

I am often asked these days what Czechoslovak writers will write now that the revolution is over. I usually reply that such questions are based on the false assumption that writers, especially banned writers, wrote mainly about repression, the secret police, prison and the cruel and bizarre practices of the communist regime. Not at all: they wrote mostly about the same things as writers everywhere, the only difference being, perhaps, that life sometimes put them in situations writers in a free country almost never experience. That can add colour to writing, nothing more. Something of this book is linked to a reality that (fortunately) belongs to the past. I believe, however, that most of what I have written does not rely on the existence of any particular regime; it is linked to our human existence, to our civilization and its problems. Whether I am right or wrong is something readers must judge for themselves.

Ivan Klíma, Prague, May 1992